GLACIER RUN

Glacier Run

PHYLLIDA BARSTOW

CENTURY PUBLISHING
LONDON

First published in Great Britain in 1983 by

Century Publishing Co. Ltd,

76 Old Compton Street, London W1V 5 PA

ISBN 0 7126 0156 2

Photoset in Great Britain by
Rowland Phototypesetting Ltd, Bury St Edmunds, Suffolk
and printed by St Edmundsbury Press
Bury St Edmunds, Suffolk

For my nephew, Jamie Lindsay

Chapter One

I sat suspended twenty feet above the snow, with tendrils of cloud swirling damply about me and fingers and toes turning rapidly to ice, and cursed ski-lift operators who failed to maintain their machinery. Twice already on this top leg of the Mont du Diamant hoist the line of chairs attached to an overhead cable had slowed and stopped, swinging gently in sudden silence; each time it had been three or four minutes before power whirred through the lines again and the chairs jerked onward.

This time whatever was causing the breakdown seemed more serious. I was too cold to take off my glove to look at my watch, but guessed that I'd been sitting there at least five minutes already and that – on a mid-March day in the French Alps at a height of three thousand-plus metres, with only a cotton poloneck and duvet waistcoat for warmth – was definitely five minutes too long. On the lower slopes it had been sunny, even hot. Too late now to regret the vanity that had prevented me from wearing the woolly hat that did so little for my looks: I hadn't got it and that was that. Rowan, fortunately, had more sense. I had seen the shocking-pink balaclava helmet that made her look like an unusually attractive Crusader bobbing merrily in front of me up the chair-lift.

She'd been quite a way in front of me, because the surly unshaven lift operator whom I'd mentally christened Shaggy had allowed her aboard and then, without explanation, roped off my section of the queue, and gestured to a whole gang of his mates to go in front of me. Bronzed, wind-beaten mountaineers, with heavily muscled legs encased in dangerously stretched ski-pants embossed with great show-off pads at the knee, they had swaggered through without paying in a jostling macho group. They were probably local lads who worked long hours making the ski-slopes safe for winter sports visitors like myself, and as such perfectly entitled to ride free on the lifts and jostle *les Anglaises* out of their way; nevertheless I ground my teeth a little as I was obliged to wait while Rowan, serenely unconscious that I wasn't following, disappeared into the cloud above.

As the delay stretched out and numbness invaded my body from the extremities inward, I transferred my curses from lift operators in general to this particular one. Shaggy must have failed to count the number of chairs coming empty down the cable, and stopped the machine before I reached the top. It was late in the afternoon: he had probably boarded up his little wooden hut for the night and shot off home, leaving me stranded.

I shivered and peered down through the cloud, wondering what my chances would be if I simply dropped off into the snow. Even a broken leg would be preferable to freezing solid.

I twisted to look behind me. Not a single chair in the line that stretched down the mountainside was occupied, and the same went for the four I could see in front of me. Shaggy had been speaking on his telephone when the last of the local lads swung off up the hill. A gap had developed before he graciously allowed me on to a chair, with the result that there was no one either behind or in front of me. I was totally alone in my predicament. The dead, muffling chill of the mountain seemed to be creeping into my innermost soul. From being annoyed I began to feel frightened. Soon I would be too cold to move even if I wanted to – and then what?

I twitched my toes inside the heavy, rigid ski-boots, themselves weighed down by the drag of my fibreglass skis dangling uselessly in the void, unsupported by a footrest. I huffed and puffed into my padded gloves and tried isometric exercises, shoving one palm against the other until the muscles ached, clamping my legs together to make contact between ankles, calves and knees at the same time, counting twenty and then relaxing. It didn't warm me in the least. I stared into the gloom below, hoping for a glimpse of Rowan.

The piste crossed beneath the ski-lift; if I could attract her attention I could tell her what had happened and rely on her to raise hell until the machinery was restarted. Minutes crawled past and I knew I was too late. Rowan must have started down alone, confident that I would soon catch her up. She wouldn't realise what had happened until I failed to turn up at the café for our ritual *goûter* of hot chocolate and sticky gâteaux.

For a moment the cloud lifted, showing the majestic triple peak of La Sorcière, La Grande Aiguille, and Mont du Diamant dominating the whole semicircle of Val du Loup. They stood out jaggedly against their blue backdrop, white and impregnable. I could see the hut of the top station no more than three hundred yards away across two small ridges. And, like a beacon of hope, I also saw a small brightly-clad figure gliding down the slope towards me, steering what looked like a small coracle in front of him. One of the local lads bringing down the 'blood-wagon' for the night.

But being a local lad who probably learned to ski before he could walk, he wasn't bothering to stick to the piste. He was taking a direct line from top station to bottom, fizzing along with soft powder-snow spraying up to bury his skis and the lower half of his legs. The coracle-like sledge known as the blood-wagon in which injured skiers were transported off the slopes plummeted towards the valley floor. Casualties were customarily carried with their heads pointing downhill, I'd heard, on the principle that a heart attack might be added to their troubles if they could see the route their rescuers were taking. I was too far away to distinguish anything clearly, but I thought I could make out a shape strapped in the little canoe.

I waved my ski-sticks and shouted at the top of my voice.

'Stop! *Au secours!* Help! *Halt!*'

The speeding figure was hunched slightly forward to grasp the handles of the blood-wagon and he gave no sign of having heard me. He was probably aware of nothing but the hiss and roar of his own skis, with an occasional grate against rock or ice as he pursued his reckless course down the mountain. A thread of sound floated back to me, a cheerful, familiar, whistled tune common to both our countries; simple, repetitive, the sort of thing one whistled with one's mind in neutral. The words I would put to it were 'For He's a Jolly Good Fellow' or perhaps 'The Bear went over the Mountain' but no doubt the speeding blood-wagoner called it 'Malbrouk s'en va t'en Guerre'.

I cupped my freezing hands round my mouth and shouted again and again until my throat was raw and my lungs bursting.

Only when the diminishing figure finally vanished over the shoulder of the hill did I give up hope.

I couldn't stay where I was any longer. Hypothermia had me in its grip, numbing my will as well as my body. There was nothing for it but to drop off the lift into the snow and pray that I landed soft and the right way up. For a moment I debated whether or not to take my skis off first. There was no telling the depth of the snow directly underneath me. It could be a few inches or a few feet. I might smash into rocks or plummet helplessly into a snow-filled ravine. Skis were hard, spiky, awkward contrivances with lots of sharp edges, uncomfortable to land on but absolutely essential to getting downhill in deep snow. Walking without them was out of the question. In the end I decided not to risk getting parted from them, but to drop a ski-stick first in the hope that it would give me some idea of the depth of the snow.

Leaning out over the edge of the chair, I threw my left-hand ski-stick like a javelin, point down, as hard as I could, but it was not quite heavy enough to penetrate the snow's crust. It landed on its point and toppled sideways, leaving me none the wiser. I would simply have to jump and trust to luck.

With clumsy fumbling fingers I unclipped the safety-chain across the front of the chair. I was swinging my ski-burdened boots, about to launch myself into space, when the overhead cable hummed and vibrated and, with a jerk that nearly pitched me headfirst after my ski-stick, the chair began to move. Weak with relief, I clung to the armrests; in seconds, it seemed, I was approaching the little hut at the end of the hoist, with its great revolving drum round which the empty chairs rattled on their downward journey.

My legs were nearly too cold to support me as I slid on to the platform of hard-packed snow, and the feeling of solid ground under my feet again was an inexpressible relief. I kicked off my skis and jumped and stamped and beat crossed arms around my ribs, whimpering with pain as circulation crept back into fingers and toes. The cloud had evaporated and the ring of peaks blazed orange in the last rays of the sun, but already the lower slopes looked dark. High time to get down to the valley. I stamped on my skis once more and shuffled to the top of the piste.

It was an unpleasant surprise to find it barred off. Crossed piste-markers reinforced by a disc saying *PASSAGE INTER-DIT* informed me bluntly that this run had been closed until conditions improved. No doubt that was another little chore the local lads had discharged before setting off on their homeward joyride. It was no comfort for me to know that Rowan had been able to use the run. I should have to find another way down, and that meant a long slow trek round the back of the ridge, following the blue markers that signalled an easy descent to the neighbouring village of Castelgard. From there I could catch a bus back to the purpose-built ski-condominium of Les Loups, where Rowan and I had rented an apartment.

I cursed, greatly tempted to ignore the warning sign and follow Rowan down the run as planned. It seemed unlikely that whatever danger had necessitated its closure would have increased dramatically during the quarter hour in which I'd languished on the chair-lift. Besides, I needed my ski-stick. As soon as I started down the slope I realised how horribly lopsided I felt without it. I took the first gentle curve of the piste as slowly as possible, watching out for the clump of boulders which I had used to mark my position when dropping the stick in the snow.

The piste was in perfect condition, smooth and shiny as icing sugar with just a light scuffle of powder on top to make turning easy. I had spotted my boulders and decided to risk following the forbidden run all the way to the bottom, when a short sturdy figure in baggy old-fashioned ski-pants, a shapeless black anorak and pale blue wool cap pulled well down over most of his face glided out from behind the rocks and came straight for me.

'*Votre baton, mademoiselle!*' He handed me the missing ski-stick but no trace of a smile softened his weathered mahogany features. He was old and gnarled and looked as bleak as the mountains themselves.

'*Merci, monsieur.*' I took it and immediately felt better-balanced. I wondered if he had watched my lonely vigil on the chair-lift, and if so why the hell hadn't he done anything to help? And did he know the run was closed? As soon as I started to ski quietly away down the undulating piste it was plain that he did. He cut in front of me with a dash that spoke of a lifetime with boards attached to his boots, blocking the way and gesticulating.

'*Non, mademoiselle*, the run is closed. Danger of avalanche.' His French was thick and blurred with patois but the meaning was clear enough. 'You must take the other route.'

'But I can't go back to the top now. Besides, I don't know another route. I must return to Les Loups where my friend is waiting. She will be worried. I will continue this way, with the greatest care, I assure you.'

I smiled but he was impervious to charm. He became stern. '*Non, mademoiselle*. It is forbidden. I will show you the way to Castelgard. From there you may take the autobus to Les Loups. *Pas de problème*. To continue on a piste that is closed is *formellement interdit* – strictly forbidden. *Suivez-moi, mademoiselle, s'il vous plait.*'

And follow him I had to, like it or not. He led me round the shoulder of the hill in an easy traverse, frequently glancing back to be sure I hadn't given him the slip. Muttering curses against mountain gnomes who wouldn't believe people could take care of themselves, I placed my skis in his tracks and went after him. In half a mile we picked up the blue markers and I tried to shake off his unwelcome company, but he refused to take the hint. Like a superannuated sheepdog, he insisted on herding me right down to the main street of Castelgard. It was several miles; before the lights of the village came twinkling to greet us, it was very nearly dark.

Then, without waiting for thanks or farewells he vanished as suddenly as he had appeared. One minute he was gliding down the snow-covered ramp that ended in the street: the next there wasn't a sign of him. He had left me without a word, mingling with the homegoing crowds of skiers and shoppers.

Puzzled but relieved, I stood myself a long overdue cup of hot chocolate plus two chocolate éclairs oozing whipped cream, and then, feeling slightly queasy, made my way to the village square and boarded the bus for Les Loups.

Rowan's key wasn't on its hook at the *conciergerie* so I knew she must have come back and would let me into the apartment. I hammered on the door and yodelled through the keyhole but got no answer. Finally I was obliged to toil down six flights of concrete steps yet again and ask the *concierge* for a duplicate key.

True to form, the supercilious brunette on duty made her usual fuss about issuing one, grumbling that clients were

12

supposed to return their keys to her whenever they went out and not to leave the building with them in their pockets in case they fell into the hands of undesirable characters who could then steal from the apartments, bringing blame on the management for what was *évidemment* the fault of the occupant.

Évidemment. I listened with feigned politeness, having heard it all before, knowing full well that the latent Anglophobia poorly concealed in every French breast would come out fighting if I tried to throw my weight around; in the end my self-restraint was rewarded when she grudgingly produced a duplicate key.

Once more I waited for the lift while the economy-conscious passage light faithfully extinguished itself every twenty seconds and the brunette watched me sardonically and applied another coat to her long red fingernails. Her expression suggested that it would be quicker to walk but she would let me work that out for myself. The lift arrived just before I had given it up as a bad job, and I rode up to the sixth floor, with the key in my hand and visions of hot showers, whisky and inspection of the day's crop of bruises in my mind.

'I'm back!' I called, pushing open the door.

Silence greeted me. No splash and gurgle from the microscopic bathroom; no snore or yawn from the bedroom, no tinkle of ice-on-glass from the living room.

'Rowan?' I said uncertainly, standing at the bedroom door and wondering why the place looked different. Larger, somehow. Tidier. Then it struck me that there was only half the usual clutter of bottles and pots on the dressing table, and those that were left were mine. Rowan's makeup had vanished. I checked the bathroom. One shower-cap. One toothbrush. No contraceptive pills. No Rowan. While I was making my slow way down the mountain escorted by the officious old gnome, she had packed her possessions and gone.

Chapter Two

I wasn't unduly surprised. This was part of Rowan's plan – the reason she had wanted me to join her on this trip. All the same, I couldn't help feeling rebuffed. She might have given me a word of warning.

I shrugged mentally and reminded myself that every cloud had a silver lining. At least for once there'd be no need to hurry with my bath. Ten minutes later I was twiddling the hot tap with my toes, snuggling my shoulders under Floris-scented water, and letting my mind drift idly back to my first meeting with Rowan. I'd been eighteen, abroad on my own for the first time, about to join a ten-week art course in Venice. After an all-night, most-of-the-next-day train journey, I'd struggled up to the fourth floor of the little hotel behind the Piazza San Marco, carrying the last of my luggage, only to find a dark-haired, olive-skinned girl of about my own age busily removing all the cases I'd already deposited in my bedroom, dumping them in the corridor and carting in mountains of her own baggage from the lift, whose door she had wedged open. So that was why I'd had to climb the stairs.

For a moment I'd watched her. Trunks and tape-recorders. Carrier bags emblazoned *Harrods* and *Gucci*. Beauty cases and cameras and shoulderbags and handbags. It looked like two of everything and one for the pot: how she thought she was going to fit that lot into half a room ten feet by twelve, I couldn't imagine.

'Hey!' I said at last.

She turned, revealing a handsome, strong-boned face, dramatically slanted eyebrows and flashing dark eyes. 'What do you mean – "Hey!" '

'I'm sleeping there, too. Leave my stuff where it is.'

'Sorry, there's no room. Two into one won't go.'

'Only because you've got too much. You must have known you'd be sharing.'

'They said sharing a *room*. Not a rabbit hutch.'

'Tough luck, Bunny.'

Her big eyes flashed. 'Don't call me that. I'm Rowan Henschel.'

'Hello. I'm Catherine Chiltern, Catta for short.'

'I saw your name on the notice board.' She spread despairing hands in an exotic gesture. 'So what are we going to do?'

'We'll leave your surplus gear in the passage.'

'Someone's bound to pinch it!'

'Why did you bring so much?'

She shrugged. 'I didn't know what to bring, so I brought everything.'

Hands on hips, she surveyed the dark little room with its scuffed lino and dingy curtains. It certainly wasn't what the art course brochure had promised, yet the manager insisted it was the room the *studenti* always used. Suddenly she began to laugh. 'If my father could see this he'd have a fit. He's staying at the Gritti.'

'Why not move in with him?'

'God, no! I'm planning to have *fun* while I'm here.' Abruptly she snapped into action, slinging my cases back into the room on top of hers. When she had finished, there was hardly room to stand, let alone lie down. We both began to giggle.

'There's only one thing we can do, and that's make a scene,' I said at last.

'Oh, I love making scenes.'

'Great.' I reached for the telephone. 'Here goes. Give it everything you've got. *Troppo piccolo* is the key phrase. *Molto troppo piccolo*: got it?'

The manager came on the line, brisk and unsympathetic. Trouble in Room 48? Too small? Nonsense! He was a busy man. He had no time to listen to imaginary complaints from *studenti*: What kind of trouble?

'Come and see,' I invited, and hung up.

Five minutes later he bustled up like a terrier poised to crunch a pair of unsuspecting rabbits. Ten minutes after that he blundered from the room with a glazed, almost cowed look. The rabbits had turned out to be the very prickliest type of hedgehog, and quite without meaning to he had promised them his second-best apartment with bathroom en suite, the one

15

which he had planned to reserve for a rich American desperate for lodgings during the *Carnivale*.

Rowan had put up a magnificent performance: she glowed with triumph. Later I sometimes wondered if, like the keeper who allows the tigress her first taste of human blood, I was responsible for turning her into a maneater. I don't think so; the taste was there, lying dormant. I just happened to be around when it flowered.

I topped up the cooling bath-water, inspected my bruises, and went on thinking.

For ten weeks we'd shared that second-best apartment, to the mingled amusement and envy of our fellow-students who hadn't bluffed the manager into providing better rooms. We went to lectures and parties together, and were soon labelled the Terrible Twins, which I didn't care for, though oddly enough Rowan liked it. I gathered that as the only child of divorced parents she'd had a lonely, fragmented childhood, and now she jumped at the chance of attaching herself to a friend. We weren't really alike, apart from a general similarity of build and colouring, but she played it up by copying my hairstyle, buying clothes that matched mine, and started to imitate the way I spoke. That was too much for me. Even if imitation is the sincerest form of flattery, I found it irritating.

'*You* don't think we look alike, do you?' I complained to Jean-Pierre, my man of the moment.

I wanted him to say no, I was far more attractive, but instead he gave me a long, thoughtful look.

'There is a resemblance, certainly,' he said eventually, 'but there is also one big difference.'

'What's that?'

He laughed. 'Rowan has *le regard sauvage* – a fierce look. You have *le regard doux*.'

A gentle look. A tame look. It wasn't at all what I'd hoped he'd say. The next day I went to a hairdresser and had my long hair cropped spikily short, and Rowan wailed when she saw it.

'I can't do that! Daddy'd have a fit.'

'Too bad,' I said complacently, patting the fringe into place. 'At least no one can say we look alike now.'

'Beast . . .'

It was the end of the Terrible Twins phase, but not the end of our friendship, which I soon grew to value quite as much as she did. Three years later, when I left art school and set up in a dressmaking business of my own, it was Rowan who launched me on the road to success.

Not only was she generous and energetic and full of good ideas, she was also – and it took me some time to realise this fully – quite astonishingly rich. In the bleak early days when fashion editors were too busy to accept invitations to my shows – or accepted them and didn't turn up – and buyers scoffed at my romantic ballgowns, Rowan backed me every inch of the way. She put up two thirds of the capital I needed. She bought my dresses and persuaded her friends to buy them too. She went to work with a will on promoting my label with the result that now, with my most ambitious collection still on the drawing board, I had as many orders as my small staff could cope with. I was even thinking of branching out into cosmetics and jewellery.

Friends like Rowan don't grow on trees. Without her enthusiasm and steady patronage my little venture would almost certainly have collapsed before it had a chance to get going. On the financial side I was as green as grass, and without the patient help of Paul Lomax, the accountant recommended, needless to say, by Rowan, I'd soon have been in cash-flow difficulties. The materials I used were expensive. Nor had I the least idea of how to publicise my clothes, talk to journalists, lunch with buyers and get their orders. Rowan saw to this as well. She claimed she enjoyed the haggling. 'I adore selling things, darling: it's the ultimate thrill when they reach for their chequebooks. Sometimes I wish Henschels' would go broke. Then I'd really show what I can do.'

Fortunately there was no danger of such a fate overtaking her family business. When punitive taxation obliged her father, Benjamin Henschel, to seek voluntary exile in Geneva, he made over the bulk of his British assets to Rowan, and since these were hedged about with every tax-dodging device known to the legal mind, they continued to provide his only daughter with quite as much money as was necessary or, indeed, good for her.

Since our days in Venice, she had lost her teenage puppy fat and now with her slim height, photogenic bone structure and huge slanting eyes, she was considered beautiful by most men if a trifle overpowering by some. She was no intellectual, but nobody's fool either, having inherited her father's excellent business brain and some of his yearning after creative artistry as well.

I always suspected that Ben Henschel, himself a generous patron of the arts, would have liked his only daughter to marry a struggling genius whose work she could have brought to flower through her money and connections. Instead, with typical perversity, she chose the man to whom I'd already lost my heart, Charles Dawson.

Even now I found it painful to remember how I'd made the classic blunder of introducing my best boyfriend to my best girlfriend. If I'd had the sense of a louse I'd have locked them into separate compartments of my life so that never the twain should meet. Charles was more than just a boyfriend for me: he was part of my childhood – part of my life. The brother I'd never had transformed into the lover of my dreams. More than dreams, in fact, though Rowan – to be perfectly fair – was never aware of this.

At fourteen he saved my life when a rowing boat I'd borrowed broke a rowlock and drifted out to sea. At fifteen I was so infatuated that I became scarlet and speechless whenever he entered the room. All my fantasies that summer, as I toiled away at my O-levels, featured myself and Charles in a series of closely-linked situations ranging from my acceptance of his heirloom ring to the birth of our first son amid the popping of champagne corks and the scent of mimosa.

My mother always said it was a miracle Charles wasn't spoiled rotten. 'That boy! Jim and Denise don't know how to say No to him.' But the slightly wistful note in her voice told me plainly that if she herself had been lucky enough to have a son like Charles instead of three widely-spaced daughters, she would have indulged him every bit as much as his doting parents did. Mother was always susceptible to attractive males, and even as a child Charles knew how to twist women round his little finger.

Tall, slim, and a natural at most games, with a fresh complexion and thick, dark-blond hair, Charles was remarkably good-looking. He had strong, clean-cut features, a square jaw, and very bright sapphire-blue eyes which crinkled into a smile that frequently saved him from trouble. His school career was full of scrapes and escapades which delighted his father, and when he achieved the honour of being appointed Games Captain as well as Victor Ludorum, the old Colonel was ready to burst with pride. The fact that Charles' academic record was less than glorious worried his father not at all. 'I never passed an exam in my life. Never had to,' I heard him telling my father. 'Charles's done well enough. Last thing I want's a boy with his head for ever stuck in a book.'

To me, struggling with teenage puppy fat and spots, Charles seemed a prince, an unattainable beau ideal, and although my hero worship must have been tiresome at times, he was always kind to me. My parents rented the coach house of his father's farm during the holidays, and living so close I would agonise over the procession of beautiful girls with shining hair and long slim legs I saw being loaded into Charles' green E-type and whisked off to sample who knew what forbidden delights. Often in the early hours, headlights would scythe across my ceiling and these would be abruptly doused, the engine's growl hushed as it passed the coach house. The car would glide, dark and silent, across the courtyard to its own back door. If I leaned right out of my window I sometimes caught a tantalizing glimpse of entwined figures swaying up the steps; heard whispers and muffled giggles. Then Charles and his girl would vanish indoors and, with a last despairing glance in my mirror, I would return to my chilly bed, praying without much hope for a miracle.

Then, as the years passed, the miracle happened. Quite suddenly, it seemed, Charles began to notice me, not as a substitute sister to be treated with friendly patronage ('If you'll mend this jacket I'll let you drive my car') but as a grown-up, desirable female. ('Doing anything tonight? How about a spot of dinner?') Nor did his proposals for fun stop at dinner. I was reluctant at first, well aware that my parents wouldn't approve, but when Charles said he'd loved me for years and all the other girls had been stopgaps while he waited for me to grow up, it seemed to make everything all right.

For three glorious, deliriously happy months I thought all my fantasies were destined to be fulfilled. Then Rowan asked us to make up a foursome on the river at Henley during the Regatta. She had everything organised: a boat, wine, strawberries and cream. The taste of strawberries still makes me feel sick, just as it did when Rowan gave Charles a considering look from sultry, expectant eyes, and said that as I was staying the night with my parents and she had to get back to London, perhaps Charles would drive her home?

And Charles, instead of saying he'd been invited to stay with me, looked back at her with the mesmerized stare of Galahad confronted with the Grail, and said Yes, he'd like to very much. Perhaps they should leave before the traffic got any worse.

So I was left with the disgruntled bearded poet who had brought Rowan down from London, plus the unattractive remains of the picnic, sitting dismally in a traffic jam on Henley bridge without a word to say to one another.

It was, up to that point, the bitterest moment of my life; rapidly succeeded by one far more bitter when three months later I watched Rowan, in a cloud of white tulle, float down the aisle of St Martin-in-the-Fields, veil thrown back to reveal her radiant face, the heirloom sapphire sparkling on her finger and Charles, lost to me for ever, on her arm.

Or her on his: oddly enough it never appeared to be that way round. She wanted him; she took him. I never felt that Charles had much say in the matter.

No one could deny that they made a handsome pair. I congratulated them, cried till I had no tears left, endured a bracing talk from my father (who didn't want his investment in Damask Designs wasted) and a sympathetic one from my mother (who turned out to know quite a bit about unrequited love herself) and decided that I would forget all about men and marriage and concentrate on my career.

It didn't work exactly as I planned, of course. Even in the rag trade there are men, and some of them are attractive, but I never made the mistake of losing my heart again. And my career blossomed. A slightly altered form of friendship with Rowan survived, probably because she didn't know and I didn't tell her how deep was the wound she had inflicted on me. She continued to buy my clothes in lavish quantities and recommend me to her friends: thanks to her, business boomed.

Sometimes I sensed she was puzzled by my unvarying refusal of invitations that might bring me face to face with Charles, but finally she stopped issuing them and the last hiccup in our relationship smoothed itself out.

I couldn't avoid hearing her talk about him: that would have been carrying self-denial altogether too far, and I hungered for news of him as a dog yearns for a bone. In the next nine years, as Rowan flitted in and out of our workrooms like a beautiful exotic butterfly, I learned of their visits to St Moritz and Monte Carlo, Royal Ascot, Cowes, the grouse moors of Perthshire and the banks of County Westmeath. The births of two adorable babies briefly curtailed Rowan's participation in these sporting delights, but Charles had taken to the rich man's life like a duck to water, and his annual merry-go-round of the international fun spots left him no time for more than the briefest of appearances in the Henschels' boardroom to which Rowan, in the first flush of wedded bliss, had caused him to be appointed.

Jet-setting is a strenuous occupation. I wasn't all that surprised when Charles resigned his commission in the Brigade of Guards. 'He simply hadn't time for all that soldiering, darling,' explained Rowan. 'They're sending his battalion to Ulster – I ask you!' Was there the tiniest hint of defensiveness in her voice? At the time I wasn't sure, but later I believed it was about then that the picture began to change. The rosy glow faded. Photographs appeared in the glossier magazines showing Rowan at charity balls, first nights . . . without Charles.

She became restless. Twice she moved house. Blonde streaks appeared in her dark hair: they weren't an improvement on Nature's handiwork. She grew demanding to the point of fussiness over her clothes and lost several pounds. Her slanting eyes began to remind me of a hunting lioness's: hungry, compelling, *driven*. She seemed to be searching for something that was always just out of reach. Poor Charles, I thought. Poor children. Rowan's threshold of boredom had never been high. I guessed she was tired of domesticity, looking for something new.

Then, last week, there'd been the telephone call.

Even before I picked up the receiver, cradling it against my shoulder with my mouth full of pins and the *toile* I was working on slipping to the floor, I was sure it was Rowan. My parents knew better than to ring when I was in the last stage of labour with a new Collection, and no one else had the number of my

Islington bolthole. Her voice in my ear was husky, urgent.

'Can I come round, darling? Are you busy?'

'Up to my eyes. Won't it keep?'

'Actually, no.'

'All right,' I said resignedly. The clean, uncluttered image I'd had in my head had begun to fade the moment the telephone rang, anyway. It was happening too often recently. Any interruption could destroy my concentration. I was haunted by the fear that I was losing my touch.

'I'll be with you in half an hour,' she said, and rang off.

I spent the time recognizing that inspiration had well and truly fled, clearing a corner of the cluttered work table, and brewing a pot of tea. I wasn't in the best of tempers when she arrived, and had a number of pithy remarks on the tip of my tongue about the delicacy of the artistic temperament and its need for peace and quiet. But when she announced that she wanted me to join her in a fortnight's skiing in the Alps – not in a month's time, not next week, but *tomorrow* – the power of speech temporarily deserted me.

'I've booked the car onto the overnight ferry. Southampton – Le Havre: it's much the most comfortable and it'll give us a flying start in the morning. It docks at seven,' she said, as if it was the most reasonable thing in the world to snatch me away from the show that would make or break my reputation, to satisfy her whim. It wasn't that she was insensitive, exactly. It was simply that, for Rowan, her own problems came first and other people's, if they existed at all, a very poor second. Though I'd known this ever since I met her, the sheer egocentricity of it took my breath away.

'Well? How about it?' She drummed impatient fingers on the table.

Useless to explain why I couldn't go, but that didn't stop me trying. One day the message might get through to her that most of the world's population had to work to eat.

I said, 'Did I forget to send you an invitation to my show, then?'

'No, I told Ginette to accept for me.' She looked puzzled. 'What about it?' Impatiently she prowled the studio, scrutinizing sketches, fingering materials. With difficulty I controlled my irritation. 'How can I possibly down tools and disappear on a fortnight's jaunt? My Collection's nowhere near finished. Some of the models are still on the drawing board. That, for instance.'

I pointed to a midnight-blue, off the shoulder confection which I had, in fact, designed with Rowan in mind.

She studied the sketch. 'Oh, that's nice. Rather my style, wouldn't you say? I think I'd like it better in green. A real emerald.'

I made a mental note to change the colour before having it made up; then she gave me another jolt by adding casually, 'The trouble is, darling, all these clothes are very much on the same lines as your last lot. You need fresh ideas: that's why a holiday now would be so good for you. I mean –' she hesitated a little ' – we don't want people to say you're in a rut.'

With unerring aim she had struck at my most vulnerable spot, voiced the secret fear that had given me sleepless nights ever since I went to work on this collection. For the first time it had seemed a labour. I'd told myself work was like that: ninety per cent perspiration to ten per cent inspiration, but deep down I'd known it wasn't true. What used to be my pleasure, my passion, had suddenly become a chore.

'Do they really look like that to you?'

It was difficult to disguise my dismay and Rowan picked it up at once.

'Don't take it the wrong way, darling. These are very good of their kind. No one else does a Romantic look that comes within a mile of yours. It's just that these – ' she waved a hand at the models that had cost me such sweat and blood ' – these aren't exactly modern, are they? More – well – nostalgic. À la recherche du temps perdu rather than Space Age.'

I knew exactly what she meant and she was spot on: that was the worst of it. At a stroke she had undermined my professional morale, shown me that the clothes I'd secretly hoped would be show-stoppers were no more than elaborations of ones I'd made earlier. More embroidery, more lavish use of lace and appliqué and sequins, leather and velvet trimmings, but the shape – the all-important line – remained stubbornly unaltered. There was nothing in this collection of mine to give the fashion journalists material for headlines: nothing to satisfy the public's lust for novelty. Rowan had called it nostalgic. My rivals would be less tactful. 'Dated' would be the kindest of their epithets.

'That's how everyone will see it,' I said, downcast. 'Old hat. Stale buns. Rehash of last season.'

'No, they won't. I'll see to that,' she said quickly.

'Rave reviews from your tame hacks don't count,' I said ungratefully. 'If the clothes aren't good enough to stand on their own, I'd better scrap them.'

'Such pride!' Her smile mocked me. 'Don't be an idiot, Catta. The clothes are all right – I've already told you so – but you do need a break. You look as if a wind would blow through you. You've been slaving away in this stuffy hole all winter. No wonder things are getting on top of you. Now.' She pushed me into a chair and shunted the tea tray in my direction. 'Do pour me a cup, I'm gasping. How are you fixed for ski clothes? We have to check in at the ferry before nine in the evening, so if you want to work tomorrow, I'll buy anything you need. I know what you like . . .'

I put my hands over my ears. 'Rowan – stop!'

'Stop what?'

'Planning. Pushing me around. I can't come with you.'

'But you'll enjoy it. You just admitted you were in a rut . . .'

'*You* said that,' I corrected. 'I said – and I mean it – that I'm far too busy even to think of leaving London. Why d'you want me, anyway? Why not one of your rich friends who hasn't got a living to earn?'

For a moment she stopped fiddling with the book of samples and looked at me directly. I noticed for the first time the blue smudges under her eyes, the tightly drawn skin. 'Because you're the only person I can trust,' she said quietly.

Oh, typical Rowan! I thought. Playing for effect. Hinting at high drama. Purest flattery, of course, but I couldn't help feeling a small glow.

'Why d'you have to trust anyone?'

She hesitated, and I could almost see the wheels spinning in her brain, choosing the best way to manoeuvre me where she wanted.

'It's Charles,' she said, and the little catch in her voice put me instantly on guard. 'We've had the most awful row. I've got to get away. Daddy was right all along. He doesn't love me: he only married me for my money.'

Laughter rose spontaneously in my throat, but I managed to turn it into a cough. Rowan took the state of her heart as seriously as a Frenchman takes the state of his liver. She'd never have forgiven me for laughing at it. But now she was launched on her big scene there was no need for me to do anything but listen and reflect what an actress Victorian melodrama had missed. Poor Charles! He couldn't have known what he was taking on. It must be exhausting to live at such high emotional intensity.

Out it all poured: the quarrel, the sulks, the insults and recriminations. Charles' extravagance – 'He feeds that woolly brute of his on rump steak, two pounds a day! I asked him what was wrong with dogmeat, and he said, 'What's the use of having money unless you spend it on the people you love?' No suggestion of spending it on me, of course. He forgot my birthday last week though I dropped hints a two-year-old could have picked up. And now he's gone and bought a ride-on mower, despite the fact that old Hoppy has the kiss of death on machinery and it's better for his arthritis to walk about the lawn instead of sitting on his ass massacring the gearbox.'

Like many rich people, Rowan had unexpected areas of economy. I didn't think Charles' extravagance sounded too hair-raising. 'Is that all?' I asked.

'*All!*' Rowan filled her lungs and was off on the in-breath as well as the out. Of course it wasn't all. Neglecting her, shouting at the children, never at home when she was, hopeless in bed.

This was more serious. The desire to laugh left me. Bed was surely an area in which Charles could be guaranteed to please the most demanding woman. In bed he was an artist, a virtuoso: handsome, virile, full of appetite. Not according to Rowan.

'AC–DC,' she said sombrely. 'He used to pretend, but now he doesn't even bother.'

'I don't believe it,' I said flatly. My mind flew back to the hotel bedroom where Charles had relieved me of my virginity. I could even remember the shape of the cracks in the ceiling. He had been so gentle, so reassuring. When I squeaked and protested he'd hugged me. 'Don't worry,' he'd said. 'Lots of girls don't like it at first. It gets better gradually.'

I'd been glad to hear that because I hadn't liked it at all.

Rowan looked curiously at me. 'What's the matter? Does it embarrass you to hear all this?'

'God, no,' I said hastily. 'I just don't believe it.'

'You'll believe it all right when you meet his latest – an awful little creep. My dear, such a pretty boy!' She flapped a hand, wrist bent. 'I call him Goldilocks. He looks as if he's crawled out from under a stone. His father's some millionaire who believes in the work ethic and won't give him a bean, so Goldie's always nagging at Charles, trying to get his hands on my money. When Charles tried to infiltrate him into the house I really let fly. I told him I wanted a divorce.'

'Oh, no!' I exclaimed involuntarily.

'Oh, yes.'

'What did he say?'

' "I'll see you in hell first." '

I thought she'd been watching too many B movies. It didn't sound at all the kind of thing Charles would say. As a child, I'd found it almost impossible to provoke him into quarrelling. He'd laugh and say he couldn't be bothered to get angry. Sensing my disbelief, Rowan hurried on, 'He said two could play at that game and I needn't imagine he'd leave Ivan and Lorna in my clutches. I wasn't fit to bring up children. There wasn't a judge in the country who'd give me custody when he heard of my goings-on.' Her voice rose indignantly. 'He called me an adulteress – a whore! I wish I'd been quick enough to get it on tape.'

'Is there – ' I asked delicately ' – any truth in his allegations?'

'Of course not.'

I was silent, thinking of pictures in glossies.

'Well, not much,' she amended after a pause. 'Good Lord! Does he expect me to sit at home knitting while he shacks up with Goldilocks? Not to mention blackening my name to *all* my friends.'

'You mean, there's another man?'

Her silence was answer enough. The picture became suddenly clearer. 'So you want to divorce Charles in order to marry someone else?'

'Yes, I do,' she said defiantly. 'You'd think if Charles was any sort of gentleman he'd push off instead of standing in my way. But he isn't. The swine won't even move out of my house. He says possession is nine points of the law and if I don't want to live with him I can move somewhere else. I don't want to move. It's *my* house.' Her outrage was almost funny.

I thought that Charles was behaving with sense and restraint. Rowan changed her mind as easily as she changed her clothes, and no doubt he believed that if he sat it out long enough she would tire of her new man and come back to him. It was certainly worth trying.

She was watching my expression closely. She said on a plaintive note, 'You see? You think I'm making it all up. You feel sorry for Charles, just like all the rest of them. You don't care a damn about me.'

'He's an old friend of mine, remember?'

She gave me a curious look. 'Was he your lover?'

Not even to Rowan would I admit that. 'More like a brother,' I said lightly. 'OK, forget the rights and wrongs for a minute and tell me why you want to drag me all the way to the Alps at the drop of a hat? Why don't you go alone?'

'Because if I did, Charles would immediately jump to the conclusion that I was going to meet . . . well, the man we were talking about. He'd probably have me followed.'

'Would he be right?'

Her laugh sounded forced. 'What's this – the Inquisition?'

'I can't help wondering why you're telling me all this. There must be some reason.'

She shrugged. 'All right, since you've more or less guessed, I might as well tell you. The thing is, this man I'm in love with lives out there, and I'm desperate to see him. Simple.'

'Without Charles knowing.'

'Yes. That's where you come in. I've told Charles that we're sharing a self-catering flat in Val du Loup, just the two of us.'

'You told him *before* asking me?'

She had the grace to look a little guilty. 'Well, yes. It just sort of slipped out before I realized what I was saying, and then, of course, I couldn't take it back.'

It was no use being angry, so I laughed instead. Rowan's face cleared magically. 'I knew you wouldn't mind. Charles thinks you're so marvellous – if I'd said I was going with anyone else he might have made a fuss. He's always telling me how clever you

27

are and what strength of character you've got, and how I ought to see more of you.'

'Oh?'

'I think he only does it to make me jealous. That's why I asked if you'd ever been lovers. Actually, I thought it was pretty unlikely.'

'Thanks,' I said dryly. 'So my role in this expedition would be to allay Charles' suspicions while you galloped off into the sunset with your new flame. Right? What if Charles guessed what you were up to and decided to come and see you?'

'He wouldn't,' she said promptly. 'Nothing in the world would make him miss Cheltenham when he's got a horse running. That's why I chose to go now. The worst he might do would be to ring up, and you could always say I was in bed with a sore throat or something.'

Or something.

I said slowly, 'Can you give me one good reason why I should drop my work and drive halfway across Europe to Val du . . . Val du what?'

'Val du Loup. Wolf Valley. Everyone's there this year for the Hollenberg Ski Championships.'

'Right. To Val du Loup, to tell lies on your behalf?'

She smiled. 'One reason? I can give you a dozen.'

'Go ahead.'

'Well, you're my friend, aren't you? I'd do the same for you.'

'The situation,' I said carefully, 'is not likely to arise.'

'Also, quite apart from being your friend, I must be one of your best customers. You wouldn't kill the golden goose.'

'Is that a threat?'

'Not if you do as I ask.'

I'd have given a lot, at that point, to flash my eyes and stamp my foot and tell her proudly to take her filthy money elsewhere, but that would have been cutting off my nose to spite my face. Deprived of Rowan's backing, I was painfully aware that Damask Designs might sink without trace.

'So you'll come?' she urged.

'I can't.'

'Listen, sweetie,' she said with unusual earnestness, 'it's for your own good. If you spend another ten days cooped up in this claustrophobic little box worrying about your damned collection, one of two things is going to happen. Either you'll ruin every one of your designs, or you'll go off your rocker. You say you haven't got time to finish the clothes. *I* say you've got far too much time. Your models are brilliant until you begin to fuss and fiddle with them – then they lose their flair and end up looking like secondhand ready-to-wear rip-offs. The best things you've ever done have been flung together at top speed – admit it.'

There was a lot in what she said. Encouraged by my silence she went on, 'A holiday now will give you a whole new perspective. You'll come back full of beans, fizzing with ideas to make the buyers sit up.'

Put like that, the idea was seductive. I wavered. Then she spoilt it by saying, 'You needn't worry about Paul kicking up a fuss. I'll fix him.'

'Don't bother.'

'But he'll – '

'You're out of date. Mr Lomax and I have agreed to go our separate ways,' I said with a certain gloomy satisfaction.

'But *why?*'

'These things happen.' There was really no need to tell her Paul had complained that now he knew what it was like to sleep with an Oxfam ad.

Rowan pretended to be shocked. 'Already! Really, darling, I can't keep pace with your love life. Men may come and men may go . . . Aren't you lucky to have me going on for ever?'

'At least I don't marry my men and then pester my friends to get me out of the mess,' I said unkindly.

She gave me a sidelong glance. 'There you are: a perfect example of why I need you. If anyone else said that I'd see red.'

I laughed. 'What are you seeing now?'

'Palest, *palest* pink.'

For the first time my curiosity stirred. 'Tell me about your new man. Who is he?'

She closed her eyes with a look of exaggerated bliss. 'He's – he's wonderful. How can I describe him? He's the only man in the world for me.'

I felt a sharp pang – for myself as well as Charles. 'Pity you didn't discover that sooner.'

'I know,' she said dreamily. 'I realised we were made for one another the moment I set eyes on him. I thought, "This is *it*. This is the man I've been waiting for all my life." And – would you believe it? – he felt *exactly* the same!'

'Incredible!'

She opened her eyes. 'You may think it's corny – '

'I do.'

'But for the first time *ever* I feel wanted. He needs me as much as I need him. We belong together like – '

'Bacon and eggs,' I suggested. I couldn't take much more of this. 'Milk and honey. Arsenic and old lace. All right, I get the picture. Love's Young Dream. And what does he do for a living?'

She hesitated. 'Well, not exactly for a living, but he paints.'

'Houses or pictures?'

'Pictures, of course.'

'Have I heard of him?'

'*Nobody*'s heard of him – yet. But they will. I'm going to organize an exhibition for him this summer. I'll take all the business worries off his shoulders so that he's free to express himself in the way he wants to.'

Who was I to scoff? She'd done the same for me, after all.

She said excitedly, 'He'll be famous. He's got a – a kind of vision. He sees things differently.'

'Another Picasso?'

'I was going to say Van Gogh. Oh, Catta, you will come, won't you? I don't think I can survive another whole week without seeing him.'

'No way,' I said.

Two days later we were driving across France in her silver Mercedes.

Chapter Three

Despite my misgivings, the journey had been fun. Rowan was a fast competent driver, and on the poplar-lined autoroutes the miles melted behind us. Once I'd agreed to come, her spirits soared. She believed in doing herself well, and as the first three-starred meal ended in the first *fine*, I found myself relaxing and beginning to share her enjoyment. For the first time for many weeks the spectre of my incomplete, uninspired collection retreated to the back of my mind while pleasanter preoccupations such as whether to choose *Huitres tièdes au sabayon de citron vert* or *Mousseline de brochet et homard* claimed the front of it.

At the Hotel de la Tour in Macon, she'd been greeted as an old friend, and we shared an excellent bottle of Nuits St Georges, basking in spring sunshine by the ancient ivy-covered tower. As the mountains closed in and the day darkened, we arrived in Albertville in the Alpine foothills and here, too, the staff of the family hotel gave her a warm welcome.

'But you are late this year, *Madame!*' exclaimed the aproned proprietor, beaming all over his face. 'We had begun to fear you could not honour us with a visit.'

They gave us the best bedroom in the hotel, and over a dinner of fresh trout and mountain lamb we gossiped and giggled till nearly midnight, but still she refused to give me any further clues to the identity of the man she was going to meet.

'It's better if you don't know,' she said firmly. 'You'll sound more convincing if you have to cover up for me.'

'Don't you trust me?'

'Of course I do. But you know how easy it is to let things slip out, and until my divorce is in the bag I've got to be frightfully careful. I can't risk the judge getting the wrong impression.'

She wouldn't be budged from this point of view, so I'd left the subject alone, confident that sooner or later Rowan – herself the one who found secrets hard to keep – would let something slip.

'When will you join him?' I asked instead.

'Oh . . . it depends. As soon as he's free.'

'*Free*? You mean he's married too?'

She smiled. 'Not exactly.'

I guessed it would be at least a week before her plan was put into operation, but I was wrong.

We arrived in Val du Loup after a twisting, engine-straining ascent of continuous hairpin bends, at noon on a perfect blue, white and gold Alpine day. The air stung the skin like Cologne, the snowy slopes beckoned.

Rowan parked the Mercedes among a couple of hundred snow-covered humps looking like huge Danish pastries, and a porter carried our bags fifty yards to the enormous central lift that whisked us straight from car-park level to the heart of the ski-village.

Towering apartment blocks like slabs of chocolate set on end had been built round a central *place* which was rather too carefully symmetrical to resemble a genuine village square. There were arcaded shops selling and hiring out ski gear at prices that made me blink, terraces for sunbathing where the deck-chairs shrieked *Bergasol*, and cafés where patient St Bernard dogs waited to be photographed with toddlers' arms clasped round their necks. A complex network of pylons and overhead cables completed the architectural eyesore. A technological miracle Val du Loup might be, but it certainly wasn't beautiful.

A few hundred yards away, lower down the hillside, the red-tiled barns and hugger-mugger ramshackle buildings of the old Alpine village could be seen: wooden chalets with logs stacked to window level, yellow-stained snow below gently-steaming middens, a blue haze of wood smoke. Though it was probably smelly and cramped and primitive, it was easier on the eye than the space age monstrosity next door.

Between the two worlds, old and new, a fairytale turreted castle rose from the snow.

'That belongs to Prince Hollenberg – the Principality that Floats on Schnapps,' said Rowan, following my glance. 'He's a marvellous publicist. He's really put this place on the map since he started to sponsor the Ski Championships. Actually he's a great dear as well. Shall I ask the Princess to invite you to her

Masked Ball? You'd enjoy it and it could be good for business. I've brought the Cleopatra dress you made me, wig, head-dress and all. Most people think it's enough to put on silly little jewelled masks that don't hide a *thing*. It takes all the fun out of guessing who's who.'

At least no one could accuse Rowan of that. She'd taken great trouble over her costume and it had cost a mint, but we were both pleased with the result.

'Let me think it over,' I said.

The apartment Rowan had rented had a living room overlooking the nursery slopes and a double bedroom whose verandah provided an excellent view of the central square. By dodging from one window to another it was possible to check exactly which of the lower ski-lifts were operating without setting foot outside. On this warm afternoon the snow of the bottom slopes had a slushy look, though higher up the pistes retained the pure white gloss of Royal icing.

Rowan poked around the apartment, opening drawers and cupboards. 'They certainly believe in cramming people in,' she commented. 'This place is meant to sleep *four*. There wouldn't be room to swing a cat! Still, it'll do for two. If I take the double bed, it gives you the choice of sleeping outside the bathroom or in the living room.' She began to pull armfuls of clothes from her handsome leather suitcase and throw them on the bed.

'Thanks,' I said dryly, reflecting that neither her packing habits nor her knack of appropriating the lion's share of available space had changed since we first met.

I didn't care where I slept. The pull of the snowy slopes was too strong to waste another moment indoors.

'Come on,' I urged, 'let's get going. We can unpack and sort things out later.'

To my surprise, she shook her head. 'You go on and explore, darling. I'm going to have a sleep – all that driving!'

It was true that she'd done most of it. Although I'd offered to take the wheel she had only allowed me to spell her for a couple of hours on the autoroute. 'Off you go,' she said, smiling. 'Let's meet back here around five. You'll be pooped by then. It always takes a few days to get fit.'

33

An hour later I'd succeeded in equipping myself with a fourteen-day ski pass entitling me to travel on all *monteurs mécaniques*, or lifts, in this valley and its neighbour, and hired boots and skis from the busy shop next to the ski-school.

'*Expert? Débutante?*' enquired the friendly boy behind the counter. He had a complexion the colour and texture of a gingernut, and hair cropped so brutally short that his scalp was sunburnt through the stubble.

'*Moyenne*,' I said modestly. 'Medium length, please.'

He chose me a pair of sleek, fibreglass Head skis that reached just to the tip of my nose, adjusted the bindings to fit my chosen Laser boots with deft, economical movements, and presented them across the counter with a flourish.

'*Voila, mademoiselle!* If in a few days you wish to exchange them for longer ones, there will be no problem. Enjoy your holiday!'

I thanked him, left my passport at the cash desk as a hostage, and clumped out into the snow, skis balanced awkwardly over my shoulder, sticks dangling, boots pressing painfully against shinbones unaccustomed to their rigidity and weight. I knew that in a couple of days' time they would seem the most normal of footgear, but for the first hundred yards or so I was as ungainly as a penguin out of water.

The moment I put the skis on, though, all reservations about the size and shape of the modern ski-boot vanished. Attached to the skis, they held my feet in a comforting vicelike grip, hugging my shins halfway up to the knee and forcing my legs to bend at the correct angle. It gave one confidence to know that in the event of an awkward fall, the bindings would release automatically, being precisely adjusted to snap just before the human shinbone did; and that the built-in brakes would spring free to stop the ski from continuing its downward path like an unguided missile.

It was all of five years since I'd last skied, and I wondered how much I'd forgotten, but physical memory came back with a rush as soon as skis and boots were united. There was nothing – simply *nothing* – to beat the sensation of swooping downhill over smooth hardpacked snow, skis hissing, sun tingling on my forehead and chin, zigzagging through the quilted stretches known, oddly, as moguls – crouching to lessen wind resistance on long straight *Schusses*. At least, that's what I thought until the thunderbolt struck me.

It was during my first descent of La Sorcière. The great jagged rampart overshadowing Val du Loup had – I discovered from the excellent tourist map – three main peaks: La Grande Aiguille, with its needle point; Col du Diamant – a broken square sparkling in the sun – and La Sorcière, a magnificent chain of rocky ledges rising to a crenellated witch's tower.

Behind each peak stretched a maze of small steep valleys, each linked to its neighbours by a system of interconnecting lifts. It was a piste-basher's paradise. One could ski all day without repeating the same run.

I decided to start at the right-hand end of the rampart and work my way across from La Sorcière to La Grande Aiguille, taking in the Col du Diamant en route. That way I'd soon get to know the layout. I pushed on to the big cable-car packed with laughing, chattering skiers, bodies brilliant as hummingbirds in stretched and padded clothes, faces clownishly grotesque with white, goggle-marked eyes and smeary mouths. Barrier cream does little for anyone's looks.

When the cable-car reached its terminus in a long high shed full of clanking wheels and rattling drums, I got out and skied down to join the much smaller queue for the three-seater chair-lift that ascended to the very summit of La Sorcière.

The view was breathtaking, provided you kept your eyes well away from the ugly conglomeration of buildings at the foot of the valley – the only blot on a perfect landscape. In fact, I was so busy staring around that I nearly missed my turn on the lift. You had to be quite nippy about shuffling into position as the three-seater swung round its drum, and it could easily catch you a numbing blow behind the knees unless you broke its force with a cushioning hand.

'*Attention, mademoiselle!*' piped a warning treble, and I came back to earth just in time to seize the seat and be whisked aloft, skis dangling, towards the high peak.

One of my companions pulled forward the safety bar; the other gently disentangled his ski-sticks from mine, and we all grinned and settled down to enjoy the ride.

Forced into sudden shoulder-to-shoulder intimacy with total

strangers, with the strange sense of isolation which being suspended high above the snow gives one, national behaviour usually runs true to type. The English observe total silence until the end of the lift comes in sight, when they may venture a comment on the weather. The French do their best to impress on any foreigner that he is an interloper and a second-class citizen to boot by chatting to one another across him, and rebuffing in a painful travesty of his own language any attempt he may make to join the conversation. Germans, like the English, keep the exchange of views to a minimum and Americans embark on an exciting monologue about their own skiing exploits which they carry on regardless of whether their listeners can understand or not.

I glanced briefly at my two companions and then took a surprised longer look. I might have been seeing double. Two boys in brilliant green anoraks, their denim jeans reinforced by long waterproof gaiters. Beneath identical protective helmets two pairs of bright dark eyes in smooth brown faces surveyed me with lively curiosity. I judged them to be about eleven years old.

'Are you twins?' I said, almost without meaning to, and they laughed delightedly.

'*Ça se voit!* Pretty obvious, isn't it?'

It was indeed. No question of breaking the ice, either: they ignored all the rules and started to fire questions at me like a double-barrelled machine gun. Was this my first visit to Val du Loup? Did I like it? Where did I live? Was I a teacher? Ah, a *couturière* – they understood. Like Dior, perhaps? Courrèges?

Modestly I disclaimed Dior status, and they said comfortingly that it took time to get established, evidently. One day I would doubtless be as famous as Dior.

It was my turn for a question. 'Do you go to ski-school?' I asked at random.

They looked down identical freckled noses. 'Competition,' the right-hand twin murmured, with a precise imitation of my own professional modesty. I looked at their crash helmets with new respect. Olympics '88? I wondered.

They gave simultaneous squeaks of excitement and pointed ahead. '*Régardez, mademoiselle! Le Delta va voler!*'

I followed their pointing fingers. On a ledge just below the summit, a large yellow triangle fluttered in the wind, and as we

36

approached from beneath, I realized that this was a hang-glider about to be launched. People were pouring out of the summit restaurant to watch: there were several men holding ropes against which the triangular wing tugged impatiently.

I looked at the drop below it, the jagged spine of rocks reaching down to the valley, and my stomach turned over. 'It's impossible!' I exclaimed. 'They must be mad.'

The anchormen stepped back, the absurdly fragile contraption moved rapidly downhill for fifty yards and lifted into the air. Human bodies hung suspended below the wing like the legs of a cranefly. The boys whooped with delight.

I shut my eyes, feeling sick.

Claude, the left-hand twin, nudged me and grinned. 'Would you like to do that?'

'I'd die of fright. Would you?'

Very much, they said, looking mournful. Unhappily the Englishman was not permitted to take children in the Deltas. It was a question of insurance. It was also most unfair. They had spoken with him about it, pointing out that since they were lighter than adults it would be less dangerous to take them, but neither their father nor *l'Anglais* would agree.

Parent Power Rules OK, I thought. 'And your mother?'

'Mothers worry too much,' said Claude sagely. 'One must not recount everything to them.'

'You say that's an Englishman?' I pointed to the yellow speck vanishing below us. The twins nodded, eager to tell all they knew.

It appeared that in the days before the ski resort was developed, an Englishman had bought the little chalet known as the Eagle's Nest: 'for his health, you understand? One of his lungs was destroyed in the war. He needed to breathe mountain air. When Monsieur Kronsky decided to build his apartments at Val du Loup and develop the valley, he tried to buy the Eagle's Nest, but the Englishman refused to sell it. Monsieur Kronsky offered *des milliards de francs* – much more than the house was worth, but each bid was turned down. The Englishman did not want to sell his home.'

'So he started hang-gliding?' I suggested.

Two heads were shaken. No, the *pauvre type* had died. It was his sons who began the hang-gliding enterprise, only last year.

It was having *un succès fou* – everyone wanted to try it. This didn't please M. Kronsky, apparently. He had done his best to get the council to ban the sport, saying it would draw custom away from the ski-school.

'And does it?' I asked.

They laughed. *'Au contraire.'* In the estimation of their father, added the right-hand twin, Jean-Louis, the opening of the hang-gliding centre had attracted more visitors than ever to the resort, and therefore actually improved attendance at the ski-school. If anyone knew the truth of such matters, it was their papa.

I asked why.

'He is the chief *moniteur* – the senior instructor. He knows everything that happens in Val du Loup – even better than M. Kronsky,' said Claude proudly.

The top of the ski-lift was in sight. Jean-Louis lifted the safety-bar, and we shuffled forward on our behinds ready to ground our skis the second we arrived.

'What will you be when you grow up?' I couldn't resist asking.

'Pilote d'avion!' they declared with one voice. 'Happy skiing, *mademoiselle.'* They vanished down the slope like a couple of green tracer bullets.

I consulted the signboard and my map and chose a run code-named *Gentian*. A Blue run – Fairly Easy. It was nice to be alone: if Rowan had been with me she would have scorned anything less than the more demanding Red. The sun shone, the snow sparkled. There was no need to hurry, no need to show off to anyone, I thought happily, and set off downhill. The upper stretch of *Gentian*, well marked with blue discs, was a long, gentle, but rather narrow piste, with a rock face on one side and a precipitous drop on the other. In summer it might well have turned out to be a cart track. I took it slowly, stopping now and again to consult the map where other runs forked or crossed the *Gentian*. Despite the beautiful weather there were few skiers about, and I revelled in the mountain silence.

It is a sad fact about skiing that to do it well you need the adrenalin fizzing. The moment you relax things are apt to go wrong. As I mooched along the *Gentian*, turning at my leisure, admiring the view with my mind, I must admit, in neutral,

38

there was a sudden hiss behind me and a young woman whose sugar-pink one-piece ski-suit seemed moulded to her slender body, her long blonde hair caught back in a ballerina's ponytail, flashed past between me and the rock wall. Taken by surprise, I turned sharply outwards, and was instantly caught up in a swarm of small dragonflies following her – a dozen or more children hot on one another's heels, stick-like legs bent, arms waving, faces intent, laughing and squealing as they zoomed after their *monitrice* in a brilliantly coloured snake.

Better wait till they've gone, I thought, and made a parallel turn to halt on the outer edge of the track. A voice yelled a warning – too late. Before I could even glance back, the breath was knocked out of me with ferocious force as someone crashed into me from behind. Skis appeared on either side of mine; arms caught me just before I spun forward over the edge, and for a terrifying moment we shot forward locked together, towards what seemed certain death.

I don't know if I actually blacked out: certainly I couldn't speak or breathe. I have no recollection of being hauled back onto the piste, but when I gathered my wits again I was sitting in the snow a hundred yards lower down, minus both skis, which my attacker was leaping back uphill to retrieve. I have never seen anyone climb so fast.

He scooped the first one from its resting place against the rock wall, tucked it under his arm and scrabbled beneath the snow for the other, which had embedded itself below the crust. All his movements were rapid and economical; he carried them down to me and stuck them in the snow with a flourish.

'*Ça va, mademoiselle?*' he enquired. 'Are you all right?' He wore shiny reflecting goggles which obscured much of his face, but his mouth was visible and to my fury it was laughing.

Vainly I tried to draw breath into my lungs to tell him exactly what I thought of him. If he'd been in my place it wouldn't seem so damned funny. My mouth opened and shut like a stranded fish, but no sound came out of it.

'*Allez!* On your feet!' he said good-humouredly, bending down to pull me upright. In the brown face his teeth looked very white, very even, and perfectly infuriating.

'*Salaud!*' I managed to hiss, and he drew back as if a snake had struck at him. The grin vanished abruptly.

'People like you should be equipped with brake lights, *mademoiselle*,' he remarked with maddening composure. 'What happened was entirely your own fault.'

'People like you should be banned from the piste,' I snapped back. 'Crazy speed-merchants who don't look where they're going . . .' As usual in moments of stress, my French deserted me.

'I beg your pardon?' he said politely, *'Je m'excuse de vous avoir dérangé.'* Though his mouth no longer smiled, I sensed that behind the shiny goggles his eyes were still laughing at me.

'You're the one who's deranged, mate,' I muttered in English. 'Only a madman would ski like that, coming down behind me without warning.'

For some reason this seemed to amuse him. Then a little sob attracted his attention. A couple of hundred feet below, at the bottom of a steep series of moguls, the sugar-pink instructor was reassembling her snake of children, waiting for those who had fallen to pick themselves up and join her. But one very small girl in a bright red ski-suit lay upside down in a drift quite near the top of the slope, kicking valiantly as she tried to disentangle skis and sticks from the snow. She must have been just out of sight of Sugar Pink, who started off downhill again at the head of her snake, apparently unaware that the back-marker was missing.

'Attendez, Caroline!' shouted my attacker. 'Wait, you're scattering your brood all over the slopes.'

Sugar Pink continued on her way, oblivious, and he cursed softly. With a couple of swift swoops he reached the sobbing child and pulled her out of the drift. *'Allez, mignonne,'* I heard him scold. 'Come on, poppet, big girls like you mustn't cry. What's the matter? Are you hurt?'

'They've gone. I'll never catch them up now,' she said despairingly, and he laughed.

'Oh, yes, you will. You and I will get to the bottom long before they do. Give me your sticks – there. *En avant!'*

He put his skis either side of the little girl's, holding her between his knees, and set off downhill in a series of lightning turns that brought my heart to my mouth. The child's shrill laughter floated back to me.

'Madman!' I said again, but with less conviction.

The sun had vanished. The deserted hillside looked bleak. I shivered, suddenly cold and stiff and tired. I decided to scrap my last run and go back to the apartment. I could hardly wait to show Rowan my bruises.

'Stop it!' she said the moment I walked into the living room.

Puzzled, I stared at her. She was dressed to kill in a clinging silver lamé catsuit, with huge knee-length moonboots in simulated mink which emphasized the slenderness of the thighs above them. Fat glossy curls, newly-washed, bounced on her shoulders, and her nails glowed like rubies. Evidently body maintenance had occupied her afternoon.

'Stop what?' I asked.

'Stop worrying about your wretched clothes. I brought you here for a change of scene, remember? I don't want you glooming about worrying over the same old things.'

For a moment I couldn't think what on earth she was talking about. Then I focused and laughed. 'To tell you the truth, I haven't given my collection a single thought all day long. What an admission!'

'Then why the look?'

'What look?'

'Oh, you know! Remote, abstracted, mind on higher things. It's how you always look when you're trying to work something out.'

I was surprised and rather touched by her concern. 'My mind's all right,' I assured her. 'It's my body that's taken a pounding. I feel as if a dozen elephants have been dancing on my ribcage.'

'My God! Why?'

I told her about my great fall, and she was properly indignant. 'People like that are an absolute menace! They've no business to ski at all. How typically French! To knock you over and then laugh! If it had been me, I'd have blown him sky high. Half these people haven't the first idea how to control their skis.'

'It wasn't so much that he couldn't ski. Actually, he looked rather good.'

'Then he can't have been looking where he was going. It boils down to the same thing,' she said. 'Let's see the damage.'

We inspected my bruises, which were disappointing. 'Give them a day or two,' said Rowan. 'They'll show up better when the greens and yellows develop. The trouble is that your skin's not pale enough for really *spectacular* bruises. Never mind: I've got some marvellous stuff to put in your bath. In ten minutes' time you won't feel a thing. Shall I turn it on for you? I'm just going to ring Daddy in Geneva to let him know I've arrived. He may want me to drive over and see him: he hasn't been at all well lately. You have a bath and change, then we'll find something to eat and see what the nightlife's like this year.'

My hopes of an early night faded.

'All right.' I went into the bathroom. Through the noise of running water I heard Rowan's voice rising and falling on the telephone, but it didn't sound to me as if she was speaking to her father.

In the matter of eating-places, Rowan proved hard to please that first evening. We tried the bar opposite, all dark beams and pewter mugs, but that was no good. 'I've tasted better daiquiris in darkest Surrey,' she said contemptuously after one sip and pushed the drink away. She stared round the crowded tables and got down from her stool. 'Come on, let's go.'

We went out into the snowy square.

'What about the Troika?' I suggested, drawn by the appetizing whiff of grilled cheese wafting from the doorway. I was hungry.

'Instant typhoid,' she said, hustling me past. 'I know what – we'll go to the Laughing Yeti. I remember it was good last year.'

But no sooner had we elbowed our way through the crowd at the bar and actually found an unoccupied table for two than she changed her mind again.

'Too noisy. That's the trouble with these places. You've got to find them *before* they become fashionable. Come on.'

'Rowan, I'm starving,' I protested. 'Surely this isn't too bad?'

'It'll take a month of Sundays to get served.'

'No – look. The waiter's just coming.'

Too late. She was already on her way to the door and the waiter shrugged and turned to another table. I hurried after her, hunger making me irritable.

'I'm damned well going to eat in the next place, no matter what it's like. After all, we can always . . .'

Rowan wasn't listening. She had pushed open the door of yet another little eating-place, the Phoenix Bar, and stood scanning the tables, oblivious of the cold air pouring in on other diners. It occurred to me that she might be searching for someone.

I remained in the doorway, sniffing the mouthwatering aromas of grilled meat and garlicky sauces, and watched her make a tour of the room, threading her way between the tightly-packed tables. It hardly seemed worth my while to follow. Despite my ultimatum – perhaps because of it – she would probably decide this wouldn't do either.

I became aware of watching eyes. I looked round and met the assessing gaze of a man sitting at the corner table, half-concealed by a pillar and the opening door. He was in his early thirties, I judged; squarely, even stockily built, with the sort of olive complexion that tans in two minutes flat and the bright, narrow dark eyes that often go with it. His thick brown hair was cut short and brushed straight back, and his lips had the amused, slightly cynical twist that sits so naturally on French mouths.

He wasn't alone. Beside him was perched a slim, small-boned blonde with a pointed, elfin face. Her straight shoulder-length hair was parted dead centre and swung forward to frame her features. She wore a dark dress with a demure white Puritan collar, which contrasted oddly with her slanted eyes and wide, reckless mouth. She leaned forward to speak earnestly to the other man at the table, of whom I could see little but fair hair curling over a red roll-collar, and hunched shoulders.

As my eyes met those of the brown-haired man I felt a kind of shock, and all my bruises began to ache again.

He smiled, showing very white, very even teeth. Then he pushed back his chair and stood up. 'Did you get your brake lights fixed?' he asked.

'You're English!' I exclaimed in some indignation.

He ducked his head in acknowledgment, half-bow, half-nod. 'Right. You know, I owe you an apology. Will you have a glass of wine with me to even the score?'

He *looked* French: that was what had misled me. The bright eyes and dark complexion definitely looked foreign. Not hand-

43

some nor – judging by performance to date – particularly reliable. All the same, a glass of wine was a glass of wine, and it would have been churlish to refuse such an olive branch. Anything was better than standing in a doorway waiting for Rowan to make up her mind where to eat. The blonde girl moved to the other side of the pillar to make room for me, and I smiled and thanked them and sat down.

'I should have known my sins would find me out,' he said, pouring wine for me. 'My name's Richard Labouchere. This is Gina van Lawick – ' the blonde girl gave me a brief nod ' – and my brother Robin. We live up at the Eagle's Nest, above the village.'

'I'm Catherine Chiltern.' I looked at them with new interest. So these were the Englishmen the twins had spoken of: perhaps it was Richard himself I'd seen dangling from the hang-glider? No, I thought. It couldn't have been, because he'd knocked me flying only minutes later. More likely he'd been hurrying down to see the glider land and collect the bits.

I turned to Robin, who sat at the end of the table. He was younger than his brother and much slighter: lean and rangy with the fine-drawn look of a greyhound. He had fair, floppy hair parted on the side, an angular face with a long narrow jaw and hollows under the cheekbones, and his movements were quick and nervous, almost irritable. He was fiddling with a fork, digging patterns in the tablecloth; I couldn't tell why, but I felt an immediate desire to put him at ease and draw him into the conversation.

'Was it you I saw flying a hang-glider over the valley this afternoon?' I asked; and when, after a moment, he didn't respond, I went on, 'The boys who were with me on the ski-lift told me the hang-gliders belonged to some Englishmen. I watched the takeoff. It looked terrifying.'

'Not really,' he muttered, glancing at me for a second, then back at the tablecloth. It was difficult to tell if the curt answer was due to shyness or deliberate rudeness: whichever it was, I felt rebuffed.

To cover the awkward moment I picked up my glass. 'Well, here's to my brake lights!' I said, and Richard laughed.

'I'll drink to that. Never stop in the middle of the piste: there might be a lunatic behind you!'

I took a reviving swig, and at that moment Rowan spoke just behind me.

'Ah, there you are, Catta. I thought I'd lost you.'

The effect on my companions was startling. Their heads jerked up to stare at her, and Gina gave a suppressed gasp. For a moment no one spoke.

Rowan surveyed the table, then her mouth curved in a smile I knew too well: a smile that meant mischief.

'Well, well! Look who's here! I didn't expect to find *you* on holiday, Gina. Doesn't my father require your services any longer? I suppose that's a good thing.'

'I'm working for Richard now,' said Gina.

'I see. Mind if I join the party?' Without waiting for permission she pulled an empty chair from a neighbouring table and inserted it on the corner between Gina and Robin.

It was easy to see that Gina wasn't pleased with this arrangement, and equally clear that Rowan didn't intend her to be. They looked at one another sideways, like hostile cats, and I wondered whose claws would first be unsheathed.

Richard spoke quickly as if he, too, sensed their antagonism.

'You're not the only one who's surprised, Rowan. I was told you couldn't get here before the Finals. Does your father know you've arrived? I spoke to him this afternoon and he didn't mention it.'

'Oh, I don't tell Daddy everything,' said Rowan. 'It would only worry him if I said I was coming and then got delayed for some reason. Actually you're right. This was a last-minute decision. My original idea was to come later, but then Catta persuaded me to bring the date forward, so I managed to alter my plans.'

I caught my breath at the casual falsification, and as if warning me not to contradict her, she turned towards me and rattled on, 'Richard's my father's lawyer, you see, so he likes to keep a check on my movements.' Her eyebrows rose questioningly. 'I'd no idea *you* knew him . . .?'

I glanced at Richard, whose eyes glinted with amusement.

'We don't really know each other. Not well, I mean.'

'We happened to bump into one another on the ski slopes,' he corroborated gravely.

Rowan looked blank. 'Bump?'

'Literally.'

Her mouth opened a little; then as she realized what I meant she threw back her head and laughed exaggeratedly. 'Oh, *no!* You don't mean to tell me that *Richard*'s the speed-merchant who knocked you down this afternoon? The one who couldn't control his skis? It's *too* funny. Richard, you'll never live this down.'

'Not if you have anything to do with it,' he said dryly.

'People will die of laughter!'

I thought she was overdoing it. 'It's not that funny – ' I began, but she cut me short.

'Oh, it is, it is! I'll tell you why. You see, Richard's a brilliant skier. He's one of Europe's leading exponents of *le ski artistique* – otherwise known as "hot-dogging".'

She saw my bafflement and added impatiently, 'You must have seen films of it: skiing backwards and turning somersaults and spinning round like a demented grasshopper. It looks like skating – on skis. It's very big in the States . . . wasn't that where you acquired your famous technique, Richard?'

'Such as it is,' he agreed pleasantly enough, though I sensed an underlying grittiness. There was a silence.

Then Gina leaned forward and said in her high, slightly drawling voice, 'Where's Charles, Rocky? Didn't you include him in this trip? Don't tell me you left him behind to look after the children while you're enjoying yourself?'

Her tone suggested she knew very well that Charles hadn't come.

'Oh, he was far too busy, said Rowan lightly. 'His horse is running at Cheltenham, so of course that takes priority over skiing.'

Gina's laugh tinkled artificially. 'Poor Rocky – what a shame! It can't be much fun playing second fiddle to a horse. I'm surprised you put up with it. So you came all on your little lonesome? Won't you find that terribly boring?'

'Don't worry, Catta and I will amuse ourselves somehow,' said Rowan with dangerous sweetness, and I wished that Gina had more sense than to cross swords with her. Rowan hated the nickname the gossip writers had wished on her, and Gina's deliberate use of it indicated that she meant to be offensive.

For Rowan, the means of punishing her was close at hand. I

saw her big slanted eyes fasten on Robin, who had stopped digging at the tablecloth and was watching her and Gina with an expression I found hard to read. Alarm? Anticipation? Perhaps a bit of both. Rowan switched on her electric smile, and he blinked just as if a searchlight had dazzled him.

'Tell me all the news, Robin,' she said, putting her hand on his arm with a pretty, appealing gesture. 'I feel quite out of touch. I haven't had a chance to read a paper for two days. How's the racing going? Are you still favourite for the Men's Downhill?'

'Don't!' he protested. He stared at her hand with the big solitaire diamond lying on his sleeve as if he couldn't think what it was or how it had appeared there. I thought for a moment he was going to shake it off.

'Do tell me.'

'I – I'd rather not talk about it,' he muttered.

'Don't be silly!' Her smile robbed the words of any sting. 'You're going to win it – you've got to. I've had the most enormous bet on you, and I absolutely forbid you to let me down!'

'Oh, *Rowan!*' he said uncomfortably.

'Why d'you suppose I've come out here a whole week early?' she went on with her own special brand of teasing ruthlessness. 'To see you, of course. To watch you win and be first in the queue for your autograph. Just think of it: you'll be the only Englishman who's ever won the Hollenberg Trophy, and we'll all be proud to know you.'

Robin's jaw tightened, and I waited for him to snap out some curt retort to her foolishness, but he didn't. Instead his mouth gave an uncertain twitch that was first cousin to a smile.

'You make it sound so easy,' he said.

'It's what's going to happen,' said Rowan confidently. 'I'd never risk my money on anything that wasn't a certainty. I never back horses – far too chancy – but I'm backing you.'

This time Robin really did smile. Fascinated, I watched as Rowan settled down to enslave him, just as she felt compelled to enslave any male between nine and ninety who showed the least sign of indifference to her charm. Or the least sign of belonging to some other woman. In this case, I could see that Gina's smouldering presence added spice to the conquest.

My attention was divided, since Richard, on the other side of the pillar, couldn't take part in the conversation the far end of the table and was therefore obliged to entertain me. He was a good talker, but must have found me poor company as I answered at random while straining my ears to catch what Rowan was saying to Robin. I could tell she was behaving outrageously. She flirted and teased, flattered and provoked, made wild statements and hung on his words when he corrected her. Anyone with half an eye could see that the whole performance was aimed at annoying Gina; blatant though it seemed to me, I had to admit that it worked wonders with Robin.

His angular face lost its look of sullen introspection and became animated, almost handsome. He stopped fiddling with the cutlery and glaring at the tablecloth; by degrees his answers to Rowan's questions became longer and longer until he was doing most of the talking.

I became aware that Richard had asked a question and was waiting for an answer; I wrenched my attention back to him.

'Sorry. What did you say?'

'I wondered how long you'd known Rowan?'

'Oh ages. We were friends before she married.'

'You know Charles, of course.'

It was a statement, not a question. I nodded as unconcernedly as I could, trying to ignore the little stab of pain I felt when he was mentioned.

'Have you seen him recently?'

'No, not for some time. I've been busy . . .' No need to tell this stranger that I'd avoided meeting Charles since his wedding day; I could just imagine how the lively, inquisitive mind behind those lively, inquisitive eyes would interpret such an admission. For a moment I feared he was going to pursue the subject; then to my relief he began instead to tell me about the Hollenberg Championships, and assess his brother's chances in the gruelling speed contest, the Men's Downhill. The draw was a crucial factor. Robin preferred to make his run early, without the added pressure of knowing the time he had to beat. From this and my own observation I deduced that Robin had his fair share of temperament, and hoped he wouldn't get carried away by Rowan's sudden interest. Few men were proof against her charm when she chose to turn it on, and it would be a pity if she spoilt Robin's chances in the big race just for the satisfaction of annoying Gina.

Judging by the way he was monopolizing the conversation at the end of the table, Robin had already succumbed: I might have felt inclined to applaud Rowan's success in bringing him out of his shell if it hadn't been for Gina's set, humiliated face as she tried unavailingly to deflect his attention to herself. She looked just as I'd felt all those years ago when Rowan used the same tactics to wrest Charles away from me. Although in a way she'd asked for it, I couldn't help feeling sorry for her.

The waiter appeared with coffee for the Laboucheres and a plate of steaming goulash which he plonked in front of me. I realized with a flicker of indignation that Rowan must have ordered it without consulting me.

'That'll do for you, won't it?' she called down the table; and because I was hungry and the food had arrived, I said it was fine, although it was the last thing I'd have chosen.

'D'you always let Rowan push you around?' asked Richard curiously.

'Oh, we're old friends. She knows my taste in food,' I said, instantly defensive. I scooped up a forkful of the orange gunge, trying to look as if I liked it.

'And that's one of them?' I thought he shuddered. 'Have some wine to help it down.'

He refilled my glass and started to tell me about the hang-gliding enterprise. He was astonished by its success. People were queuing to pay five hundred francs for a single joyride.

'Money for jam,' he said cheerfully. 'We'll have to take on a few more instructors if it goes on like this.'

I did a rough calculation. 'Forty pounds for how long?'

'Oh, eight to ten minutes, I suppose.'

'They must be out of their minds,' I said abstractedly, shovelling down the glutinous goulash and wondering how I could persuade Rowan to leave. Robin was hanging on her words, now, and Gina looked ripe for murder.

'I'll take *you* up, if you like,' Richard offered. 'Special reduction. Ten pounds off the usual rate.'

'No, thanks! Skiing's quite exciting enough for me . . .'

49

I tried to catch Rowan's eye but she ignored me. I could hear Robin making much the same offer to her, with very different results.

'Would you really?' she said enthusiastically. 'I'd love to try . . . so long as you promise to bring me down safely.'

'I promise,' he said solemnly.

Rowan's eyes danced. 'When can we go? You're racing tomorrow, so that's no good. What about the day after tomorrow – Tuesday? Let's say Tuesday.'

'You mean it? You really want to?'

'Of course I do. I wouldn't miss such a chance for anything.'

Gina tried again to break into the conversation, but they ignored her. I wondered why Rowan had this compulsion to take men away from other women. A psychiatrist might say it was due to a deep-rooted insecurity, but Gina's explanation, I felt sure, would be very different. Then I wondered what excuse Rowan would find to duck out of the hang-gliding date when Tuesday dawned. I knew her enthusiasm was faked because when I'd described the hang-glider I'd seen, she said wild horses wouldn't drag her onto one of those contraptions.

To my relief I saw that Richard had summoned the waiter and was paying the bill.

'We'll have to go,' he said. 'Sorry to rush away before you've finished, but it takes over half an hour to get back to the Eagle's Nest by car. During the daytime we use the ski-lift which is much quicker, but that stops at five, and after that it's a question of driving. Anyway, nice to meet you, and no doubt we'll see more of you both when the races are over.' He stood up. 'Ready, Gina? Robin?'

'You can't go yet!' Rowan wailed like a spoilt child. 'I'm just catching up on all the news. It's still quite early, and Robin says–'

'Sorry, Rowan. Another time. Robin's racing tomorrow, don't forget. No distractions allowed at this stage of the game.'

'Are you calling me a distraction?' She flashed him a bright, angry glance, and Gina's wide mouth curved.

'He's right, Rocky,' she cooed. 'I know it seems early to you, but *we* all need plenty of sleep. Never mind, I'm sure you'll see lots of other friends here if you look around. Come on, Robin. We'll leave the night owls to their revelry.'

The proprietorial tone grated on me and Rowan, whose

flashpoint was even lower than mine, bit her lip: a sign of rising temper. But providentially at that moment the street door was flung open and a party of Italians swaggered in as if they owned the place. Heads turned to watch as they threw off their outer layers and called loudly for a table. Three men, two women: vivid as parakeets in their couture *après-ski* gear, and about as raucous. One of the women spotted Rowan and screeched with delight.

'*Ciao, bimba!* Where have you been hiding? We looked everywhere and could not find you. Ah, Ricardo, going so soon? And Robin, *va bene?* You are ready for the big effort tomorrow? Good, good. The best of fortune go with you. *Allora*, Rowan, come and sit by me. We want to know everything, everything . . .'

The men clustered round her, kissing and exclaiming. Abruptly she lost interest in baiting Gina and allowed herself to be swept away.

'Come on, Catta,' she said gaily, 'we must leave the athletes to their beauty sleep. Happy dreams, Robin! Don't forget my shirt will be on you tomorrow, and I don't want to lose it!'

She blew them an airy kiss and waltzed away to join the Italians, leaving me to settle our bill. I liked Rowan. She'd been a good friend to me and I enjoyed her company. But I couldn't help reflecting, as I watched her plunge merrily into her new party without a backward glance at the one she'd quitted, that anyone who stayed married to her for nine long years must have the patience of a saint, and if this was her idea of an evening's entertainment it was hardly surprising that every now and then Charles felt the need of a carefree night out with the boys.

Chapter Four

Pulpy washerwoman's fingers were a clear indication that I'd been wallowing too long. I always did if there was no one to bang on the bathroom door and urge me to hurry. No Paul. No Rowan. Although I'd been expecting her to disappear like this, I hadn't imagined it would be so soon, or that she'd give me no indication at all of where I could get in touch with her. Suppose Charles telephoned to say that one of the children was ill and needed her? I felt like someone who'd been left holding a broom with a bucket of whitewash balanced on it. One false move, and the whole lot would come down on my head.

Problems crowded in. This evening, after supper, we were expected to make up a four at bridge with Rupert Harlow, a London art-gallery owner and his wife, who were renting an apartment below ours. It was Rowan who'd wanted to go; had she forgotten?

Then there was the matter of Jerome, the ball-of-fire ski instructor she'd hired to give us private lessons. I didn't much enjoy these sessions; I preferred to go at my own speed and sort out my own mistakes, but Rowan had insisted. She had booked Jerome's exclusive services every morning for a week. Now I should be obliged to suffer his hectoring alone and trust that Rowan would reappear in time to pay him off. I couldn't possibly afford to.

My hand was hovering over the telephone, about to cry off the bridge party, when it rang.

'Hello?'

'Oh!' The caller was young, male, hesitant. No prizes for guessing who it might be. 'Sorry to bother you. Can I – er – speak to . . . to Rowan?'

Now for it. I made an effort to gather my wits. Whatever I said now, I must stick to until Rowan returned.

'I'm sorry, she's asleep. She didn't feel at all well when we came down from skiing this afternoon. Her throat was very sore, so she went to the doctor and he's given her antibiotics.

She's taken them and gone out like a light.'

'Oh no! What wretched luck! Just when . . .' His voice faded despondently, but he didn't ring off.

'Shall I give her a message?'

'Yes, please. It's Robin – Robin Labouchere. We met – '

'I remember. How did you get on today?'

'Oh. Well, I won my heat. It was a close thing, though. I hoped that Rowan would be able to come and watch. I got her a special pass. When she didn't turn up, I – Oh, well, it doesn't matter.'

I cursed Rowan's compulsion to charm temperamental young men.

'She's got quite a high temperature, and the doctor advised her to stay in bed for several days.'

'Oh dear. I was going to take her hang-gliding.' A long pause. 'Perhaps if I ring tomorrow?'

His persistence was tiresome. Maybe I was using too much soft pedal. 'Better not,' I said briskly. 'She's lost her voice. She can hardly whisper.'

'Oh, I see.' He sounded so downcast that I nearly offered to come and watch him race or hang-glide or whatever myself, but that wouldn't have been the same. I hadn't Rowan's knack of charming temperamental young men. So I said nothing, and after a long, painful pause he muttered, 'Well, goodbye,' and hung up.

I drew a deep, calming breath and reviewed what I'd told him. There must be no variation in my cover story. In this place, gossip spread like wildfire. High temperature, voice reduced to a whisper, antibiotics, complete rest. Yes, that was all safe enough.

I inspected the fridge and store cupboard, and decided to stock up as if for a siege. That would give colour to the story that Rowan was ill. As I waited outside the apartment for the lift, the telephone began to ring again, but I ignored it and went on my way to the shops.

At six thirty the supermarket was thronged with improvident skiers who had left their provisioning until the last possible moment. As usual there were no trolleys. I snapped up the last wire basket under the nose of a broad-beamed blonde *Hausfrau*, and used it as a battering ram to force a path through to the delicatessen counter.

The crowd jostled and swayed, muttering insults in a variety of tongues. In ski-lift queues and supermarkets, xenophobia flourished. Dazed-looking English couples with brick-red faces stared at the wine display like Sahara travellers confronted with a mirage. Sharp-featured French housewives pinched avocado pears with cruel, questing fingers, and bearded young Germans shouted to one another across the display stands, while cramming into their baskets enough cheese to feed a plague of rodents.

Inevitably the queue for the check-out stretched halfway round the shop, and for the third day in succession I vowed to come earlier in future.

Friends of Rowan's greeted me on all sides.

'Excuse me, but aren't you sharing a flat with Ro?' asked a big busty blonde wearing orange lipstick and a king's ransom in pearls. 'Would you be an angel and tell her I'll take ten tickets for the Greensleeves Ball? I know she's on the committee. Moyra Percy. Where is she, by the way?'

I launched into my spiel about the sore throat, and had hardly finished before a round-faced, chunkily-built man in a white silk poloneck tapped me on the shoulder. I recognized him as Edward Williams, a former brother-officer of Charles'. 'Where's Rowan? Trust her to skive out of the shopping! Are you both coming over to Lionel's this evening?'

Again I explained.

By the time I had worked up to the front of the queue I reckoned that everyone in the supermarket with even a smattering of English must be aware that the popular Rowan Dawson née Henschel was ill in bed and out of circulation for several days. I made the confinement longer, the doctor's diagnosis more serious, gaining confidence as the story became familiar. I almost believed it myself.

'Rotten luck,' was the general verdict. 'These high-altitude bugs can really knock you for six. Remember poor Ronnie last year at Avoriaz? Took to his bed on the second day and stayed there until it was time to leave.'

'Ah, but not alone,' chipped in a high, carrying voice. 'Cas was fool enough to leave her Swedish au pair to look after him. Ronnie was happy as a sandboy . . .'

'Now, Sal . . .!'

'I don't suppose Ro's suffering from that kind of bug?' The woman called Sal raised a sly, interrogative eyebrow. 'I mean, things haven't been too rosy of late, and what with poor old Charles being left at home . . .!'

This was too close for comfort and I was glad to sling my purchases into a box and make my escape. Clearly the tide of opinion ran strongly in Charles' favour. Again I cursed Rowan for leaving me to hold what had begun to feel like an extremely slippery baby. I hoped she would turn up before I ran out of excuses. Three days in Val du Loup had been enough to convince me that as far as Rowan was concerned, the world was a very small place.

Two days passed, alternately dragging and spurting. The evenings dragged worst, because I could hardly go out leaving Rowan to her supposed sufferings; besides, there was always the danger that someone would call to see her. In such a tiny apartment it was unrealistic to pretend that the doorbell could go unheard. Once word got around that Rowan wasn't there, the game would be up.

So I stayed in and ate solitary meals with the yellow pine panelling closing in on me like prison walls, listening to laughter in the square outside, lonely and bored to the point when I began to wonder if I'd been a fool to kick Paul out of my life. Just because he wasn't Charles. Just because I couldn't have Charles.

The boredom was punctuated with spurts of panic when the telephone rang or friends of Rowan's came to the door with sympathetic requests to see her. Once Gina van Lawick turned up armed with a bottle of some potent patent medicine which she said would kill any bug between New York and New Delhi. I had the greatest difficulty preventing her pushing past me into the double bedroom. She hardly seemed to listen to me.

'I'm sorry,' I insisted. 'The doctor says she mustn't see anyone. It's extremely catching. Anyway, she's just dropped off to sleep. She had a wretched night.'

Not only did Gina stand her ground; she even advanced a little. She had that trick of crowding nearer as she spoke, forcing her listener to retreat. 'What about you? Aren't you afraid you'll catch it?'

I shrugged. 'Too late to worry about that. Actually I think she got it from me in the first place.'

'Come on, she can't be *that* bad. Do let me in. I'm immune to most things, honestly.'

Including hints, I thought, keeping my hand firmly on the door and my body planted across the opening. 'Better not. You don't want to breathe germs all over the hang-gliding customers, do you? Very bad for business.'

'Just let me have a peek at poor old Rocky. I won't wake her, I promise.'

'Sorry. Doctor's orders.'

Short of pushing me aside and marching in, there wasn't much she could do, but I had a nasty feeling that she smelt a rat. With bad grace she left, promising – or threatening – to come again soon, and I heaved a sigh of relief as the lift took her down to ground level. With any luck, by the time she called back Rowan would be able to deal with her in person.

Three days passed without a word from Rowan. I began to be seriously worried. I couldn't pretend she was ill for much longer.

On Thursday evening Richard Labouchere telephoned to ask me out to dinner. I declined the invitation.

'Sorry. I can't leave Rowan.'

'What about a drink? I'd like to talk to you.'

That sounded ominous. I could make a fair guess what it would be about. Again I said, 'Sorry.'

'Oh, come on,' he said impatiently. 'You don't have to hold her hand all the time. This'll take half an hour, maximum.'

'I can't, Richard. Really. It's not only Rowan: I'm busy, as a matter of fact. I can't spare the time.'

'Half an hour!'

'Listen,' I said, trying hard to sound reasonable, 'I can guess what's worrying you.'

'Been looking in your crystal ball?'

I sighed. 'Call it deduction. Anyway, you can take it from me that – that the scene in the Phoenix Bar won't be repeated. All right? Then, when he didn't say anything, I added, 'Rowan won't . . . um . . . bother your brother any more.'

'How d'you know?'

'Well, if you really want to know, I told her not to.'

'Oh, did you?' He didn't sound precisely overjoyed. 'So that's the message I'm supposed to give him?'

'Please yourself.' I thought of Rowan smiling at Robin, egging him on. The dazzled look on his face. I said defensively, 'She was only being friendly. She doesn't realize how over-whelming the cumulative effect can be.'

'You can say *that* again. So, having *overwhelmed* my brother, Rowan has decided she doesn't want to see him again. Is that right?'

'That's about it,' I agreed. I thought he was making absurdly heavy weather of a little flirtation. Robin would have to grow up some time, and the longer his big brother insisted on fighting his battles for him, the slower that process would be.

'Well, damn you both for a brace of heartless bitches,' said Richard suddenly and violently, and the line went dead against my ear. Unprovoked rudeness is always a shock. I noticed that my hand was trembling as I replaced the receiver.

I began to heat up a soothing cup of chocolate, wandering round in my bra and pants as I prepared for bed; the telephone rang again. Abstractedly I picked it up, my attention still on the milk as it came near to the boil.

'Your call to Grandes Alpes,' said an English voice. 'Go ahead, caller.'

Instinct shrieked a warning. For a panicky moment I thought of hanging up on him, but that was no solution. He would keep on trying, perhaps all night.

'Hello?' My voice reflected nothing of inner turmoil.

'Catta, darling! Lovely to hear you. I'd know your voice a million miles away.' He might have been in the next room. 'Listen, sweetheart, can I have a word with Rowan? Is she there?'

Resentment battled with pleasure and resentment lost. How dare he lavish endearments on me, whom he'd upped and left without a backward glance when Rowan beckoned? Who'd seen neither hide nor hair of him for nine weary years? But oh, how lovely it was that he remembered my voice as well as I did his; that he still called me 'sweetheart'.

'Are you there? Can I speak to Ro?'

'Sorry, Charles.' I jerked myself back to the present. 'Just a minute, the milk's boiling over.' As I pulled the saucepan to safety my mind was running like a computer, sorting out what to say.

'All right, panic over. Yes, Rowan's here, but there's a problem about speaking to her. She's lost her voice. Completely. She can hardly make a sound. The doctor says it's an infection of her vocal cords, and she mustn't strain them. Can I relay a message? Is it about the children?'

'No, the children are fine. Well . . .' He hesitated. 'It's a bit complicated. Business, you know. I ought to speak to her direct.'

'Sorry,' I said with real regret. I hated deceiving him, but I'd had so much practice in dealing with this request over the past seventy-two hours that the words almost said themselves. 'She's just taken a dose of the sedative the doctor prescribed for her, and it's put her out like a light. Even if I got her out of bed to speak – or rather listen – to you, I doubt if she'd take in a word.'

'Christ! It sounds really serious. Ought she to be in a proper nursing home?'

Hastily I made calming noises. I didn't want him panicking, calling in specialists. 'Oh, no. There's an excellent doctor here who knows all about this sort of thing. According to him it won't last more than a few days. Nasty, brutish, and short.'

Charles' laugh woke memories I'd thought buried for ever. If he'd been there in person it would have been the excuse for an arm round my shouders, a bear hug. He used to find it amusing that I instinctively pulled away. 'My little Puritan. Just like a snail: touch her and she shoots into her shell.'

I pushed such thoughts away. They made it more difficult than ever to lie to him. Charles was the most open of men. He said what he thought as and when he thought it. Rowan mocked at such transparency – but she wasn't above taking advantage of it, I thought angrily. Whose side was I on, anyway?

Carefully I chose the subject most likely to distract him. 'How did your horse run? Did he win?'

'How on earth . . .? Oh, I suppose Rowan told you. Actually his race is tomorrow.'

'Best of luck, then.' Something nagged at me: something that didn't quite fit, but I was too relieved to hear he'd be fully occupied to examine the feeling closely.

'Well, if you're sure Rowan's all right, I suppose the business will have to wait.'

'Oh, she'll be fine in a day or so. I'll tell her you rang.'

'I'm so glad you're with her.' His voice faded, then came back strongly. 'I can trust you to look after her. Give her my love when she wakes up – oh, and keep a big hug for yourself . . .'

'Goodbye, Charles,' I said quickly, and hung up before he could tell me when he'd call again. That was another trick I'd learned in the past three days.

Evasion and deception. I stared at the panelled walls and they seemed to move nearer, shutting me in. Claustrophobia threatened. I went hastily on to the balcony and gulped lungfuls of stinging frosty air, looking down at the lights and strolling couples, children throwing snowballs, an Alsatian walking stiff-legged round a Pyrenean mountain dog. All jolly and ordinary, the smiling face of a purpose-built winter fun-spot.

But the towering peaks above the valley weren't jolly at all. They were savage, inimical, one of the most formidable barriers on earth. The dwelling place of barbaric gods whose pleasure was to hurl hailstones and blizzards, avalanches and thunderbolts against the mortals who invaded their sanctuaries. If I stared too long, those jagged masses would begin to march towards me; they would crush the steel-and-concrete buildings as a vice crushes an eggshell.

I shivered. Enough of such fancies – the empty flat and worry about Rowan were getting on top of me. I wished the whole business was over. I wished I'd never become involved. Charles would certainly ring again tomorrow. Before I spoke to him I must discover where Rowan had gone, because it seemed to me that every lie I told, every fantasy I invented, was tangling us both in a net from which it might prove difficult to escape.

The key to Rowan's Mercedes still lay on her dressing table. My first move the following morning was to go down to the car park and search the car for some clue to where she had gone and with whom. There was nothing.

Then I flung reticence aside and went through her bedroom with a toothcomb. Nothing. I even forced the lock off the little

59

Morocco writing-case she'd brought, and found a letter dated the day we'd arrived in Val du Loup.

It began *Carissimo* . . . but that was no help. *Carissimo* Who? My mind leapt to the Italians who had swept her away from the Laboucheres' table that first evening. Three men, two women – but I couldn't remember their names or even what they'd looked like. Perhaps the spare man was Rowan's lover.

Since it was the only lead I had, I decided to look for those Italians. Anything was better than staring at the panelling, dreading the shrill of the telephone. Snippets of that evening's conversation came back to me. One of the women had mentioned taking lessons from a private instructor called Victor.

First stop the Ski School. The girl at the bureau was prepared to be helpful, but she told me there was no Victor among the Val du Loup *moniteurs*. Dead end. Then she flicked back her beautifully cut dark hair and said she was almost sure that a guide by that name worked in the neighbouring village of Caravosse. Would I like her to check?

I would.

Her colleague in Caravosse confirmed her guess, but produced a new problem. Their ski school had two instructors called Victor. Which did I want?

'I don't know. I'll have to talk to them myself,' I told the helpful girl, and she smoothed her hair and gave me exact instructions for getting to Caravosse. It sounded a day's trek. First a bus, then a train . . .

It *was* a day's trek. By the time I'd run the second Victor to ground on the nursery slopes and heard from his own lips that he taught children only, I was tired and dispirited. A whole day had been wasted and I was no further on.

I caught the afternoon bus back to Val du Loup and stumbled upstairs to the apartment in my heavy ski-boots, cursing the lift which was out of order yet again.

The front door was ajar. In an instant I forgot the day's worries and toils in a wave of relief.

'You're back!' I exclaimed, and flung open the living room door.

A figure rose from an armchair to greet me, but it wasn't Rowan.

'Where is she?' said Charles in a tight, hard voice I'd never heard him use before. He loomed over me, large and menacing, his shoulders blocking out the light.

I stood stock still, mind frozen, unable to utter a word.

'Don't bother to think up a pack of lies, because I won't believe them. Save yourself the trouble and just tell me one thing. Where the bloody hell is my wife?'

I found my voice. 'Steady on. What's all this about? What are you doing here – how did you get in? I thought you had a horse running – '

As I spoke I realized what had struck me as odd the previous evening. Today was Friday. The Cheltenham meeting ended on Thursday. His horse couldn't have been due to race there today.

Charles turned on me with something close to a snarl. I saw how pale he was, and that his suit was creased and his shirt collar curling. That told me more about his state of mind than any words could.

'Answer my question, damn you! Where's Rowan?'

'All right, all right. Take it easy. Just let me get these boots off, they're killing me.'

'*I'll* kill you if you don't stop stalling.'

'Charles!'

'I want the truth about what's going on here. What the hell d'you mean by telling me Rowan was ill in bed when she's not even here? Where is she?'

I undid the last clamp on my boots and thankfully freed my mashed feet. There was no point in pretending any longer. Charles would have to be told. In a way it was a relief to know that I needn't shoulder the burden of worry alone.

'I don't know,' I said slowly. 'She didn't tell me where she was going.'

'What?' He took me roughly by the arm and turned me to face the light, staring at me closely as if to detect any further attempt at prevarication. His fingers bit into the muscle of my shoulder. 'I don't believe you,' he said flatly.

'It's the truth.'

'*My God!*'

He let go of my arm and dropped into a chair. He looked so shattered that I felt doubly furious with Rowan for putting him through this and roping me in to aid and abet. I mixed him a stiff whisky and water which he accepted without a word. A moment later he said, 'How long has she been gone? How long have you been pretending she was ill?'

'Four days.'

'My God,' he said again. 'You treacherous bitch. I thought – I thought at least I could trust *you*.'

That hurt, just as he meant it to. I got up and said, 'Look, Charles, you'll have to face up to it. These things happen. I know it must be a shock if you didn't see it coming, but the best thing you can do now is go back to England and wait for her to get tired of this man, whoever he is. She'll come back to you once she's had her fling. You know that as well as I do.'

He was staring at me with an angry, puzzled look. The strong planes of his face might have served as a model for El Greco. 'What the hell are you talking about? Are you trying to tell me that – that Rowan's gone off with some man?'

'Well, yes.'

'You blithering interfering idiot! Do you suppose I'd give a brass monkey's if she slept with the entire ski-school?'

'Obviously you would,' I said coldly. I was getting tired of taking all the blame. I seemed to be on a hiding to nothing; again I regretted that I hadn't heeded my instinct and refused to get involved.

He lit a cigarette and inhaled a lungful of smoke. 'You don't understand, do you?' he said more reasonably. 'You don't know why I'm here?'

'No, I don't. Suppose you tell me?' I snapped. 'Suppose you stop biting my head off every time I open my mouth and tell me what the hell *is* bugging you? First you blast me for doing what Rowan asked me to. Then you say you don't care whom she sleeps with. I don't understand and I wish I'd never got mixed up with either of you.'

'I'm sorry, Catta.' He put a hand to his forehead in a tired gesture, pushing back the hair that always fell forward. 'All right, I see it's not exactly your fault, but I'm worried out of my mind. Without meaning to you've made matters far worse.'

'*Explain!*'

Abruptly he stood up, fishing in his jacket pocket. He pulled out a square white envelope and handed it to me. It had a first-class stamp and a London postmark and was addressed to him.

'Read that.'

I pulled out the single sheet of plain typing paper and my heart began to thunder. 'Oh, no!' I murmured.

The message was composed of printed letters cut from newspaper. The words were unevenly spaced but perfectly clear.

'It can't be real. It must be a hoax,' I said, appalled.

'It's real enough.'

'How can you tell?'

He said tightly, 'I thought it was a hoax when I rang and you told me Ro was ill. I believed you. Then this came in the morning's post.'

From his briefcase he produced a small tape recorder and took a cassette from his pocket. 'Listen.'

He switched on the machine and adjusted the volume. Rowan's husky voice filled the room – fearful, pleading – but unmistakably her voice.

'Do as they say, Charles. Pay them what they want. *Please*, Charles, I'm so . . . so scared. I'm cold and in the dark and so horribly frightened. Don't let them hurt me . . . I don't want to die. Oh!' Her voice ended in a gasp; I felt physically sick. Rowan, who had never begged anyone for anything.

I pressed my palms hard against my temples, trying to shut out the memory of that frightened voice, trying to think.

I said, 'But she went away of her own free will. That was why she made me come, so that I could cover for her. She told me she was going off with this man – '

'What man?'

'I don't *know*. I kept thinking she'd let it slip – you know what she's like about secrets – and I thought at least she'd tell me when she was coming back. But then she just vanished . . .'

'How?' he interrupted. 'Tell me every single thing you can remember.'

'It's so little.'

'Never mind. Tell me exactly how it happened.'

'Well, it was a foul afternoon, blowing and snowing . . .'

When I finished he nodded. 'Whoever abducted her moved

those piste markers to stop you following,' he said slowly. 'Would you recognize the man with the blood-wagon? Or the old boy who guided you down?'

I shook my head. 'The blood-wagon was too far away. I can't even remember what the man was wearing. You know, I was worrying about the cold and whether the lift would ever get going again. Nothing else seemed to matter.'

'I know. But sometimes if you think about it hard, something clicks.'

I thought about it hard, but the one thing that filled my mind was Rowan's pleading voice. *'Please, Charles . . .'*

'Can you pay them?' I asked abruptly.

'Can pigs fly?'

'But . . . the house. That must be worth a packet. And Rowan's trustees. Surely they could raise the money?'

'Three million francs? My dear girl, it's easier to squeeze blood from a stone than a couple of hundred out of those skinflints.'

'But if you tell them she's in danger?'

He thought it over and shook his head. 'I *daren't* tell them, Catta. You saw the letter – God! I'd never forgive myself if anything happened to Ro. It's going to be hard enough to keep her disappearance quiet as it is, with this place swarming with journalists because of the Championships.'

'And the Hollenbergs' Ball,' I reminded him.

'I know. Gossip columnists in every bar. If the Press gets wind of this story, Rowan's life won't be worth a row of beans.'

I said hesitantly, unwilling to pry but needing to know how things stood between them, 'She told me there'd been trouble . . . Some kind of row.'

His smile twisted my heart. 'Was that her excuse? I might have guessed. Marital bust-up, that kind of thing?'

'You mean there wasn't?'

He said rather wearily, 'Nothing worse than usual. Nothing that wouldn't have been forgotten in a week or so. Poor darling, she does love to keep up the drama. I'm afraid she finds a husband's dog-like devotion a bit tame at times, but I can't change any more than she can.'

'So it wasn't anything serious?'

'God, no! We have a shouting match now and again. She enjoys it – says it clears the air.'

I said slowly, 'Rowan told me you were getting a divorce.'

He shook his head. 'That's the first I've heard of it. Lord, no. She'd never do that. Quite apart from my objections, she'd never leave the children. Oh, she has a little fling now and again when she finds some fellow she fancies, but that's as far as it goes.'

'And you?'

'I try not to mind,' he said shortly, and my heart went out to him. Poor Charles! There was no point in asking how much he did mind, or if he ever regretted his marriage. Such questions were better unasked.

'So . . . what shall we do?' I said briskly to get the conversation back on the rails.

'We? You mean you'll help?'

'Idiot! Of course I'll help.'

He took a deep breath and expelled it with a sigh. 'Oh, thank you, darling. I hardly dared ask. You're an angel.'

'Steady on,' I stepped back before the automatic grabbing reflex could connect. 'I haven't done anything yet. In fact,' I added dryly, 'my performance to date hardly bears examination.'

He wasn't listening. 'Ever since that damned cassette arrived, I've been turning it over in my mind, round and round like a squirrel in a cage. I've been bashing my head against the bars until I thought I'd go crazy. I didn't know where to turn. I can't tell you the relief it is to share the burden. To know you'll back me up.'

'And I can't tell you what a relief it is to stop lying to you.'

We smiled at one another and nine years' separation vanished as if it had never happened. We were a team, Charles and I. He would lead and I would follow, and together we'd get through anything, just as we had in the old days. He was the same Charles I'd always known, although there were new lines radiating out from the corners of his eyes and his mouth had a firmer set than I remembered. No doubt he could say much the same about me. It was no good pretending the lonely years hadn't left their mark.

'Right. So what shall we do?' I said again. 'How can we raise three million francs? Rowan's father?'

'He's the only person I know with that kind of money,' said Charles slowly. 'It's going to shock him terribly, and the worst of it is that he's very frail nowadays. His heart's in a bad state. I hate having to ask him – '

'She's his daughter. You know how he adores her. Money won't count for anything beside Rowan's safety.'

'That's what you'd think,' he said sombrely. 'But the richer you are, the more you hate parting with money. If only I could see some other way.'

We sat in silence, wrestling with alternatives.

'I don't think there *is* another way,' I said at last. 'Not if it's got to be done in secret.'

'Will you come with me to ask him? Geneva's only four hours away.'

I thought that over, tempted.

'You might be able to persuade him. The trouble is, he doesn't like me,' said Charles matter-of-factly. 'He's never tried to hide it. I know he'll react against anything I suggest.'

'No,' I said regretfully. 'You'll have to go alone. It's very much a family matter. And one of us ought to stay here to fend off visitors. You can't imagine what it's been like with Rowan's friends ringing up every five minutes to ask how she is.'

'I can imagine only too well. All the same . . .'

The telephone rang and we both jumped. I reached it first. 'Hello?' I said guardedly. *Wait for further instructions . . .*

'*Allo? Ici Courier des Neiges . . .*' The local news-rag: my heart seemed to pause and then begin beating very fast. The story *couldn't* have got to them already.

A moment later my fears were dispelled. The girl reporter sounded very young, very over-awed. Definitely not a hard-bitten newshound scenting a scoop.

Would I, she asked hesitantly, have the great kindness to describe to her what manner of historical costume my friend Madame Dawson would wear to the Masked Ball which the Princess Hollenberg was to give at the end of the Ski Championships? She would be infinitely obliged.

The Cleopatra costume was one thing that hadn't vanished with Rowan. I signalled all right to Charles and launched into a seam-by-seam description. I could hear pages rustling and little gasps as the girl adapted her shorthand to my fractured French. When I finally hung up on her squeaks of gratitude, the bell instantly rang again. This time it was Gina van Lawick.

'You see?' I said when she, too, had been fed the latest bulletin. 'I simply can't come with you, much as I'd like to. I'll hold the fort here.'

'All right, I suppose I'll have to go alone. But first you must show me just where it happened. Where you last saw Rowan, and where that blood-wagon went. My father-in-law will want all the details. I'll get myself skis and boots, and we'll go up there together tomorrow morning.'

Chapter Five

It was noon next day before Charles presented himself at my apartment, but although it was a perfect morning for skiing I was glad of a rest from the slopes. Yesterday's shocks had left me feeling curiously limp.

When Charles did appear, however, he looked less strained than he had the previous evening. Blue stretch pants clung to his long legs and the matching padded jacket gave him a Superman outline. Though pale beside other skiers, already he blended more easily into his surroundings.

'Ready for action?' He smiled. 'I like your hair that way. It suits you.' It was typical of Charles to notice recent efforts with shampoo and blower. Morale soared.

'Let's go,' I agreed.

We took the big cable-car and its adjoining tow-lift, and arrived at the summit restaurant of the Col du Diamant just as the early lunchers were starting to clump off its slatted verandah, groaning as they bent to reclamp their boots before streaming back to the pistes for their afternoon dose of sun and snow. They were very different slopes from the last time I'd seen them, the day of Rowan's disappearance. Then low cloud had obscured most of the huge snow-bowl, and only the steel pylons had stood out plainly in the mist. Now the sky arched cloudless blue over the diamond-glittering snow, which was peopled with brightly-clad skiers as thick as hundreds-and-thousands on an iced cake.

Outside the restaurant, in an angle of verandah protected from the wind, a row of slim and not-so-slim girls, naked to the waist, exposed glistening faces and reddening breasts to the ultraviolet rays.

'That one's going to wish she hadn't when she gets in the bath tonight,' commented Charles, stopping for a closer look. The girl in question opened a slit of furious eye, glared at him, then resumed her rapt, sun-worshipper's pose.

'Surprising how many of them speak English,' he said, unabashed. 'Where do we go now?'

There was a considerable queue fanning out at the foot of the Trois Fontaines chair-lift behind the restaurant, but I saw at once that the operator was the same shaggy youth who had allowed his friends to queue-barge me, so separating me from Rowan. Now it occurred to me that this might have been done deliberately.

'Let's have a word with him,' said Charles, when I put forward this theory. 'Perhaps he'll remember you.'

'He might. There was practically no one else up here that day.'

We shuffled on our skis round the edge of the queue until we were close enough to call to Shaggy as he supervised his machinery. Seeing our approach, he made impatient shooing movements which said clearly, Don't bother me now.

'Perhaps we'd better wait until he's not busy.'

'We'd wait all afternoon.' Charles shoved purposefully through the roped-off enclosure. '*Un moment, monsieur,*' he said distinctly. 'I'd like a word with you.'

Again the shooing gesture.

'It's important. *Très urgent!*' Charles shouted over the clatter of chairs rolling round the drum. Interested faces turned towards us.

The shaggy youth looked exasperated. '*Fou-moi le camp!*' he yelled in a flat, toneless voice, and turned his back.

'That famed Gallic courtesy,' remarked Charles. He reached out his ski-stick and poked Shaggy between the shoulder blades. '*Urgent!*' he shouted.

Inside the dark little cabin beside the lift there was a quick movement and I had the impression that someone was leaning forward only a few feet away, listening intently, but against the light I could see nothing.

The shaggy youth switched off the lift and there was a groan from the queueing skiers. In a couple of strides he reached Charles and grasped him roughly by the shoulders, turning him round. 'It is forbidden to speak with the operator,' he shouted angrily. 'Go away. Make the queue like everyone else.'

There was a loud murmur of approval from the crowd, accompanied by a perfect barrage of remarks injurious to

British pride. There was nothing for it but to withdraw.

'Come on,' I said, tugging at Charles' sleeve. 'We won't get any change out of him while he's on duty. Perhaps we can soften him up with a drink later. Let's go up to the top.'

'Typical French bureaucrat,' grumbled Charles, and raised two fingers towards the affronted queue. *'Vive le Marché Commun!'*

Ignoring muttered rebukes from people around us, we pushed into the queue and eventually reached the front. But just as we and a svelte pink-suited Frenchwoman stood waiting our turn to climb aboard, there was a commotion in the crowd at our backs. Loud curses and squeals were accompanied by the clatter of skis tramping over other skis. I looked round.

The next minute, Charles lay flat on the ground under the chair-lift, the Frenchwoman and I had swung aboard, and so had a thickset young man in dark clothes and huge goggles, who had mysteriously appeared beside me.

Had he deliberately pushed Charles over? I'd seen nothing, but the shocking-pink Frenchwoman had no doubts about it. All the way to the top she heaped invective on his unresponsive head, comparing him with the lower farmyard animals in terms which were hardly fair to our four-footed friends. He said nothing, turning his face away in surly silence and burrowing his blue chin deep into the collar of his anorak.

Just as we reached the summit, however, he jostled roughly against me, feeling in his pocket. Nervously I edged away, unable to move far because my pink neighbour had already raised the safety bar. To my relief the young man merely seemed in need of more elbow room. We grounded our skis, stood up in unison, and as we did so he thrust a folded piece of paper into my gloved hand.

Then he shot off downhill at speed I couldn't hope to match, leaving me staring at the message he had delivered. It was in French, short, unsigned, and to the point.

If you wish to hear of your friend, come ALONE to the Café Belle Hélène, at nine tonight. Tell no one. Ask to speak with Bubu.

A variety of emotions – shock, worry, fear – battled within me, quickly followed by a spate of questions. Was it from the kidnapper? Why give me the message rather than Charles? Who was Bubu? Should I tell Charles? After four days in Val du Loup I knew the simply-planned streets well and was sure there was no café called the Belle Hélène.

My reflections were interrupted when Charles erupted from a following chair, snow-covered and furious.

'Where's that bastard? Did you see him push me over?'

'It's true, I saw it myself,' corroborated a pretty curly-haired brunette who had just got off the lift. She had sharp features and an air of lively curiosity. 'He attacked you deliberately. Typical German, always pushing to get in front.'

Charles' anger was always short-lived. He smiled at the girl. 'We were just going to have a drink. Will you join us?'

The girl accepted with an alacrity I found suspicious. 'You are Monsieur Dawson, *oui*?' she said brightly, when he had ordered three *vin chauds* and settled us at a table. 'I am sorry to hear your wife is ill. Everyone here is looking forward to her appearance as Cleopatra at the famous Ball! Tell me, how is she today?'

One of Rowan's friends? Somehow she didn't strike quite the right note. She was too inquisitive, too *professional* . . . She went on prattling gaily and with a sinking feeling I realized where her questions were leading. A rumoured estrangement between M. Dawson and his wife? How pleased she was to hear this was merely a fabrication. Yes, he could rest assured that she would let this be known. And Mademoiselle Chiltern? The keen profile turned in my direction. We were no doubt all good friends?

'My childhood sweetheart,' said Charles blandly, and I kicked him on the ankle. Surely he could see . . .? 'She makes all those clothes my wife spends a fortune on. You must have heard of her?'

'Ah, *that* Catherine Chiltern! The *couturière* – fantastic!'

I looked at Charles in despair. Why couldn't he keep his mouth shut?

Presently the keen-featured girl left us, full of smiles and thanks, no doubt to phone her editor from the nearest callbox. I rounded on Charles fiercely. 'Why did you tell her all that?'

'If you try to dodge the Press it makes them think you've something to hide. If you actually volunteer information, ten to

71

one they won't use it,' he said calmly. 'Don't worry, darling. I'm not going to throw you to the wolves. Yes: I recognized that little bitch. She's a stringer for *Paris-Presse*, always hanging round racecourse bars and charity balls to see what she can pick up. Some of the English agencies use her stuff, too. It seemed a good opportunity to put down smoke.'

'You might have warned me.'

'If I had, you'd have shot back into your shell and clammed up so tight she'd have smelt a rat at once,' he said, and I had to recognize the truth of this. 'These gossip stringers get a nose like a bloodhound's, but if you lead them away on a false scent you can often make them play things your way.'

'Personally, I'd avoid the lot of them like the plague.'

'That doesn't work.' He watched my face. 'Trust me, darling. I've had a fair bit of experience in handling this sort of situation. One gets to know when to bluff and when to show one's hand. Just trust me and follow my lead.'

'You haven't given me much chance to do anything else.' I still felt ruffled. 'And less of the "darling" bit, if you don't mind. It gives the wrong impression.'

Charles grinned. 'Old habits die hard.'

'If you want my help, you'd better put that one out of its agony,' I said tartly.

'Darling Catta!' His hand came down to cover mine.

'Stop it!' I looked at my watch. Four fifteen. The chair-lift closed in ten minutes' time. If we wanted to catch Shaggy as he came off duty, we would have to hurry.

I drained my *vin chaud*, tasting the grittiness of cinnamon in the dregs, and went over to the snowbank in which I'd stuck my skis. Without looking to see if Charles was following I kicked them on and set off downhill.

'Such dynamism!' he protested, half-laughing, as he caught me up and took the lead once more. 'You've changed, Catta. You've changed a lot.'

You've only yourself to blame if I have, I thought bleakly. Did you expect me to remain a hero-worshipping teenager for ever?

His smile flashed back over the sky-blue padded shoulder. 'Remember how I used to tell you to *make* things happen instead of *letting* them happen?'

72

I used the excuse of a fork in the piste to pretend I hadn't heard. I chose the easy zigzag route to the foot of the chair-lift, but Charles took it straight from impossibly high up, shooting down the last steep sheet of ice at breakneck speed, his long body bent chin on knees. Within inches of the wooden cabin he skidded to a dramatic halt in a flurry of snow. *You* haven't changed much, I thought.

Crossed ski sticks across the chair-lift entrance told us that our timing was impeccable: it had just closed for the night. The line of chairs hung stationary from their cable, the rattling drum at last was silent.

'Don't let him see you,' murmured Charles in my ear. 'We'll nab him after he's shut up shop.'

We withdrew to a row of deckchairs in front of a little bar, and sat awkwardly, skis still attached to boots, watching like cats at a mousehole while the shaggy youth tucked up his machine for the night. To and fro he bustled, in and out of the little cabin, checking and locking, shovelling away packed snow from the duckboards, putting things ready for the morning.

The summons to the Café Belle Hélène seemed to burn in my pocket. I struggled with the urge to tell Charles about it – ask his advice. The instruction to come alone had been clear, and yet . . . As the sun slipped behind the Sorcière peak and dark shadow crept upward to engulf the rose-tinted snow-bowl, I shivered, not entirely from cold. I began to rehearse French phrases, thinking out what to say to the shaggy youth, how to waken his memory of Rowan's last ride up the mountain. Was it remotely possible that he'd remember one glamorous girl among the thousands he watched board his lift, day in, day out?

'Now!' said Charles, and pushed himself upright. Shaggy had come out of the cabin once more, dressed for departure. Skis on shoulder, he walked a few yards on to flat ground, dropped the skis and kicked them on. All his movements were brisk yet automatic. He had the air of a working man on his way home.

Charles had already halved the distance between them when Shaggy looked up and saw him: his response was instantaneous and I realized that the question was not whether he would remember Rowan, but whether we would get near enough to

73

ask. He gave Charles one swift, startled glance, and took off downhill like an arrow from a bow.

I turned and cut across the slope at an angle to intercept him. 'Wait!' I called.

Charles skied well for an Englishman; but like most Englishmen he had to rely heavily on courage and strength as substitutes for agility and control. Twice I saw him overshoot Shaggy's route as the youth doubled like a hare back and forth across the steep shoulder above the tree-line. Taking appalling risks, going twice his speed, Charles went straight where Shaggy turned, and only a good deal of luck prevented him ending upside down in a snowdrift. Still he could not catch him.

'Wait!' I heard his long-drawn-out yell. 'Wait! I must speak to you.'

Without a backward glance, Shaggy zigzagged down the slope, heading for the dark trees.

I followed, hopelessly outclassed, taking the shortest possible route towards the serpentine piste code-named *Primule* for which I guessed our quarry must be making. At the bottom of the *Primule* there was a sort of ski-crossroads: a clearing with a big relief map of the area. Beside it stood a fingerpost pointing out five or six different descent-routes, all named after mountain flowers. If I could get there first and see which way he went . . .

I felt like a Shetland pony pursuing two thoroughbreds, but by making quick turns on my short, easily manoeuvrable skis, I was actually getting downhill faster than either of the two speed-merchants, who were still outrunning one another in wide swoops across the empty snow-bowl. They were out of sight, but after my early intensive exploration of these slopes, I was prepared to gamble that once he reckoned he'd shaken off his tail, Shaggy would double back to the crossroads in order to get down to the village.

Gasping for breath, legs quivering like jellies, I reached the fingerpost and leaned forward on my sticks to ease the stitch in my side. There was no sign of the men.

Down here among the dark trees it was very quiet. Snow-laden branches drooped low; now and again one shed its burden with a soft rustle. The temperature must be rising. When this happened all down my neck, I went and stood close against a trunk, my dark clothes making me invisible in the gloom. I strained my ears for the telltale hiss of skis: was I too late? Was there another way down which I didn't know about? It seemed an age that I stood there watching and listening, though it was probably no more than five minutes.

Both Shaggy and Charles had been moving so fast that it began to seem unlikely they hadn't reached this point yet. Either they were still playing hide and seek above me; or Charles had managed to catch up and persuade Shaggy to talk; or they were already below me and I was wasting my time. Three possibilities and no way of knowing which was correct.

I was on the point of giving up when I heard the sound I'd been waiting for: the soft shushing of skis over wet snow. Shaggy appeared, alone, and christied to a stop. I froze against my tree trunk. He was older than I'd thought at first, twenty-five at least, stocky and powerfully built, with a broad, typically Alpine face, low-browed, blunt-featured, head set close onto bulky shoulders without much benefit of a neck. He looked stubborn, nervous and rather stupid, like a bullock.

He glanced back up the track as if to confirm that he'd outdistanced pursuit, and humped his rucksack higher on his back. He was evidently about to move on.

I slid forward to block his path. *'S'il vous plait, monsieur,'* I began soothingly. I got no further.

As if the bullock had brushed against an electric fence, he started and ducked his head. *'Merde!'* he grunted. Then he turned at right angles to the piste and went over the lip into the trees, down a slope – a veritable precipice – thickly set with thick straight trunks: a slope that only someone who'd been born on skis would dream of tackling. The twin tracks of his departure reproached me as I stared at them. I hoped I hadn't driven the poor fellow to his doom. I was still staring at them when Charles skidded to a halt beside me, scarlet-faced and panting.

'Gave me the slip,' he gasped. 'Where's he gone?'

I pointed to the twin tracks.

'Oh, hell!' he exclaimed. We looked at one another and he shrugged. 'That's the end of it, then. We'd better go on down. I suppose we *might* still bump into him . . .'

75

'I doubt it. Why wouldn't he stop? Why's he scared to talk to us?'

'Search me. Unless he had something to do with Rowan's disappearance.'

'That's what I was thinking.'

I went on thinking about it as we skied down the long winding piste code-named *Tulipe*, heading for Val du Loup. My thighs ached from the short fierce descent to the crossroads. Charles waited for me to catch up every few hundred yards, but even so I was forcing the pace.

'You go on,' I said eventually. 'I'm tired. I'll come down at my own speed.'

'You're sure? All right. I'll wait for you at that café – what's it called?'

'Rumpelstiltskin.'

'Right. Two éclairs and an Espresso?'

How well he knew my weaknesses! I waved him off and he sped showily away at a pace more suited to his temperament. I stopped trying to hurry and continued alone.

The sedentary winter at my drawing board was having its revenge. In the short time since we arrived, I'd taken more exercise than in the past four months, and quite suddenly my leg muscles packed up on me. The snow on these lower slopes was heavy and slushy, so that my skis kept sticking instead of gliding, and every time it happened I fell over. Getting up after a fall is much the most exhausting part of skiing. The effort of unscrambling limbs and equipment from whatever unsuitable position they've come to rest in, then heaving your whole weight upright, takes more out of you than any other man-oeuvre.

After five falls in close succession I had lost all rhythm, all confidence. Night was closing in; the trail winding down between the trees seemed endless. I wished I'd taken the short way instead of blindly following Charles' lead.

Below me lights twinkled and my spirits revived. I wasn't so far from the bottom after all. The low growl of an engine reached me: a couple of bends lower down I could see a slow-moving yellow machine grinding laboriously uphill. It was one of the piste-bullies – immense snow crawlers with cater-pillar tracks, carrying a ten-foot-wide angled blade on hydraulically operated arms in front, and a roller-cum-harrow behind. A wonderfully versatile machine that could go up or down almost any slope, equally adept at scraping flat the tiresome quilted moguls that built up where skiers turned, clearing freshly-fallen snow from the pistes, or shovelling it away from the bottoms of lifts. An admirable vehicle – but one to which it was advisable to give a wide berth. It was no doubt for this reason that this piste-bully's driver had waited until dusk, when skiers could reasonably be expected to have left the slopes, before making his ascent of this narrow track. Anyone who collided with such a monster would inevitably come off second best.

It flashed through my mind that here I was, dark-clothed and probably practically invisible, with a sheer rock wall on my left-hand side and an equally sheer drop on my right; but then I measured the width of the track with my eye and decided there was no cause for alarm. There was plenty of room for the bully to pass. In fact, there was really no need even to stop and flatten myself against the wall, in which position I would be harder to see than if I continued boldly down the middle of the track.

So continue down the track-middle I did, still feeling wobbly after so many falls, approaching each corner with care, ready to take evasive action if I found myself eyeball to eyeball with the machine.

Our confrontation, when it occurred, was on a relatively straight stretch. As I rounded one corner, the bully crawled round another about seventy yards away, headlights blazing, snowplough blade raised, and as I came within range of those probing lights, the blade descended on its hydraulic arms, filling most of the track. Even at the time, this struck me as odd. The snow was already thin: it made no sense to scrape more of it away. With the lights glaring at me like angry eyes, it was difficult to judge the width of the blade, but even so there was enough room to pass. I stayed in the middle of the track until I was sure the driver had seen me, then swerved to my left, against the rock wall, to let him go by.

At once the headlights swung in the same direction. The blade scraped along the wall so close that I heard it clang against rock and saw sparks fly. Wrong side of the road, I thought, hastily veering across his front. Continentals drive on the right. Again the headlights swerved to follow me.

It was a nightmare version of that sidestepping manoeuvre on crowded pavements. You step one way to dodge someone who does the same, perhaps two or three times before one of you has the sense to stand still.

Twice the deadly *pas de deux* was repeated. Swing to the left. Blocked. Swing to the right. Blocked again. Was the driver mad? I thought frenziedly, changing sides once more. Was this his idea of a game?

My mouth was dry, tiredness forgotten as I realized he didn't intend to let me pass. His aim was to squash me against the rock or drive me over the edge. We were only a few yards apart. The wide, curved blade of the snowplough looked like a shark's jaw, reaching out for me.

With nerves screaming, I clung to the rock wall until the last possible second and then, with the blade practically on top of me, turned square across the front of the bully, trying to get past on the outside before the driver had time to swing the blade.

I very nearly made it. As the driver realized I'd tricked him, his machine veered round like a rearing horse to cut off my retreat, and in my anxiety to get clear of the blade, I let one ski slide off the edge of the piste. Instinctively and fatally I leaned inward. Next moment I'd lost my balance and was falling head over skis towards a terrifying drop, my nylon clothes skidding over the snow and my scrabbling hands unable to check the slide.

Everything seemed to happen in slow motion. Trees slid past just out of reach. Lumps of rock came away in my hand. Every movement I made accelerated my descent. I could see the lip of the precipice only feet away: a craggy rock face with jumbled boulders at the bottom of the shadowed ravine below.

Then my skis caught in something and the slide was arrested, leaving me hanging very close to the edge.

Cautiously I reached up a hand and found the tree root which had saved me. I prayed that the quick-release bindings on the skis would hold firm and, still with the utmost care, pulled myself round until I was half-sitting, half-lying against the slope. On the track above, the noise of the piste-bully's engine faded, replaced by eerie silence.

I tried to move farther away from the edge and felt a sickening slip as the tree root shifted. Panic threatened. At any minute my sole support might give way. Then I heard a different sound: the rustle of snow-laden branches, a man's rasping breath. Slowly and carefully someone was climbing down to me.

Rescue! I thought, and kept very still.

A hand gripped my shoulder. I looked up to smile my relief and got a shock. A black hood like an executioner's covered my rescuer's entire head. Eyes gleamed through narrow slits, the mouth was a thin horizontal slash.

Rescuer? I wasn't left in doubt for long. With one arm hooked round a tree for support, the hooded man leaned down and tried to drag me towards him.

'It's my ski,' I said in shaky French. 'It's caught.'

He edged closer, gloved fingers scrabbling for the release toggles. He yanked them both and the skis popped off. Without further delay, he gave me a powerful shove which would have sent me over the edge to eternity if I hadn't clung to the tree root with all my might.

'Merde!' He pushed again.

I let rip with a scream that woke thin, high echoes across the valley. He hit me across the mouth and by reflex I grabbed his arm. He tried one-handedly to shake me off but I hung on like a bulldog, determined that if I went over the edge I'd take him with me. I hooked my hands through the tough nylon pouch strapped to his arm, and knew with a sense of grim triumph that like this I was as strong as he was. Without letting go of the tree he could not shake me off.

'Charles!' I screamed, knowing it was futile. 'Charles! Help!'

'Hang on, I'm coming,' said a voice above us.

Another pair of hands gripped my shoulders, and this time there was no question: they were drawing me away from the brink. I tried to help, edging uphill on elbows and knees to the accompaniment of staccato French orders and exclamations; but when at last I lay gasping on the comforting solidity of the piste, only one person knelt beside me.

'That was a near thing,' said Richard Labouchere. 'Isn't the piste wide enough for you? What the hell are you doing up here so late, anyway? Don't you know it's dangerous to ski in the dark?'

I struggled into a sitting position. The hooded man had gone.

'Where is he?' I gasped. 'Stop him. Don't let him escape.'

'If you're looking for the chap who saved you, I'm afraid you're too late. He's pushed off. Never mind, I expect he'll survive without your thanks.'

I took a deep breath, knowing it would be fatal to sound hysterical. 'That man was trying to kill me.'

'Don't be absurd.'

The words were like icy water hitting my midriff. Too late I remembered his hostility to Rowan, his rudeness on the telephone.

'It's true,' I insisted. 'He was driving the piste-bully. He – he pushed me over the edge. He was trying to finish me off when you arrived.'

'*Finish you off?*' He looked at me curiously. 'Have you been drinking? Sorry, wrong question. I mean, *what* have you been drinking? It's lucky I found you rather than some officious *moniteur*. They take a poor view of foreigners who go looking for trouble.'

'I wasn't looking for trouble. I tell you, he chased me with that machine. He drove straight at me . . .'

'Steady on. Before you make any more wild accusations I ought to point out to you that skiing after sunset is extremely dangerous, particularly if you've a skinful of alcohol on board.'

It was no use losing my temper, though this accusation coming on top of the most frightening few minutes of my life taxed my self-control severely.

'Listen,' I said.

'I'm listening.'

'I haven't been drinking.'

'Were you just admiring the view in the Soleil Bar?'

'One single solitary *vin chaud*,' I said through gritted teeth. 'Not enough to cloud my judgment or stimulate delusions.'

'I'm not so sure. Altitude doubles the effect of alcohol,' he said. 'People often don't realize it until they find they can't control their skis.'

I glared at him. 'My skis were under perfectly good control until that – that madman drove his machine straight at me.'

'I saw you fall over half a dozen times. That's why I stayed behind to keep an eye on you.'

'Then it's a pity you didn't watch a bit more closely or you'd have seen that maniac weaving about until he pushed me off the track. I tell you, he was trying to kill me.'

'Why on earth should he want to do that?'

'I don't know.' I felt suddenly exhausted. Whatever I said, he wouldn't believe me. I was wasting my breath. 'Why are *you* up here so late, anyway?' I added.

'I told you. I saw you crashing about and falling over every few yards, and thought I'd better see you got home safely. Besides, there's something I want to ask you.'

'Ask away.'

'How's your friend Rowan?'

The same old question, but I didn't quite like the way he said 'your friend.' The words had an ironic, faintly mocking inflection, as if he knew our relationship was not just as it appeared. It warned me to edit my usual answer.

'She's a bit better today,' I said cautiously. 'Of course, that sort of bug leaves you feeling pretty weak.'

'Of course. And you've probably been giving her all sorts of drugs to cure her, and those are apt to have a debilitating effect, too.'

I stared at him in the gathering gloom. 'Well, yes. The doctor's given her various pills.'

'And you make sure she takes them?'

What was he getting at? I said rather sharply, 'Rowan's grown up, you know. She knows what's best for her.'

'Delighted to hear it. Is she well enough to come to the telephone?'

'Hardly. The doctor says she oughtn't to use her voice at all.' I forced a laugh. 'She's being very good about it, though it's a nuisance as you can imagine. We have to communicate on paper when sign language gives out.'

'Ah. Then d'you think you could shove pencil and paper in her hands and get her to write a couple of lines to my brother? Just to put his mind at rest, you know?'

'What's worrying him?'

'Oh, he's a great worrier, my brother. He thinks you're telling him a pack of lies,' said Richard steadily. 'He thinks Rowan isn't ill in bed – she's not even there – and you're pretending she is in order to hide the fact that you're having it off with her husband. What d'you say to that?'

81

'I say it's none of his bloody business!' I exploded, with cold fingers of fear behind my anger. 'You tell your nosy little brother to stick to his skiing and – and hang-gliding, and keep out of other people's affairs. Just because Rowan was kind enough to encourage him –'

'Kind enough?' The dark eyes were hard as black glass. 'Is that really your idea of kindness? To pick someone up and drop him flat a couple of minutes later? Come on,' he said roughly. 'You've told me what I want to know. Get your skis on and start moving unless you want to spend the night up here.'

'Wait,' I protested. 'I'll explain . . .'

But he had already moved off.

'I thought you were never coming,' said Charles. Two cigarette butts lay in the ashtray in front of him; two crumb-sprinkled paper lozenges on his plate.

'You've eaten my éclairs!'

'I'll get you some more. What kept you?'

When I told him, his face darkened. 'The bloody fool! He drove it straight *at* you? The man must be crazy.'

I said slowly, 'I don't think he was crazy.'

'You mean it was deliberate?' He looked up sharply. 'Did you recognize him?'

'He was wearing a hood. I couldn't see his face. But all the same there was something about the way he came for me . . . something deliberate.' I shivered. 'I think he recognized me . . .'

Charles was silent, drawing on his cigarette. His clear blue eyes searched my face. At last he said, 'Promise me you'll be careful while I'm away in Geneva? I don't like leaving you behind, especially after this. Change your mind and come too. Then I'll know you're safe.'

'Caution is my middle name.' I bit into the replacement éclair. It was delicious.

Charles laughed. 'If it is, you've changed more than I imagined.'

'Don't worry, I'll take care,' I assured him. 'How long will you be away?'

He grimaced, stubbing out the cigarette. 'It'll depend on how my father-in-law reacts – and how quickly he can raise the cash.

I don't suppose even he keeps the odd three million lying idle in case of emergencies. Two days, I suppose, at least.'

My heart sank; it seemed an eternity. 'What if the kidnapper tries to contact you?'

'I'll have to rely on you to handle that. Play it by ear. But for heaven's sake get in touch with me as quickly as you can. You've got Ben's number? Don't go playing a solo hand.'

The crumpled note seemed to burn my pocket. I was on the point of mentioning it when he added, 'Now, how about a spot of dinner? We ought to give the gossip writers something to fill their columns.'

But I couldn't share his delight in playing Tom Tiddler's Ground with the Press. 'I'm tired,' I said. 'I'll have an early night.'

'Poor darling, you've been overdoing it.' He looked at me with a strange, reluctant half-smile. 'What you need is – ' He paused.

'What do I need?'

'I was going to say you need someone to look after you.'

'Don't tell me you're offering your services?'

I meant it as a joke to relieve the tension between us, but his half-smile faded. His hand came down over mine as it lay on the table, gripping it so hard that it hurt.

'If only I could,' he said, as if to himself. 'Christ! If only I could!'

Chapter Six

Pushing open the swing door of the Café Belle Hélène a few hours later, I walked into a wall of hostility so intense that it was almost tangible.

This was no glossy chrome-and-vinyl eaterie for winter sportsmen, nor even one of the fake olde-worlde mountain inns with darkened beams and barrels cut in half to sit on. The Belle Hélène looked like a genuine relic of the days before the tiny farming community was overrun by winter holidaymakers. It had probably been the villagers' sole source of gossip and entertainment for a couple of centuries, and the unfriendly stares of the regulars playing draughts or drinking at the scarred, scrubbed ancient tables told me plainly that I was unwelcome.

I felt horribly conspicuous as I walked forward into the sudden hush and chose a corner table; but after a minute or two the dour faces turned once more to their games and gossip and I was able to take stock of my surroundings.

The room was low and dingy to the point of dirtiness, with yellow-grey walls haphazardly adorned with 'Fifties pin-ups, all bosom and fluttering doe eyes. There had been music before I entered, chatter and a certain gaiety; now the wizened accordion player shut up his instrument with wheezing finality, and the aproned *patron* said something that provoked further stares at me.

Most of the men looked like farmers: a few silver or horn-buttoned waistcoats their only concession to evening wear, and the women were anything but dressy – hobnailed boots showed beneath ankle-length serge skirts, and woolly shawls covered wispy locks. But what the company lacked in youth and beauty, it made up for in appetite. Huge plates of fried potatoes, hunks of meat swimming in gravy were being shovelled down those weathered throats, and waiters scurried here and there with loaded trays. Evidently the Belle Hélène's kitchen enjoyed a good reputation.

When at last a waiter stopped at my table, having avoided my signals for as long as he saw fit, I ordered a cup of chocolate.

'We don't serve chocolate.' The fact seemed to give him satisfaction.

'A glass of red wine, then.'

He brought me a tumbler of thin, sour stuff which would have done well for removing tarnish from brightwork. I wondered gloomily what it would do to the lining of my stomach. He charged six francs, which was ridiculous considering you could get a whole bottle of better stuff for four, but I paid up rather than antagonize him further. As he fumbled for change in his grubby apron pocket I asked if I might speak to Bubu.

He gave me an unfriendly look. 'I know no one of that name, *mademoiselle*.'

From his tone I was sure he was lying.

'Perhaps this will assist your memory?'

I tried to slip him a five francs, but he pushed it back at me, saying, 'I tell you there is no one by that name here.'

This was a setback I hadn't anticipated. The waiter began to move away.

'One minute, please.' I dug in my pocket and found the crumpled note. He read it carefully, lips moving over the words. Then he shrugged and handed it back.

'This *is* the Café Belle Hélène?'

'*Oui, mademoiselle.*'

'Is there another by the same name?'

'*Non, mademoiselle.*' He turned. 'Now, you will excuse me: I have work to do.'

He vanished into the kitchen leaving me staring in perplexity at the paper. Bubu must be here – or was it all a hoax? I looked up and met a familiar lizard-like gaze. Immediately the old man dropped his eyes, but not before I'd recognized him. It was the officious ancient gnome who had guided me home the afternoon Rowan vanished. Excitement sent me straight across the room to him.

'Good evening, *monsieur*. I'm so glad to find you again. I have been wanting to thank you for helping me.'

The diamond-shaped eyes in their network of wrinkles continued to stare down at his glass of wine like a necromancer

85

consulting a crystal ball. He gave not the slightest sign of having heard me.

'Good evening, *monsieur*,' I repeated with rather less confidence.

A clawlike hand descended on my shoulder: an old woman with apple-red cheeks and a tight, buttoned mouth. 'He is deaf, *mademoiselle*. Completely deaf, poor man. He cannot hear a word you say.'

'He wasn't the last time I saw him.' Frustration made me reckless. Were *all* these people in a conspiracy against me? If they weren't going to talk to me, why had they asked me to come here? The time was correct: I'd arrived on the dot of nine as instructed. The place was right: everyone assured me this was the one and only Café Belle Hélène. So what the hell was wrong and where was Bubu?

I retreated to my own table, deciding as I went that I'd give him another ten minutes and that was all. If, at the end of that time, Bubu hadn't contacted me, I was going home to bed. Only the memory of Rowan's frightened voice kept me there at all. I sat down and sipped the sour wine, trying to ignore the hostile looks and half-heard mutterings.

Five minutes crawled past. Out of the corner of my eye I was aware of much nudging and whispering from a group of young men at the table to my left. They were an unprepossessing bunch of thugs and I took care not to look at them directly, but instinct told me I was the object of their attention.

Eventually one of them, stocky, swarthy and bearded, swaggered across to lean over my table, poisoning the atmosphere with his personal aroma of garlic, black tobacco and sweat.

'*Mademoiselle* is lonely?' he leered.

Could this be Bubu? He was so obviously bent on picking me up for a dare that I decided he could have nothing to do with my mission. I surveyed his pock-marked, brutal features and sly eyes and resolved to see him off as fast as I could.

'I'm waiting for a friend. He's a boxer.'

He laughed, showing stained teeth. 'Your friend appears to have forgotten his appointment.'

I hoped my silence would discourage him, but it didn't. Egged on by the whistles and guffaws of his friends, he plonked himself uninvited at my table and reached out a thick arm to encircle my shoulders.

'I will be your friend, English Miss,' he said, pulling me roughly towards him and looking round at his friends for applause.

His proximity was disgusting. Without considering the pros and cons of such an action, I slapped him smartly across his hairy jowl and, as he released me with a grunt of displeasure, caught up my handbag and made an ignominious bolt for the door, stumbling over the legs outstretched to trip me.

Outside, the narrow alley was very dark. As I stood blinking on the step, zipping up my anorak with shaking fingers, a block of shadow seemed to detach itself from a doorway and move smoothly towards me.

My nerve gave. I gasped and started to run; heard the footsteps behind me quicken, and missed my footing on the packed snow. I sprawled full length.

'Catta! What *are* you doing?' said Charles, bending to help me up, and at the sound of his voice I nearly cried with relief. 'Didn't you hear me? What made you take off like a scalded cat?'

I shook my head, speechless. 'Come on,' he said, taking my arm in a firm, comforting grip. 'You ought to be in bed. I thought you wanted an early night? I happened to be on my balcony and saw you go out, but even then I had the devil's own job to find you. I must have looked in a dozen bars . . . Why did you pick that grotty little joint?'

Of course, I thought, it was Charles who had prevented Bubu from showing himself. No doubt he'd been scared to approach. Charles' protectiveness, though kindly meant, had undoubtedly cost me the contact. Quickly I spun him the first story that occurred to me.

'It wasn't my choice. Jerome – our ski instructor – invited me and Rowan to meet him there for a drink and I thought I'd better go in case he got suspicious.'

'But why there? Why not in the ski-village?'

I shrugged. 'I think that café belongs to his second cousin once removed. I certainly didn't see him pay for anything.'

'And what made you rush off like that?'

I hesitated. 'It was getting a bit steamy. Jerome thinks he's God's gift to English girls.'

Charles' laugh was warm, amused. 'Still my little Puritan? Now listen to me, Catta darling, and pay attention this time. I asked you to be careful, didn't I?'

'Well, yes.'

'Wandering about alone in the old part of the village is not my idea of being careful. Why didn't you tell me where you were going? Jerome wouldn't have got steamy with me around.'

'No, but . . .'

'Of course he wouldn't. So will you please have a bit more sense and do as I tell you?'

'All right.' We walked on in silence, but a tiny spark of resentment had begun to smoulder within me. It had been all very well for Charles to lay down the law to me when I was fifteen, but a good deal of water had flowed under the bridge since then. Without his interference tonight I might have found out something useful. I couldn't tell him without risking another lecture. Nevertheless, his criticism rankled.

We reached my apartment block. Standing in the lobby waiting for the lift, he smiled and said, 'Don't get uptight about this. I'm only thinking of your safety. May I come up for a bit?'

The smile disarmed me, but the tiny resentful spark prompted me to shake my head. 'You've got an early start. Better to go to bed at once.'

'That's what I meant.'

'Sorry.'

'Oh, come on. Why sleep alone?'

If he could see no reason, why should I? Rowan apparently slept around as a matter of course. All the same, an obscure feeling of loyalty to her made me say No again, and get into the lift as if temptation didn't exist. Charles caught the door before I could shut it.

'I'll keep asking.'

'And I'll keep refusing.'

He laughed. 'Trying to excite my hunting instincts?'

'If I was, would I tell you?'

Gently I detached his fingers from the door and, as it shut, pressed the sixth-floor button.

It took a strong effort of will to return to the Café Belle Hélène. I waited for forty minutes, fighting sleepiness with strong black coffee, until I felt confident that Charles must be tucked up, solo, in his hotel bed; then I spent another twenty persuading myself that my journey was really necessary. Even when the will was there, the way remained a problem since the last thing I wanted was for Charles, whose room overlooked the square, to see me about my nocturnal ramblings again.

It was nearly eleven before I slipped out via my neighbour's balcony and the service staircase, which smelt unattractively of rotting foodstuffs trapped in black polythene, but had the virtue of debouching into a narrow alley well out of sight of the residents' picture windows. I hurried back through the silent streets, trying not to think of the dour faces that would greet my reappearance.

The reception I got was not the one I anticipated. I was hesitating outside the swing door, listening to drink-blurred voices competing with the accordion's nostalgic lament when I sensed a presence behind me. Before I could turn, a hand was clapped over my mouth, stifling my instinctive scream, and a voice growled: 'Silence, *mademoiselle*. Bubu wishes to see you.'

Keeping his palm pressed against my mouth, he manoeuvred me sideways a few steps, swung round, and whisked me through one of the small doors set in the wall. There he released me just enough to pull a strip of material from a pocket and bind it over my eyes.

'Stop it!' I protested. 'Let me go.'

He didn't answer, but taking me roughly by the arm, he guided me through what I first thought was a courtyard and then, as the pungency of manure rose to my nostrils, identified as a farmyard complete with midden. Complete, too, with suspiciously growling dog.

On we went, through more doors, up and down steps. I lost my bearings completely and didn't enjoy the dog's close attendance on my ankles. I had begun to fear that I, too, was about to be abducted (but no one would be fool enough to hope for anything from my father's Army pension) when the journey ended in a stuffy room smelling of Gauloise cigarettes, where my guide abandoned me to the custody of the dog, which sniffed my legs and growled as if daring me to move an inch.

I didn't move an inch. Using the senses left to me, I deduced from the chink of glasses and dull rumble of voices that our roundabout trip had been designed to confuse me, for we were still quite near the café. When the faint wail of the accordion reached my ears, it confirmed this guess. Bubu lived in the warren of houses behind the Belle Hélène.

As I reached this conclusion, I sensed a new presence in the room, and felt the dog's tail wave against my legs. A moment later the blindfold was twitched away. In the glare of an unshaded bulb I blinked silently at a complete stranger: a squat pasty-faced toad of a woman tightly encased in shiny black satin. Hard jet eyes matched the beads round her thick neck. Grey-streaked hair was drawn back severely from a centre parting and twisted into a bun.

'I told you to come alone.' Her voice was harsh as a crow's.

'I tried to. I didn't know my friend had followed me.'

'He is your lover?'

Rather too emphatically I said, 'Certainly not! Charles is the husband of my friend.'

'*Hein!*' The hard black eyes bored into me. 'Where is she, your friend?'

'You tell me,' I countered, wondering how much this hostile old toad knew. Dare I admit to her that Rowan was missing? What if she should contact one of the news agencies? A single telephone call, and they'd pounce onto the story.

She waddled a step nearer, her beady gaze still fixed on my face. 'If your friend never returned, you would be pleased to marry this Charles, *n'est-ce pas?*' she said softly. 'Shall I arrange that for you, *mademoiselle?*'

The old witch! 'Don't be absurd!' I snapped. 'Look here, *madame*, if you have anything to tell me concerning my friend, I'd be glad to hear it. If not, I'd like to go.' I paused, then added, 'If any harm comes to her, be assured that I will tell the police of your part in it.' I searched my vocabulary for the translations of 'aiding and abetting', and 'accessory before the fact' but legal terminology was beyond me. 'I'll go to the police,' I repeated.

She sneered. '*Ça, je m'en doute.*'

We regarded one another with acute dislike. 'Why did you ask me to come here if you've nothing to tell me?' I demanded. 'Why the secrecy? What concern is it of yours?'

'Kindly allow me to ask the questions, *mademoiselle*,' she barked back like a Nazi wardress. 'Let's say that I am angered when people break promises.'

'I haven't broken any promises. I told you: I didn't know Charles was following.'

'Oh, not you, *mademoiselle*. *You* have broken nothing – except your friend's marriage.'

'That's not true.'

Her eyebrows lifted. '*Non?*'

'Charles is an old friend from my childhood,' I insisted. 'Almost a brother.'

'It is fraternal affection that makes him follow you?' she said sceptically – that very special disbelieving tone the French are so good at.

'Yes.' It gave me the creeps to think that the old toad must have been observing me and Charles, spying on us. What else had she seen?

Before she could speak again the door opened to admit a broad-shouldered young man. I recognized Bubu's errand boy: the one who'd pushed Charles off the chair-lift. He spoke to her in a low, urgent tone, and abruptly her manner changed.

'Very well, *mademoiselle*; now listen carefully. If you wish to learn more concerning your friend, you must take the *téléférique* to the restaurant that stands above the Poste de Secours on the Col du Diamant tomorrow morning.'

My heart leapt: at last I was getting somewhere. 'May Charles come too?'

'*Absolument pas*. It is essential that you go alone. My son will be waiting. If anyone follows, he will not keep the rendezvous.'

I asked cautiously, 'Will he take me to Rowan?'

'That is for my son to decide.' For the first time her peremptory manner changed; a certain greasy expectancy crept into it. 'No doubt a suitable recompense will be offered to those who assist in restoring her to freedom.'

'No doubt,' I said dryly.

'Something in the region of a million francs?' she hazarded.

Her greedy eyes revolted me, but it seemed imprudent to haggle. Better pass the buck to Charles, who would no doubt hand it straight on to Ben Henschel.

'I really can't say. Her husband must be consulted . . .'

'*Non!*' The interdiction came sharply, like a slamming door. '*You* must promise us the money, *mademoiselle.*'

A million francs . . . Clearly it was no use expecting Rowan's release to come cheap, whether the money was paid to the kidnapper or his rivals. Nevertheless I had no doubt of what Ben Henschel would want me to say.

'All right. I promise . . . on condition that you give me a guarantee that she will be returned alive and well.'

'Agreed. Be at the restaurant at ten tomorrow. Enter the door beside the bar, and my son will meet you there.'

Nine o'clock the following morning found me among the earliest birds to queue on the steps of the *téléférique*, waiting for it to start its daily grind up and down the Col du Diamant. It was another bright, brilliant day, with sun just melting the crusty edge of night-frozen snow, but the forecast had spoken of localized storms, a prediction confirmed by the thin layer of mackerel cloud around La Sorcière's peak.

Ahead of me were perhaps two dozen skiers, mostly men, some clear-eyed, chatting idly, others with the dogged, stunned look of sufferers from cheap-wine hangovers. A girl with shoulder-length blonde hair turned suddenly, registered surprise, and smiled widely.

'Hi, Catta! How's Rocky today?'

Outwardly I smiled: inwardly I cursed. Just my luck to run into Gina van Lawick when I wanted to be alone. 'She really *is* a bit better at last,' I said cautiously.

'But not up to skiing?'

'Oh, no. She'll have to take it easy for a day or two.'

'So you're on your own . . .' The green eyes surveyed me coolly, assessingly. In the soft light of the Phoenix Bar I'd thought her face elfin: here in the sun's harsh glare it looked more like a hatchet – cold, sharp, potentially dangerous. She said, 'Why don't we ski together today? I know plenty of runs right off the beaten track. Places you'd never find without a guide. I've got a free day. I'll take you on a Grand Tour.'

How the hell could I refuse?

Gina awaited my answer with an attention I found unnerving, her fingers plucking at the ski-pass she wore strapped with elastic round one arm. Since this was the bottom lift, passengers were required to display their passes.

'I'd enjoy that,' I said, patting my pockets, first abstractedly, then gradually letting a look of concern cloud my face. This I stepped up to Shock-Horror as I investigated the last hiding place in my anorak, the front pouch. 'Damn! I've left my pass behind. I'll have to go back.'

'How maddening. Never mind, I'll wait.'

'God, no. I wouldn't dream of keeping you here. You go on to the top. Maybe we can ski together another day.'

Gina didn't move. 'It's all right, I'm in no hurry. You pop on back and fetch the wretched thing – I don't mind waiting. It's lovely here in the sun.'

But as I took off my skis outside the apartment block a few minutes later, I saw that far from sunbathing, she had moved up the steps to a patch of shadow from which she could keep me under observation every inch of the way.

I went in through the front and out at the back, thinking furiously how to shake her off. The last thing I wanted was her company. Using the big cable-car on its first ascent of the morning, I could have reached the summit restaurant with time to spare. To get there by the only other possible route – using a series of different tows and chair-lifts – would be a close-run thing, and the first leg of such a route was well within Gina's field of vision.

In the lobby I stripped off my anorak and reversed it from green to yellow, then put on my unflattering and little-worn teacosy hat pulled well down to meet my goggles. Trying not to look towards the steps where Gina stood, I strolled nonchalantly, skis on shoulder, to join the short queue at the Nursery Slopes chair-lift, and hid myself behind a burly Frenchman with a pack of children at his heels. While I waited, I kept a wary eye on Gina. She shifted her position once or twice, as if wondering where I'd got to, but her attention remained fixed on the doorway from which I might be expected to emerge.

With a small glow of satisfaction I swung aboard my chair and watched her pistachio-green anorak diminish with distance.

The French schools had started their Easter holidays. The pistes were twice as crowded as usual and queues waited at the foot of every *monteur mécanique*. Pushing with a ruthlessness quite foreign to my nature, skiing faster than my skill warranted, I slid and fell, fell and slid, zigzagging across the network of lifts, blessing the time I'd spent studying the map of the area.

At last I reached the final leg of my ascent: the station from which little egg-shaped four-seater cable-cars climbed to the summit. A glance at my watch confirmed that I was already late for the rendezvous. Too bad: better arrive late than with Gina van Lawick in tow.

I shoved my skis into the holder at the front an empty 'egg', and clumped inside, collapsing onto the slatted seat with a sigh of relief. I closed my eyes. Nearly there . . . Pray heaven that Bubu's son hadn't given me up . . .

Boots stumbled over my outstretched legs as a man clambered aboard. The automatic door clamped shut, isolating us in a tiny, swaying world.

'Got you,' he said.

I opened my eyes, hardly able to believe what they saw. Richard Labouchere, goggles glinting, mouth grim as a rat trap, faced me from a distance of approximately three feet, and his next words were enough to convince me that this was no coincidence.

'Why the hell didn't you stop when I shouted?' he demanded. 'Don't pretend you didn't hear, because I saw you look round.'

I *had* turned my head, thinking I heard my name called, but then dismissed it as imagination.

'I'm in a hurry,' I said shortly, pleased to see that Richard was panting. The bits of his face that were visible shone with sweat. 'I'm late for an appointment.'

'With Charles Dawson, I suppose.'

How dared he suppose any such thing? 'Charles has gone to Geneva. On business.' I snapped out the words and turned away to stare out of the misted window. The forecaster had known his job: already the bright sky was clouding over.

'Excellent. Then perhaps I can persuade you to tell me what the hell you and he are playing at.'

'What d'you mean?'

'Take a look at this.' From his anorak pouch he pulled a folded newspaper and put it in my hands. 'Read that,' he said, and pointed.

The girl from *Paris-Presse* had wasted no time. Under the heading *Three's Company?* the paragraph read:

Is life with diamond heiress Rowan 'Rocky' Henschel losing its appeal for gambling ex-Guardee Charles Dawson? While the tempestuous beauty lies sick abed in Val du Loup, venue of this year's Hollenberg Ski Championships, Lothario Charles rekindles his old flame for Top People's designer Catta Chiltern. Will Rocky rise to find husband and dressmaker Absent Without Leave? Watch this space.

I glanced at the dateline. Today's London paper. Faking a world-weary yawn, I handed it back.

'The things papers will print!' I said lightly. I was much relieved that there was no hint that Rowan was missing.

'Is it true?'

I smiled. 'Is it any of your business?'

'I don't understand you,' he said slowly. 'I can't make you out at all.'

'Don't lose any sleep over it. After all, it's nothing to do with you.'

In the cramped cabin his presence was overwhelming. Surreptitiously I inched open the sliding window.

'That's where you're wrong,' he said.

With an effort, I looked him straight in the goggles. 'All right,' I challenged. 'What is your interest in me and Charles? Why do you keep pestering us?'

He pushed up the eclipsing goggles. I noticed for the first time that his eyebrows weren't level. The fine white line of a scar ran diagonally from the corner of his right eye to vanish in the close-cropped hair at his temple, giving a questioning lift to his right eyebrow while the left remained sternly level. He said, 'I want to find out why you're so determined to keep Robin and Rowan apart. What have you got against him?'

It was the last thing I expected him to say, and I found it difficult to answer. 'I've nothing against him. I hardly know him.'

'That's why he can't understand why you're behaving like this, choking him off when he telephones, telling him Rowan can't speak to him. Good Lord, I should have thought if you were trying to get off with her husband, you'd have been keen to have Robin take her off your hands. Instead, you're being deliberately obstructive. Since that evening at the Phoenix Bar he hasn't even spoken to her, let alone seen her.'

'But she's ill!'

'He's only your word for it. He can't even find out who's treating her. What's the doctor's name?'

I was ready for this. 'Dr Greenbergh,' I said quickly.

'Never heard of him. Where does he hang out?'

'Down in Abbeville,' I said, taking a chance. 'One of Rowan's friends recommended him – I'm not sure who.'

'I see. So this mysterious Dr Greenbergh has ordered you to keep Robin away, is that it?'

'No, of course not. I mean, he's told her not to speak to *anyone*. Not Robin, particularly.'

'I think I'd better have a talk with Dr Greenbergh,' he said thoughtfully. 'Perhaps you'd let me know where to find him?'

'You're reading too much into this,' I said quickly. 'You're making a mountain out of a molehill.'

'Robin wouldn't agree with you. His skiing's gone all to pieces since you and Rowan arrived, and it's spoiling his chance of winning the Trophy. I didn't want her to come during the Championships, anyway. I asked her to wait till Robin was free, but she swore she wouldn't distract him. She'd give him moral support . . .'

I could actually feel my mouth sagging open. Hastily I snapped it shut. 'Are you telling me,' I said carefully, 'that *Robin* is the man Rowan came here to meet?'

'Are you telling me you didn't know?'

'I didn't. I swear it. I – I can't believe it now.'

His eyes narrowed. 'You must have realized – from the things she said. From the way she behaved.'

'I didn't. I thought that was just Rowan.' I shook my head, groping for words. 'You know how she likes to play people off against one another. I thought she was getting at Gina. I promise you I had no idea Robin was her – '

'Her lover?' He looked unconvinced. 'Strange that she didn't tell you. Most of her friends seem to know all about it.'

It's disconcerting to find that you've firmly grabbed the wrong end of the stick. My mind zoomed in circles, like a bee in a greenhouse unable to find the skylight.

Richard said, 'You and Rowan seem to have remarkably little communication for such close friends. I assume you *are* close friends?'

When I said nothing, he went on, 'I've got a load of work piling up in Geneva. I ought to be back there now, but I can't leave Robin in such a state. He thinks Rowan's tired of him. That she's found herself a new man and can't bring herself to tell him. But I've known Rowan off and on ever since I started to handle her father's affairs, and whatever she is, she's not that kind of coward. So why is she hiding behind you? Or is there – ' he paused, then said quietly, 'some more sinister explanation?'

I wondered what on earth to tell him. Without Charles' approval I couldn't tell him the truth. The silence stretched out. I had to say something. I decided to stick to the official line.

'Look,' I said with an awkwardness that wasn't wholly feigned. 'I didn't want to alarm your brother because Rowan hates a fuss, but in fact she's been pretty ill. Apparently this bug can have nasty after-effects, so I've been doing everything I could to make her follow the doctor's instructions. Perhaps I've overdone it, but better safe than sorry. I had to tell Charles, of course, and when he arrived it seemed even more important that there shouldn't be a – a drama. I'm sorry Robin misunderstood. Perhaps you can explain to him better than I could.'

The level eyebrow descended a fraction. The scarred one remained in position. 'All very reasonable,' said Richard slowly. 'All very sound and sensible and above board. The trouble is, Catta, that I don't believe a word you say. I don't believe Rowan is ill: I don't believe she's even in that apartment you're guarding like a dragon. What do you say to that?'

My heart had given a nasty jolt, but I forced myself to stay calm. The cable-car station was in sight. At all costs I had to get rid of Richard before contacting Bubu's son. I shrugged. 'Please yourself what you believe. It's no skin off my nose. But if you *could* see your way to leaving Rowan and me alone for the rest of our holiday, I'd be grateful. We came here for a bit of peace and quiet . . .'

He cut me short with a hard scornful laugh. 'Don't give me that! Robin's got a sheaf of letters to prove that peace and quiet were the last things Rowan was looking forward to. If you swallowed that story you're a bigger fool than you look. Or a

97

bigger liar than I imagined. But then rich bitches like you and Rowan wouldn't know the truth if it came up and shook you by the hand.'

It was the second time he'd called me that. I hadn't liked it the first time either. To be lumped together with Rowan as a bored, idle troublemaker with more money than sense made me see red.

'Get it through your head that I work for my living,' I said between my teeth. 'Probably a good deal harder than you do.'

'I haven't the smallest doubt of it. Sponging off your rich friends while seducing their husbands must be absolutely exhausting. A lawyer's life is a rest cure compared to yours.'

'I don't sponge off my friends. Or seduce their husbands.'

'No?' He grinned, as if pleased to have got under my skin at last. 'That's better.' The approving tone made my fingers itch. 'Now you sound less like a vocalized computer and more like a woman. In a minute or two you may even start telling me the truth.'

Fortunately there was less than a minute to endure of his company. Facing forward, I could see the roof of the station about to close over us. He must have read the relief in my expression because he glanced round and frowned.

'All right, Catta, before you vanish again, there are two courses of action I'd like to suggest to you. Either you get Rowan to speak to my brother direct and put his mind at rest; or you can both leave Val du Loup and go somewhere else to finish your rest and relaxation. You've got the whole of the Alps – the whole of the world to choose from. Get out and make trouble elsewhere.'

His arrogance took my breath away. 'My God!' I breathed in simple amazement. 'What kind of dictator are you? You can't order us to leave. You can't imagine you can shoo us out like chickens that have strayed into the vegetable patch.'

'No?' The scarred eyebrow rose. 'Think it over. You'd be surprised what I can do if I put my mind to it.'

The cable-car stopped, swaying gently. The automatic door slid open. Politely he allowed me to scramble out first and handed me the ski-sticks I'd left behind in my haste. Without another word to him I wrenched my skis out of the holder and hurried away towards the entrance. Thanks to Gina and Richard's interference, I was nearly twenty minutes late for my rendezvous.

Chapter Seven

He had waited. I think he would have been prepared to wait all day, since he showed not the least sign of impatience as he sat behind the bar, whittling at a lump of yellow wood and whistling through his teeth. Shaggy, the lift operator: hairy, blunt-featured, with bull-like shoulders and short, thick neck. Bubu's son in every respect apart from the eyes. Hers had been bright, shrewd, malicious. His were dull brown pebbles, devoid of expression.

'Didier,' he said, by way of greeting. His voice had the harsh toneless timbre I remembered.

'Catherine,' I responded, and offered my hand. That, it appeared, was to be the extent of our social chitchat. He took the skis I was carrying and glanced at them, then indicated that I should remove my boots. I padded after him through a door into a well-equipped workshop with a carpenter's bench, where he went briskly to work to marry my boots to another pair of skis, longer, thinner and stiffer than my own. Trekking skis. Excitement stirred in me: excitement tinged with fear. I wondered where we were going.

Didier refused to answer my questions and after a few attempts I gave up, fearing to prejudice my chance of being taken to where Rowan was imprisoned. Even when he pushed open the door of the workshop and told me to follow him, his accent was so thick that I had difficulty understanding.

Ten minutes later we halted to survey a different world. The twentieth century had vanished, and in its place was an older, harsher landscape which Man's inventive genius had not touched, remote as the moon from the tamed snow-bowl we'd left, with its flattened pistes, pylons and cables, restaurants and sunchairs and brightly clad holidaymakers. An overcast sky turned the rocks leaden, the snow a matt opaque white which looked level but wasn't. By eye, it was curiously difficult to tell uphill from down, but my aching leg muscles had no hesitation in assuring me that we were climbing.

Didier paused to let me catch up and I stared around in wonder. Apart from our own, there wasn't a single ski-track or footprint of any kind. Great ramparts of cliff reared overhead in a long narrow valley, steep-sided and forbidding. Around the rocks, ravens and lammergeiers wheeled and cried hauntingly, but otherwise the silence was complete. It was an eerie place.

Didier hitched his rucksack higher on his shoulders and grunted. He slogged off into the white landscape, his legs moving with the regularity of pistons. Step – *slide*; step – *slide*. The pace looked as natural to him as walking. Imitating him as best I could, I followed.

The long valley branched, gave way to another, wider but equally empty. We wound through huge scattered boulders like petrified giants and I glanced nervously at the overhanging cliffs from which they had fallen. Snow floated down in large soft flakes, blotting out the view until I was aware of nothing but Didier's bent shoulders and thick legs plodding endlessly away from me.

Over the next two hours I grew to detest those tireless legs. Once Didier stopped and took from his rucksack two hunks of hard bread sandwiching a meagre slice of salami whose taste made me think of raw red hands in a greasy washing-up water. I choked it down, but it was too cold to rest for long and soon he jerked his head and set off again, always a dozen yards ahead of me, apparently oblivious to my increasing tiredness. For a time pride kept me going, but in the end even that gave out.

'Don't go so fast. I can't keep up,' I called.

His head didn't turn. I stopped mutinously. Despite the thickly falling snow it was bliss to stand still. I could see that he was heading for a narrow cleft between two cliffs but going by an unnecessarily roundabout route. If I cut across, I could save myself several hundred yards.

I turned my skis out of Didier's tracks for the first time since leaving the piste, and felt them sink unnervingly through the top crust. Pathfinding was certainly harder work than following, but if it saved distance it would be worth it. I shuffled along, feeling my way, moving at an angle to Didier's route. I couldn't see the tips of my skis, so deep were they buried, but they slid along easily enough once they were through the crust.

'*Attention!*'

The harsh shout stopped me in my tracks. As I turned to look at him enquiringly, he turned and came after me with great skating strides, covering the distance between us at unbelievable speed. He reached out a hand, grabbing my shoulder. As if on cue, a large chunk of snow beneath the tips of my skis fell forward like a hinged table flap, and collapsed into the black crevasse it had concealed. *Beneath my very feet.* I gasped with fright and moved back smartly. I hadn't realized we were crossing a glacier.

The narrow escape glued me to Didier's heels for the rest of that interminable journey, but my legs were shaking with exhaustion when at last he stopped and pointed to yet another virgin snow-bowl stretched out below us.

'*Voilà*,' he said. 'She is there.'

Forgetting my aching legs, I followed the line of his pointing hand. Through the falling snow I made out a shape which, blurred though it was, had not been put there by Nature. A house? No – a barn, long and low, drifted up to the eaves so that the roof seemed to be resting on the snow. An isolated farm building that no doubt served as a shelter for the shepherds whose flocks grazed the high pastures in summer; a store for mountain hay or refuge for sickly lambs. Anyone who chose such a place to hide a hostage must have precise local knowledge.

The falling snow thinned. Presently it stopped altogether and I saw the building clearly. It looked completely deserted.

'How d'you know she's here?'

Didier grunted, putting a finger to his lips. Not one of the world's great conversationalists, I thought. He stood motionless, shoulders hunched, neck thrust forward, watching the building with alert intensity.

It seemed a long time before he moved. Apart from the rustle of an occasional snowslip on the cliff above us and the lonely cawing of crows, the valley lay silent and empty.

At last he grunted again, satisfied.

'Wait here. Don't move,' he said curtly, and himself glided stealthily forward towards the building some fifty or sixty yards away, using rocks and snowbanks to cover his approach. When he got there, he bent down to peer through a grating or ventilation slit, and whatever he saw reassured him for the wariness left his movements. He removed his skis, and I heard a hollow *clack* as he clapped them together and stuck them upright in a snowbank, the tips resting against the barn wall. Clearly the need for silence was over. He turned to look at me and I thought he was about to wave me up to him, but instead he signalled Wait. He walked quite openly along the wall of the barn, under the eave, and disappeared round the end where, presumably, there was an entrance beneath the central gable.

I fidgeted, cold and wet and bursting with curiosity. Dared I follow? Minutes dragged past.

Just as I decided to join him and risk his displeasure, something against the wall of the barn moved, at the very edge of my vision. I turned my head sharply and stared, but all was as it had been.

A bird, I thought. Didier must have disturbed it – or perhaps snow slipped off the roof. Nothing to worry about.

Then I looked more carefully at the barn and realized with a sudden drop of the stomach that all was not quite as before. Didier's skis had vanished. My gaze remained riveted to the place where they had been as I tried to rationalize their disappearance. They must have fallen over. The movement I'd half seen had been the skis slipping sideways. But there wasn't a breath of wind and my brain still carried a clear picture of Didier clapping his skis together to knock off the snow, then jabbing them upright in a bank – an easy, efficient gesture which no doubt he used a dozen times a day. My heart began to pound. I was acutely aware of danger.

Didier reappeared, strolling casually, and made a beckoning gesture. I didn't move. He waved again, impatiently; then suddenly, he too, noticed that his skis had gone. At that distance I couldn't see his face clearly, but his movements conveyed extreme alarm, even panic. His head turned rapidly from side to side; he floundered into the snow and bent down, scrabbling as if hoping to find them buried.

At the other end of the barn, beneath the roof's overhang, a shadow moved again, closing the distance between them. I saw him clearly: black hood, black ski-suit, silver-gilt padded shoulders. The executioner, stealing up on the bending man with the inevitability of a dream, and as in a dream I watched helplessly, unable to stir hand or foot, unable to scream a warning. My throat was dry, my limbs apparently paralysed.

At the last moment the hooded man must have made some sound – perhaps he spoke – because Didier straightened up, and the yell of terror that burst from him froze my blood. He put up his hands in a futile gesture to shield his head, and in his pursuer's hand something gleamed. Almost immediately I heard two muffled plopping sounds in quick succession – sounds that seemed too small and innocuous to have the effect they did. Didier pitched forward into the snow, and a moment later the plopping sounds were repeated as the hooded man, standing over his fallen body, shot him carefully, almost thoughtfully, in the back of the neck. The ground beneath my feet seemed to tilt and there was a roaring noise in my ears as the world turned black. I shut my eyes and clung to the rock, willing myself not to faint.

When I opened my eyes again, the murderer was dragging Didier's body round the end of the barn. He disappeared from sight. As minutes passed, the nausea I'd been fighting turned to fear as I realized just how much of a fix I was in. Didier was dead, and without him to guide me I was lost – quite literally. I hadn't the least idea where I was. It was bitterly cold and already late in the afternoon. As evening drew on the temperature would drop still further, yet I dared not approach the barn. I had been standing still for the best part of twenty minutes, and fingers and toes were numb. Without shelter I would die of exposure, yet to venture into the only shelter in sight, where Didier's murderer lurked, was unthinkable. The horrid casualness with which the hooded killer had pumped bullets into a defenceless man told me all too plainly that he wouldn't think twice about doing the same to me. His attack with the piste-bully had failed: he'd be careful to make no mistake next time.

Before I could decide whether I preferred to face the gun or the glacier, the black-clad figure reappeared from the front of the barn, carrying skis. I watched, shivering, hardly daring to hope that he was going away, but a moment later I realized he was. He stamped on his skis, grasped his poles, and began to climb the slope behind the barn, leaving a neat herringbone pattern in the snow.

He was going to pass my hiding place. I shrank still further back beneath the overhang, desperate to see yet not be seen. As he came closer I heard his regular panting breath, saw that he was slim, of medium height, with graceful, well-coordinated movements – a neat, strong, racing-whip of a man . . . with no face. The black hood covered his head completely.

I watched in utter despair as he trudged past, knowing I could never pick him out or describe his appearance. He had no distinguishing marks at all.

Yet as he reached the downward slope and began to glide swiftly away, a faint thread of tune floated back to me, the chirpy, repetitive song that branded him as Rowan's kidnapper:

> *Malbrouk s'en va t'en guerre,*
> *Mirotan, mirotan, mirotaine!*
> *Malbrouk s'en va t'en guerre,*
> *Ne sait quand reviendra!*

I steeled myself to wait for ten freezing minutes after he was out of sight before stumbling on numbed legs to the barn, using every scrap of cover to conceal my approach, just as Didier had done. Fire from the dying sun bathed the irregular clinker-built walls in a rosy light, but the ventilation slits in the barn showed no answering gleam. If there was anyone inside, he or she was in darkness.

Reluctant to abandon my skis in case a quick getaway was needed, I made a slow circuit of the barn, dreading every minute to stumble over Didier's body. But the trail of flattened snow led away from the building, and almost without thinking I found myself at the entrance beneath the gable: a stable door of which both top and bottom halves were bolted on the outside.

My heart leapt. Outside bolts meant one of two things. Either the barn was empty, in which case I could shelter safely, or . . .

'*Elle est là,*' Didier had said. 'She is there.'

After a brief struggle I shot back both bolts and opened the creaking door, peering into the dusty gloom. Inside the barn something whimpered – a small, querulous sound like a lonely puppy.

'Rowan?'

There was no answer.

'Rowan? Are you there?' Slowly I groped my way across the

hay-strewn floor, around the cobwebbed walls, hands stretched out in front like a sleepwalker's. Gradually my eyes adjusted to the gloom. The whimper came again from my left, where an old-fashioned trough manger had been covered with a plank to form a sort of shelf.

My hands touched a trailing softness – blankets – then recoiled in atavistic fear as my exploring fingers encountered the unmistakable stringy greasiness of hair. I held my breath, sensing a warmth, a human presence, then a great wave of thankfulness brought the blood rushing to my cheeks. The thousand-to-one chance had come off: I had found Rowan, and she was still alive.

She was lying on her back, tightly swaddled in a sleeping bag, over which were heaped more blankets. Hurriedly I opened the shuttered window to let in more light and what I saw shocked me inexpressibly. Rowan's eyes were covered with a black blindfold; her hair straggled over her shoulders, and her nose and chin were as sharp as an old woman's. She was unconscious, breathing shallowly, and from time to time through her parted lips came the little whimper. The tang of surgical spirit rising to my nostrils told of a recent injection. No doubt the hooded man had been jabbing her into oblivion when he detected Didier's approach.

I unwound the blindfold, talking to her, trying to rouse her, but her eyes stared straight ahead unseeing. She was alive but dead to the world, and she looked frighteningly frail, as if a puff of wind could blow her away.

Trying to lift her, I quickly discovered that this was not the case. Although she was as helpless as a baby, she was a great deal heavier. I wondered how on earth I was going to move her.

'Ro?' I said urgently, patting her cheeks and pushing back the tangled elf-locks. 'Wake up, Ro. It's me – Catta. I've come to take you home.'

She didn't respond by so much as the flicker of an eyelid. I talked to her, shook her, slapped her. I fetched handfuls of snow to rub on her face and hands in a vain attempt to rouse her but nothing I did produced any sign of animation apart from that mindless heartrending whimper.

'You've *got* to wake up, Ro!' I said in despair. Minutes were passing, the light outside was fading, and nothing I did had any effect. 'We've got to get away before he comes back. You'll have to help me.'

It was no use. There was no sign that she'd seen or heard me, or even felt my increasingly rough handling. I felt desperate. There was nothing from which to construct a sledge, and the blood-wagon on which she'd been transported to this dismal place was not to be seen. I pulled three planks out of the manger and even found a length of plastic twine with which to lash them together, but the moment I laid this rough stretcher on the snow it sank through the crust, and I knew that even unloaded it would be too heavy for me to drag. Pulling an unconscious Rowan on top of it was out of the question.

At last I faced up to the fact that I couldn't move her in this state. I'd have to leave her where she was and go for help. Provided the hooded man didn't realize that Didier hadn't been alone, there was no reason why he should suspect that I had discovered the whereabouts of his hostage. Though I hated having to do it, I replaced Rowan's blindfold, pulled up the sleeping bag, whose smell made my stomach heave, and heaped the blankets on top.

Rowan sighed slightly and settled into the position in which I'd found her: legs drawn up, arms hugging her shoulders. Below the blindfold, the angle of her jaw stood out like a skeleton's.

'I'll be back,' I said, though I knew she couldn't hear me. 'Don't worry; I'll be as quick as I can.'

Then I muffled her head in the top blanket once more, pulled the shutter closed, and stumbled through the gloom to the door. The last thing I heard as I shut and bolted it was that plaintive animal whimper.

Outside I was alarmed to see how dark it had become. Shadow from the cliff was creeping towards the barn, and although the herringbone tracks of the kidnapper's skis still showed clearly, in an hour's time it would be a different story. I imagined myself still following them as darkness fell, losing them, straying towards a crevasse . . . a precipice . . . The temptation to remain in shelter was strong. Only by deliberately envisaging how Didier had looked when the hooded man approached could I force myself to leave the barn and set off the way the murderer had gone.

As soon as I rounded the end of the cliff and the wind hit me, I realized how tired I was. The hurry to the rendezvous, the row with Richard and the long slog across the glacier had taken more out of me than I realized – or was it the shock of finding Rowan unconscious that made me feel that every step was the last I'd manage? Yet under the aching weariness I was conscious of pride. Rowan was alive and *I* had found her. Not by chance, either. If I'd obeyed Charles' instructions to do nothing until he returned, her hiding place would still be as mysterious as the identity of her abductor. Now I knew both, her rescue was only a matter of time. I bent my head against the wind and slogged on upward, following the tracks.

Chapter Eight

Stars were pricking through a pewter sky when at last the tracks
vanished. Not down a slope too steep for me to follow, as I'd
feared, but into a mass of other tracks and tyre-marks on a
snowed-over road. Roads led eventually to towns. I quickened
my pace, cheered by the thought of people, telephones, com-
munications. The notion that the murderer's tracks might lead
only to some isolated hideout had not been an attractive
one.

Lights twinkled among the trees a few hundred yards ahead,
and soon the growl of an engine in low gear reached me.
Headlights snaked uphill and turned in at tall iron gates set in a
chain link surround. The gates stayed open, so I followed the
car in.

A party was in progress. The front door stood hospitably
open and light streamed from it onto the cars parked haphazardly on a semi-circle of churned-up snow in front of a
substantial wooden chalet.

A man stood in the doorway, greeting guests with much
hearty backslapping and hand-pumping. He was tall and imposing, with a big square grey-streaked head and long-nosed
face. I thought he looked like a rather jovial wolf. I was
suddenly acutely conscious of my fatigue and dishevelment, but
before I could decide to retreat and try another house, two big
dogs bounded round the corner of the building and came
straight for me.

That settled it. I called, 'Excuse me, *monsieur* . . .' and
moved forward into the light. The grey-streaked man stopped
in the act of closing the front door.

'Who's there?' he called, puzzled; then, catching sight of me,
he roared at the dogs in a voice which stopped them in their
tracks. I went quickly towards the safety of the house, tripping
and stumbling over the rutted snow.

'Good evening, *mademoiselle*,' said the grey-streaked man
and smiled. 'Have you chosen this method of transport because

you don't trust the driving skill of my son's guests? You have my sympathy.'

Hastily I explained that I wasn't a guest but simply a benighted skier. He accepted the story without question.

'Come in, come in!' he exclaimed. 'Your companions will be worried about you. You can telephone from my house to set their minds at rest.'

'That's very kind of you.'

'Come this way, *mademoiselle*; and when you have reassured your friends, I insist that you join my guests, for a few minutes at least.' He laughed, not unkindly. 'You will excuse me if I say you have the air of a little sparrow that has flown in from the storm. Allow me at least to arrange transport back to Val du Loup. There are several of my son's friends who will be returning to the village.'

I thanked him again and he summoned a stout maid with a frilled apron over her black dress, who showed me the telephone. As soon as she left me I put a call through to Ben Henschel's apartment in Geneva, hoping desperately that Charles would be there. I couldn't wait to astonish him with my news.

But the voice that answered was that of Mario, Ben's secretary-cum-manservant. I knew him of old: a close-mouthed Italian whose puffy features bore witness to an unsuccessful career in the boxing ring. He was Ben's watchdog, guarding his master's privacy in a way which Rowan, I knew, thought ridiculously exaggerated. Now he dashed my hopes by telling me that both Charles and Signor Henschel were out.

I suppressed a groan. 'When do you expect them back?'

'I am sorry, *signorina*, but I do not know. After supper, certainly. Probably late. Signor Henschel has gone to the theatre with friends. As to Signor Dawson, he left no word of when he would return.'

'Can you give me a telephone number where Mr Henschel can be reached?'

Mario hesitated and I willed him to be helpful, but in vain. The guard-dog syndrome reasserted itself. 'I am sorry, *signorina*. Is there a message I can give him?'

'Please ask Mr Dawson to ring me in Val du Loup the

moment he returns. It's very important. I don't mind how late it is.'

'*Bene, signorina*,' said Mario woodenly, and I gave him the number and rang off, wondering how the hell I could get in touch with Charles. Every moment was vital. It would take him four hours at least to drive from Geneva up the twisting mountain road to Val du Loup. Even if Mario gave him my message immediately he could hardly get back before the lifts started at nine tomorrow morning, and then another three or four hours would be needed to slog across the glacier to Rowan's prison. The glacier itself posed an ugly question: without a guide, would I remember the route Didier had taken?

Problems . . . problems . . . All my elation at finding Rowan was draining away as I realized how far we still were from rescuing her. The thought that she must spend another night – possibly another day as well – drugged and helpless in that freezing barn filled me with foreboding. And then there was the probability of the hooded man's return. How often did he visit his captive, to top up the sedatives and check that she was still alive? Twice a day at least, I guessed. The risk of hypothermia made it essential to see her that often. Then it followed that he must make his approach the way I'd tracked him tonight rather than across the glacier: but so intent had I been on watching the imprints of his skis in the fading light that I'd taken little note of where they'd led me. Across two narrow valleys, certainly, but after that?

'*Ça va, mademoiselle?* Did you get through all right?' My kindly host stood in the doorway. Beyond him I could hear a confused babble of voices, laughter, the chink of glasses.

'Yes, thank you. I left a message.'

'Good. Now come and join the party. We will find someone to drive you home.'

'I'm very grateful, *monsieur*. I'm sorry to put you to so much trouble when you're busy.' I held out my hand. 'My name is Catherine Chiltern, from England.'

'*Enchanté, mademoiselle.* And I am Emil Kronsky.' He smiled, showing large white teeth, an orthodontist's dream. I looked at him with heightened interest. So this was Mr Big, the entrepreneur who'd designed and built Val du Loup. Whose offers for their property the Labouchere brothers had stubbornly resisted. He seemed too friendly and approachable to fit such a bloated-capitalist role.

He led the way to the large room from which the party noises were coming, introducing me to sleek jewelled women and sun-flushed men with as much formality as if I'd been a grand duchess instead of a rather bedraggled gatecrasher. The cream of Grandes Alpes society seemed to have gathered that evening in Emil Kronsky's handsome chalet overlooking the lights of the fashionable playground he had carved from a rugged mountain valley. From the picture window that extended from floor to ceiling and wall to wall, the view was spectacular: diamond-studded sky, royal icing peaks above a gaudy jewelbox of emerald, ruby, and topaz lights, all the daytime ugliness of steel and concrete architecture hidden by the black velvet night.

'Come and meet my son Maximilian. He knows who will go back to the village tonight. There he is – with the drinks.'

I looked across the room. If Emil Kronsky reminded me of a wolf, his son was more like a fox: lean, elegant, with a fine head of flaming hair swept back from a narrow, aristocratic face, whose pallor contrasted oddly with the ruddy open-air complexions of his guests. He looked the indoor type. His intelligent eyes moved here and there, seeing to the needs of his guests, flickering with laughter as he poured drinks and chatted to a couple of pretty girls. He looked the life and soul of the party, yet his father's expression, as he elbowed a courteous passage through the crowd, was resigned rather than approving. I'd seen the same look on my brother-in-law's face when his daughter brought home a bunch of friends without warning – reluctant hospitality mingled with a strong desire to throw them all out into the street – and guessed that the party had been sprung on Emil Kronsky against his wishes.

I started to follow him across the room. Before I'd gone more than a few yards, however, a hand touched my shoulder and I turned to confront Robin Labouchere. His fair complexion was flushed, almost feverish-looking, and his eyes had a hard shiny glaze.

'Where's Rowan?' he demanded.

The relief of seeing a familiar face was so intense that I nearly blurted out the truth there and then. Only recognition that the face although familiar was far from friendly kept my mouth shut.

'Where is she?' he repeated. 'Didn't she come with you?'

'No,' I said, hastily pulling myself together. 'No, I'm afraid she's not up yet. The doctor told her to stay in bed a couple more days.'

'That's a lie.'

He took a quick step forward as he spoke and I had an uncomfortable feeling that drink had so far loosened his inhibitions that it wouldn't take much to provoke him into seizing me by the scruff and shaking a more satisfactory answer out of me.

Abruptly I came to a decision. Every minute that Rowan spent in that barn increased her danger. If Charles wasn't available to help me, I must find someone else – and who better than Robin? He loved her. He was already half convinced that I was hiding something from him. If I didn't make him an ally, he might become a dangerous nuisance.

He said truculently, 'I've been to your apartment and she isn't there, so don't give me any of that crap. If you won't tell me where she's gone, I'll see what my friends in the Press can find out.'

All trace of youthful hesitancy had left his manner. He looked unpredictable and desperate, like a stag brought to bay. On either side of us people were beginning to turn and stare: I knew I must stop him talking before he did any harm.

'Have you got a car?' I asked.

'What's that got to do with it?'

'Have you?'

'Yes.'

'Give me a lift home, Robin,' I said quietly. 'There's something I want to tell you. About Rowan.'

I rang Ben Henschel's apartment at ten o'clock and eleven, and again at midnight. On each occasion Mario sounded huffier, but I was beyond caring what he thought. He assured me that he hadn't forgotten my message but there was nothing he could do: neither of the gentlemen had returned. It was not unknown, he added, for Signor Henschel to stay overnight with his friends. As for Signor Dawson, no doubt he amused himself in his own

113

fashion. There was a sneer discernible in this last remark: Mario didn't approve of Charles.

I repeated my instructions and rang off, convinced now that I'd been right to enlist Robin's help, although his reaction to my story had been unexpected, even disturbing. As he listened, his hostility had vanished and been replaced by something suspiciously like elation. He'd begun to drive recklessly, sliding his brother's heavy BMW round the snow-covered bends in a way that brought my heart to my mouth.

'I knew it!' he exclaimed. 'I knew Ricky was wrong.'

'You mustn't tell him,' I said quickly. 'It's vital that *no one* hears – particularly not the Press. She's in *danger*, Robin. The man who shut her in that barn is a criminal. A homicidal maniac. I saw him murder Didier. Until Rowan's safely out of that barn, you mustn't say a word about it to anyone.'

He grinned. I could feel I wasn't getting through to him. He seemed to have seized on the single fact that Rowan hadn't thrown him over, and nothing else would register. Too late I wondered if I'd have been better advised to go to the local police, but Charles had been dead against it, and until I could get in touch with him my hands were tied. Besides, I could imagine only too vividly how difficult it would be to convince a posse of cynical French policemen that Rowan had been kidnapped. In my mind's eye I saw the half-smoked Gauloise drooping from disillusioned French lips, heard the disbelieving voice: *'Et alors, mademoiselle,* can you provide any evidence to back up this fantasy . . .?'

The kidnapper might be watching me as well as monitoring Charles' movements. If he should see me approaching the *gendarmerie* he was likely to jump to conclusions which might mean the end of Rowan. I dared not risk it. Nevertheless, I wished with all my heart that circumstances could have provided me with a more reliable ally than Robin Labouchere.

'Are you sure you can find the barn? You know the way?' I persisted, and Robin lifted his hands from the steering wheel with a large expansive gesture before plonking them down to whip through a racing change.

'No problem! I know it like the back of my hand. Ricky and I used to camp there when we were into rock climbing a few years back. That was before the hordes invaded Val du Loup. Then a

114

couple of trekkers slipped into a crevasse and old Kronsky was so scared that the place would get a bad name that he persuaded the SAVDL to ban all skiers from the glacier. Lot of nonsense. People who can't look after themselves have got no business off the pistes anyway.'

Every word he said increased my concern. This was a very different Robin from the silent, morose figure in the Phoenix Bar; now he seemed arrogant, contemptuous, even reckless. He roared round a couple of bends, deliberately over-correcting to make the car skid, and when I clutched the grab handle he laughed aloud.

'She loves me, she don't. She'll have me, she won't . . .' he chanted, zigzagging down the line of cats' eyes as if they were slalom gates.

'Steady on!' I exclaimed; then, when he took no notice, 'why don't you let me drive the rest of the way? I didn't have time for a drink.'

'Don't worry, my reflexes are in perfect order. Richard won't let me touch alcohol when I'm in training.'

Outside my apartment block he switched off the engine and turned a flushed, excited face to me. 'I can't wait till tomorrow . . . Where shall we meet?'

'Outside the Trois Fontaines lift at nine o'clock. We'll have to go the long way round by the glacier for fear of running into the murderer on the shorter route. The problem will be carrying her back across the glacier. She's very weak . . .'

'Leave that to me. I'll bring a sledge, and blankets, champagne and caviare! You've done your bit, Catta. Now I'll take charge.'

His air of exhilaration worried me. I found it hard to believe it wasn't caused by alcohol, but why had he bothered to lie? Did he imagine I'd sneak to his brother?

I said as emphatically as I could, 'Remember, Robin, it's a matter of life and death. Don't say a word about where you're going to *anyone.*'

'All right, all right. No need to keep telling me. My love was dead and is alive again, was lost and is found!' he declaimed extravagantly. 'I've been in hell these past few days, Catta: sheer black bottomless hell. I couldn't eat or drink or sleep. I couldn't ski to save my life. Every time I heard your voice on the telephone telling me that Rowan wouldn't see me, I felt like cutting my throat. But all that's over now. I feel so happy I could shout from the rooftops. It's as if I'm soaring upwards on great wings . . .'

'Robin!' I was seriously alarmed. 'Don't talk like that. There's a long way to go before Rowan's safe. For God's sake cool it.'

'Mum's the word. My lips are sealed.' He began humming, *'With catlike tread, upon our way we steal . . .'* then broke off to clasp my hand and say laughingly, 'Don't look so worried, Catta: just think – this time tomorrow we'll be celebrating! Don't you trust me?'

He waved an airy hand and the car roared away before I could reply, which was just as well, I reflected, since the answer to his final question would have been a short and unequivocal No. I didn't trust him, nor did I understand him, and I wished very much that it was Charles, not Robin, who would meet me at the Trois Fontaines lift the following morning.

As I shut the apartment door after a miserable night worrying about Rowan, the telephone began to ring. In my haste to get back indoors and answer it, I dropped the latchkey. Precious seconds were wasted grovelling on the floor of the darkened lobby before my hand closed over it. I prayed that the caller would keep ringing. I felt certain it was Charles at last, but knowing his impatience with all things mechanical, I didn't expect him to persevere for long unless I answered. Twice already that morning I'd dialled Ben Henschel's house, only to get the engaged signal. I thought it more than likely that Mario had left the receiver off the hook.

The key stuck. I jerked it out and tried the other way up. This time it turned. Dropping everything I was carrying, I darted across the little hall and grabbed up the receiver. Too late: it buzzed at me emptily.

I took a deep breath and rang the Henschel number again: to my inexpressible relief Charles answered.

'Thank God!' I exclaimed. 'I've been trying to get hold – '

'Catta?' He sounded surprised. 'How odd, I was just ringing *you* a minute ago. Mario gave me your message when I got in last night.'

'*Last night?* Why didn't you call me?'

'Have a heart, darling. It was late – after one, anyway – and I was tired. I'd been at meetings all day with Ben, trying to raise the money. You've no idea what a business it is. I thought whatever it was you wanted would keep a few hours. What is it, anyway?'

Now I'd got him listening at last, I found it oddly difficult to tell him.

'Well? Surely you didn't haul me out of bed just to hear my voice?'

'Listen,' I said urgently. 'I've found Rowan.'

For the space of perhaps ten seconds there was silence apart from the humming on the line, then he gave a sort of half-laugh, half-groan. 'Sorry, darling, it's too early. I'm not feeling up to jokes just yet. Perhaps after a cup of strong black – '

'I'm not joking,' I said with controlled desperation. 'It's true. I've found her. She's shut up in a barn, miles away up in the hills. She's – she's unconscious. I couldn't move her. She's tied up and blindfolded and drugged . . .'

'Are you feeling all right? You sound very odd to me. Hadn't you better take a couple of aspirin and lie down?'

'Listen, you've got to believe me. I've found Rowan and she's in a bad way. I tried to get hold of you all yesterday evening –'

'Now, steady on a minute,' he cut in. 'Let me get this straight. You say you know where Rowan is – right?'

'That's what I'm *telling* you.'

'It's . . . it's incredible. I can't believe it. Tell me everything.' Like changing a radio wavelength, his voice was suddenly clear, positive, excited. 'How did you find her? What were you *doing* miles up in the hills? Begin at the beginning and tell me everything.'

The need to convince him acted as a tonic. I pulled myself together and gave him a rapid summary of yesterday's events with only one omission: to tell Rowan's husband that I'd been forced to ask her lover for help seemed an unnecessary rubbing of salt in the wound.

Apart from the occasional exclamation he listened in silence, but when I told him I was on my way back to the barn, he said sharply, 'No. Stay where you are and wait for me. If I start at once, I'll be with you by noon. Just wait and do nothing until I arrive.'

'We'd lose a whole day,' I objected. 'It takes at least three hours to cross the glacier. We'd never get there and back before dark.'

'Then we'll go tomorrow. If Ro's under sedation, as you say, it won't make any difference to her.'

'But it will! It might make all the difference. It's freezing in that barn. She could easily die before we got there. Another twenty-four hours may finish her.'

'Use your head, darling. Whoever kidnapped Ro isn't going to let her die,' he said firmly. 'She's his golden goose. He's got a vested interest in keeping her alive.'

I couldn't share his confidence. 'You haven't seen her – or him. He's mad – he must be. We can't leave Rowan there for another whole day.'

'Now listen to me, Catta.' Charles' voice took on the firm, Pack-leader tone I recognized so well. 'I absolutely forbid you to do anything until I get back. The last thing we want is some badly-organized rescue bid going off at half cock. Don't you see? It's far more dangerous from Ro's point of view than if we leave her where she is. Wait till I get there, and we'll do the thing properly – understand?'

Understanding was far from being the same as agreeing, but I knew how hopeless it was to argue with Charles once his mind was made up. He must have taken my silence for assent, for he added, 'Don't worry, darling. I'm sure she'll be all right so long as we keep our heads and don't do anything that might put the kidnapper in a panic. He doesn't know you've found her – remember? While he thinks he can negotiate with us, he'll treat her all right, believe me. It's not in his interest to hurt her.'

My brain told me he was right, but his words nevertheless set in motion a train of thought I strove unavailingly to suppress. What if I'd left some telltale evidence of my visit to the barn? It had been dark: I'd been nervous and hurried. A dropped tissue, an unbolted shutter . . . even my footprints on the dusty floor might be enough to tell the hooded man that his prisoner had been seen.

'But, Charles . . .' My voice died away.

Probably it was naive of me to hanker after approval for my

efforts to find Rowan, or even an acknowledgment that I'd done something positive towards wiping out the record of my disastrous concealment of her disappearance. When it didn't come, I said, 'At least tell me you're pleased I found her . . .'

'*Pleased*!' The explosion was like a slap in the face. 'I'm appalled. You should never have taken such risks. I told you – I *begged* you – not to do anything without telling me.'

'I tried to tell you.'

'All right, you tried. But you didn't succeed.' His tone softened. 'My darling idiot, don't you realize I'd rather pay the ransom twenty times over than have a hair of your head hurt? Or Rowan's, for that matter. Now, for the love of God, stop meddling. All this is miles out of your league. Just stay where you are until I get back and leave the negotiating to me. I'm on my way.'

He hung up before I could protest and slowly I replaced the receiver. The little spark of resentment was burning again, brighter and stronger this time. Miles out of my league, was it? It was all very well for Charles to say he'd pay twenty times the ransom, since he wasn't the one who was paying it anyway. That privilege was reserved for Rowan's father who might – I didn't say would, but might – have different ideas about shelling out three million francs unnecessarily. Charles hadn't seen Rowan's chin sharpened like a witch's, her rosy-olive complexion turned slack and grey.

I can be obstinate, too. In this instance I knew I was right and Charles desperately wrong. Another twenty-four hours of inactivity was unthinkable.

A man was waiting by the Trois Fontaines lift, his back towards me, head bent as he fiddled with a screwdriver at one of the runners of the skeleton sledge at his feet. He wore a black shiny ski-suit with chevron bands of red, yellow and green across the shoulders, and at the sight of him my heart gave a great thump. My unreliable ally had betrayed me. Robin Labouchere's brother had come in his place.

'Good morning,' said Richard, with a smile that barely touched his eyes. For a moment he looked me up and down in silence. Then he said coolly, 'Robin said you were in a hurry to catch the first cable-car, but I see the urgency has evaporated somewhat. I've been waiting here since nine.'

'I should have known better than to trust your brother. I might have guessed he'd tell you everything,' I said bitterly.

'So you should. But since you didn't, let's get on with it, shall we? We've wasted enough of the morning as it is. I take it you *do* still want to go up to Villoutrey's old barn? You haven't changed your mind about that?'

'No. Well . . .' I hesitated.

'I see. It's like that, is it? You want to go with Robin but not me.'

'No, no! I've got to go there. I'm wondering why Robin couldn't keep his mouth shut.'

'All right, then, let's be off. We can discuss Robin as we go.' He picked up my skis as well as his own and started towards the cable-station. 'I hope you realize what you've taken on; the old barn is quite a long way away. I don't want to have to carry you.'

'Nor do I.' Strangely enough, my exertions of yesterday had tired me less than I expected, or else it was my anger at Robin's loose-mouthed treachery that raised my adrenalin level. I'd have died rather than ask Richard to carry me.

'What did he tell you?' I demanded, hurrying after him. 'He promised he could keep a secret. Why can't he do anything without asking you first?'

He said in a tight, controlled voice, as if the words were being dragged out of him, 'Perhaps you'll understand when I tell you my brother's what's known as a manic depressive. It makes his moods very . . . unpredictable. All right, don't look so alarmed. It's quite a common condition – you probably know half a dozen people who have it more or less – but unfortunately Rob's case is worse than most. On the whole he copes with it quite well. It's only when people like you start pitching him tales of murder and mayhem that it upsets his equilibrium. That's why I sent him off to the races today, and told him I'd come in his place. You and Rowan, between you, have wrecked his chances in the Championship, but I wanted to make sure you didn't send him off the rails altogether.'

I stared at him speechlessly. Of course, once one knew, it made sense: Richard's overprotectiveness, Robin's silent morose look when I first met him and the contrast with yesterday's aggressive hyperactivity.

At last I said, 'Why didn't you say so before? Why did you let me go on thinking . . .?'

'Strangely enough I don't usually broadcast it from the rooftops. As I told you, he's learning to cope with it. With a mixture of drugs and a reasonable amount of care, we manage to keep his condition fairly stable. Anyway, I thought Rowan might have mentioned it to you.'

'How could she? She's disappeared. What I told Robin last night is true: she's been kidnapped –'

'By your vanishing friend in the black hood?'

His sceptical tone made me furious. 'He's not my friend. And he does exist.'

'All right, all right, tell me more.'

'He's trying to get Rowan's father to pay a ransom.'

'Strange that Ben hasn't mentioned it to me.'

'Of course it's not strange. It's a secret. The more people know, the worse danger Rowan's in.'

'So that's why you told Robin, who told me . . .' He frowned. 'Wouldn't it have been more sensible to ask her husband to help you rescue her?'

'I couldn't. He's in Geneva, trying to persuade Ben to raise the money.'

'Is that difficult?'

'Obviously it's not easy.' I went on quickly, 'Charles is desperately worried in case the papers get hold of the story. He daren't even bring the police in – in case Rowan gets hurt.'

He started to speak, changed his mind, and stared at me in silence. I had the feeling he was trying to see into my mind. At last he said, 'Have you been in touch with Dawson since you found her. Does he know?'

Should I tell him Charles had expressly forbidden any rescue attempt until he returned? I hesitated, then said, 'I spoke to him just now – that's why I was late. He's driving back at once. He'll be here in a few hours.'

'Then why not wait till he arrives?'

It was what I'd hoped he wouldn't say, but at least I was half expecting the question. I said urgently, 'Because I don't think it's safe to leave her there a moment longer. If I wait for Charles it'll be too late to cross the glacier and get back today, and that's a whole day wasted. If you'd seen what Rowan looked like yesterday you'd know why I'm worried sick. I *must* go today.'

'I suppose that makes sense – up to a point. So Dawson would like you to wait for him, but you're determined to go. Does that mean you accept responsibility for going against his wishes?'

How I hated the legal mind that reduced everything to black and white. 'Yes.'

'All right then, on your own head be it. I'll come with you. I've got to go back to Geneva tomorrow, but today's my own. We'll go and look for Rowan, but I don't mind telling you that if we find her in old Villoutrey's barn I, personally, will eat my hat.'

I glanced at his black astrakhan pillbox. *'Bon appetit!* I hope you like the taste of unborn lamb.'

'It's only nylon,' he said, and led the way to the cable-car.

From the outside, the barn looked unchanged. We had made good time across the glacier, speaking little, but although it was only a few minutes after one o'clock, the heavily overcast sky and copper-tinged clouds made it seem much later.

We stood in the shadow of the cliff, watching the barn just as Didier and I had surveyed it yesterday. The neat herringbone tracks the kidnapper had made on leaving showed clearly still.

'Come on,' I said nervously, and poled quickly across the intervening snow to the barn. I took off my skis and propped them against the wall, then hurried round to the door beneath the central gable. When I'd left, it had been bolted top and bottom. Now it stood ajar.

As I stared at it, with the first premonition of disaster touching my heart, Richard slid silently up behind me.

'What's the matter?' He gave me a curious look. 'Aren't you going in?'

'We're too late.' My words fell heavily. I felt suddenly very tired. I sat down in the snow, legs weak, an awful guilt overwhelming me. Charles had been right. I should have left well alone. My meddling had driven the kidnapper to act: it might have cost Rowan her life.

Incapable of thought, I sat and listened to Richard moving inside the barn, turning the place upside down. I stared blankly ahead, seeing from here what wasn't visible from the cliff: tracks stretching away towards the opposite side of the valley.

Single tracks inside a double: a sledge pulled by a skier.

Richard came and stood beside me. 'All right, Catta, the party's over. You can stop pretending. The old barn's been empty for years. Now suppose you tell me what the hell you mean by dragging me here?'

I got up, vaguely surprised to find my trousers soaked through, and went inside. Richard had flung open the shutters and pulled a lot of planks from the wall to expose an inner shed, like a stall, but it was all just as empty as he'd said. There was no trace of human occupation, no corner where anyone could hide, and yet . . .

'Ether!' I exclaimed. 'Surgical spirit and drugs. Surely you can smell it?'

He sniffed perfunctorily but I could tell he wasn't really trying. To me the whole barn reeked like an operating theatre: it was impossible to believe he wasn't aware of it.

'I don't smell anything like that.' He gave me a puzzled look. 'You're quite an actress, you know. Once or twice back there you almost had me worried. But you shouldn't overdo it. The best actors always know when to stop.'

I'd thought I was past caring whether he believed me or not, but now I had an overwhelming urge to break through that cynicism. I must convince him Rowan had been held captive here. I knelt down beside the manger in which she'd been huddled, scuffling through the dry musty hay at the bottom of it with fierce concentration.

'What are you doing?'

I didn't answer. I went on searching and at last found what I wanted. My fingers closed on metal and extracted it from the hay.

'Look!'

'A hair-grip?' he said blankly. 'What's that supposed to prove? That some hiker once slept in the manger? It might belong to anyone. It's probably been there for years.'

'It's Rowan's. She drops them wherever she goes. It's – it's a standing joke with people who know her. You can always tell where Rowan's been sleeping. Ask Robin.'

He frowned. 'Easy to say but pretty difficult to prove.' The sceptical mouth twisted a little. 'Come on, don't keep me in suspense. I'm longing to hear the next thrilling instalment of this fantasy. Where is she? Who's taken her away?'

Just in time I realized that to obey my impulse to scream would just confirm his opinion that I was a hysterical fantasist. As calmly as possible I said, 'I told you. It's the man in the black hood.'

'The one who drove the piste-bully at you after you'd had a few drinks?'

'One drink. Yes. The same man. He must have realized that I'd been here yesterday.'

'Perhaps you dropped a hairpin.'

I looked at him suspiciously but he wasn't smiling. His expression was serious, even worried. He said, 'One thing's been bothering me. How did you know about Villoutrey's barn – that it even existed, I mean?'

'Because I came here yesterday, of course.'

'But how did you find it? Who brought you here? Who showed you where you could cross the glacier?'

It was like having a light switched on in my head. In my worry over the disappearance of Rowan I had forgotten the only piece of solid evidence I had to back up my story.

'I'll show you,' I said, and made for the door.

Outside the snow looked flat and matt under a lowering sky. The wind had died and I had a strange feeling that the landscape was holding its breath, waiting for the onslaught. Hurriedly I kicked on my skis and poled round the barn to the corner where I'd seen Didier grovelling, begging vainly for mercy. There was the deep trough ploughed by his body as it was dragged out of my sight and there, where the sledge-track joined it, was a rusty indentation in the snow.

I turned to find Richard close behind me, staring at the mark. 'Come on,' I said, and set off following the trail the sledge had left. It must have been heavily burdened: every thirty or forty yards the puller had rested, either to adjust his load or because its weight was almost more than he could manage. Here and there the same rusty stain marked the snow.

When he reached the scatter of rocks beneath the cliff on the far side of the valley, the man pulling the sledge seemed to have decided that enough was enough. There was a trampled area and a sinister grey-white mound of stones and scree. The next snowfall would conceal it completely: we were only just in time.

I bent down and began to remove the stones, and a moment later Richard did the same.

The hooded killer hadn't gone to much trouble to bury the body. No doubt he thought the elements would soon make a proper job of it.

'You'd better not look,' said Richard, as he pulled away the scarf that had been roughly wound round the bloody head, but I ignored his advice. In death, as in life, Didier's expression was surprised, bovine and slightly resentful, his dull eyes fixed in a baffled glare at the sky; his mouth sagged open to show discoloured teeth. The exit holes of several bullets had made a mess of his lower jaw and his whole face was masked with frozen blood, but there was no question of his identity.

I sighed, mainly with relief. The continuing tracks showed that the sledge had been dragged on along the valley, its burden halved, but at least my worst fear wasn't realized. Rowan's body had not joined Didier's beneath the mound of stones.

Chapter Nine

'So that's the last of Casavargues,' said Richard, and dropped the scarf to cover his head.

'Didier,' I corrected.

'That's right. Didier Casavargues, one of the local no-good boyos, always out for a fast buck providing it didn't entail too much exertion. Well, this puts a different complexion on things. We'll have to notify the police.'

I should have guessed this would be his reaction. 'Not the police,' I said quickly. 'Not until we've found Rowan. *Please*.'

'You can't conceal a murder. It makes you an accessory –'

'I know, but just a day or two'll make no difference to him, and it could make all the difference in the world to her.'

'What about his mother? His family? They'll have to be told.'

'I don't think,' I said slowly, 'that his family are the kind of people who'd want anything to do with the police. They might even have some idea who the murderer is. I'll tell them about Didier – I'll have to – but I think I might be able to persuade them to keep their mouths shut – for the moment, at least.'

'No, you don't. You've got some fairly tricky explaining to do to the police anyway, without wading any deeper into trouble. I'm a respectable lawyer, and I'm not risking my reputation or yours by letting you break any more laws.'

'Damn your reputation. It's Rowan's life!'

The sharp crack of thunder overhead took us both by surprise. Richard glanced up quickly, and I saw his mouth open in a shout of warning just before his hand gave me a violent shove away from the makeshift grave. I staggered back, arms outstretched, trying to regain my balance.

'What the hell . . .?' I gasped, and toppled over a little bank down which I slid, my mouth full of snow and my ears of a spine-chilling soft rumble as an overhanging segment broke off the cliff above us. I could see it coming: a greyish tumbling mass like a dirty wave, rearing as it rushed downhill on a fifty-yard front, with boulders and jagged lumps of rock bounding high above the mass as if a giant was skimming ducks and drakes.

In an instant the grave was obliterated, smothered beneath hundreds of tons of scree, and I just had time to think, so that's why he buried him there, before the edge of the avalanche caught me.

An irresistible weight of snow wrapped round my legs and engulfed me up to the waist as I tried to flounder clear. Then a boulder must have hit me. Stars exploded inside my head.

I came to with bursting lungs and an awful sensation of suffocation, but almost before I'd had time to wonder how deeply I was buried and what had happened to Richard, I heard him calling. My ski-sticks were looped to my wrists, and when I cautiously poked one out in the direction where the light seemed strongest, to my immense relief it broke through the crust and I saw the sky. I gulped in air and called, 'Here I am!'

'Hang on, I'm coming. Keep waving.'

I listened to him wading through the drifts, his breathing curiously magnified, as if heard through a snorkel. Presently I felt a tug on the ski-stick, and he burrowed down until he could see me, his brown face peering at me in the strange yellowish gloom.

'Are you all right?'

'I think so.'

'Give me your other stick and I'll pull you out. No, wait. Take your skis off first.'

I moved my legs experimentally and discovered that only one was attached to a ski. It was a struggle to reach the release-toggle, and even when both boots were unencumbered I scarcely had the strength to hang on to the sticks as Richard slowly hauled me clear. The leather straps bit into my wrists, but they held; I was shaking with delayed shock and so exhausted that I couldn't even stand while Richard burrowed back into the hole to bring up my ski.

'I'll look for the other one in the morning. It's hopeless now,' he said, sticking the survivor upright to mark the spot.

'The m . . . morning?' I said through chattering teeth.

'We won't make it back tonight. It'll be dark before we're across the glacier.'

127

Thunder still rumbled among the peaks and Didier's grave had vanished completely.

'But . . . C-Charles will be . . .'

'Bad news always keeps,' said Richard firmly. 'Come on, let's get a fire going before we freeze.'

Comfortably if somewhat itchily snuggled in a nest of hay a few hours later, I watched flames flickering on the cobwebbed walls and listened to Richard's quiet breathing. In a physical sense he was close – there wasn't enough hay to be stand-offish about where we slept and I was as grateful for his body heat as no doubt he was for mine – yet mentally we might have been in different worlds.

Worry and guilt nagged at me like a pair of abcessed teeth. Worry about Rowan, guilt because I'd done so precisely what Charles had told me not to. How could I explain? What must he be thinking as he waited for me?

I moved restlessly, and the breathing ceased. Richard said, 'What's the matter? Can't you sleep?'

'I keep wondering where she is . . . what's happened to her.'

'Stop worrying. There's nothing you can do. Think about something else.'

'I can't.'

'Count sheep.'

Easy enough to say. *For I am armed so strong in honesty* . . . Lucky devil, I thought resentfully, with your clear conscience and your capacity for instant sleep. I rolled over on my other side.

'Dear God! I'd rather doss with an electric eel.'

I said, 'Tell me about Robin and Rowan. How long has it been going on?'

'How long?' The grumbling sleepiness left his voice. He sounded wide awake, on the ball. 'Difficult to say, exactly. They've known each other for years . . . Ben Henschel's been very good to Robin – to us both. He helped us over the worst patch, when we didn't know what was wrong with Robin and why he got these terrible moods, up one minute and down the next. That started during his first year at university, and he had to drop out. He never knew from one day to another whether he could work or not. His concentration was utterly destroyed and so was his self-confidence. He couldn't drive a car, go to parties . . . it was hardly safe to let him go out alone. He became completely withdrawn, and the worst of it was that he refused to see a doctor. He kept insisting he was all right.'

'It must have been terrible.'

'It was. Then Ben put me on to this marvellous doctor in Geneva – a woman called Chantal Leclerc who specializes in nervous diseases, and gradually she brought the trouble under control. That was when Robin started to paint. She suggested it would be therapeutic. That, I suppose, was where Rowan began to notice him.'

I heard the echo of her voice: 'He has a kind of vision. He sees things differently.' She'd compared him to Van Gogh.

'That's the other side of the coin,' he went on. 'Robin's work takes a bit of getting used to, but people who know tell me he's bloody good. Brilliant, even. That's to say, he could be, given the right encouragement.'

'Which Rowan could provide.'

'Yes. She didn't tell you this? Well, Ben had arranged for a friend to hold an exhibition of Robin's work in a private gallery. Just to assess people's reactions: sort of testing the water. Ben had gone to a lot of trouble and asked a whole crowd of big noises in art – and then at the last minute his heart packed up on him and he couldn't go.'

'So Rowan deputized for him?' In the dark I nodded. I could see it all. Rowan playing hostess – Rowan in her element exerting her powers of persuasion to sell Robin's pictures just as she used to promote my clothes. No doubt red stickers had appeared like measles on the frames. Small wonder if the artist had fallen in love with his lovely patroness – or at least, I thought uncharitably, realized he was on to a very good thing.

'She did. The exhibition was a success – too much of a success. Robin went on a high, and it took all sorts of adjustments to his pills before we got him on an even keel again. Chantal insisted that he had a change of scene and a rest from painting, so I thought it would do him good to spend the winter here. He likes the hang-gliding, and he's a brilliant skier – much better than I am – so although he missed both Rowan and the painting he's been reasonably happy. Until you came.'

I ignored the last remark. 'Have you been here all winter too?'

'Off and on, work permitting. When I can't be here, Gina takes over. She's a trained nurse. She looked after Ben last year, and when he didn't need her any more he suggested she came to help out with Robin.'

More impressions slotted into place. 'How did Robin react?' I asked. 'Does he mind being treated as an invalid?'

'He's been very sensible. Chantal was wonderful. Without her I'd never have been able to convince him he needed treatment.'

For a fleeting moment I allowed my thoughts to dwell on the wonderful Chantal. Richard's tone suggested warmer feelings than pure admiration for medical skill.

'She made him see that it's perfectly possible for him to get back to a normal life. That's his aim, now. He was low for the first week or two here, so she boosted his pills, and he's been up and down several times since, but Rowan kept in touch all the time – she wrote and telephoned and kept saying it wouldn't be long before she came here herself – so he had that to look forward to. With all her faults, she's very kind. Temperamentally, she'd make a better nurse than Gina.'

If Rowan was to marry Robin, there'd be nothing to stop me and Charles from . . . I pushed the thought away. As a dream, that was a non-starter.

He went on, 'She's good for him, bucks him up, stops him sliding into his private Slough of Despond. She's got so much confidence – fantastic vitality. And she can handle him when he gets aggressive. When he's on a high, he gets resentful of me, but he doesn't mind Rowan.'

'Is he on a high now?' I asked cautiously.

'I'll say! Last night he kicked over the traces and nicked my car to go up to Max Kronsky's dream palace. Not a word of warning: off he scooted with twelve thousand pounds' worth of uninsured automobile.'

The hair rose on my head. 'Uninsured!'

'He hasn't got a licence.'

'My God.' I'd have enjoyed the drive home even less if I'd known.

Richard went on, 'The trouble is, Rowan's a bit *too* exciting

130

for him at times. When her husband began ringing up and making threatening noises, I saw it was getting out of hand.'

'I don't see that you can blame Charles,' I said stiffly.

He grunted disagreement. 'That sort of crude reaction wasn't going to help anyone.'

'You call it crude. I think it's natural.'

'All right, we'll agree to differ. The point is, Robin can't cope with that sort of pressure. His mental balance is too precarious. So – on Chantal's advice – I told Rowan, I *begged* her, to stay away from him.'

He didn't sound as if begging was something that came easily. 'And she wouldn't?'

'She wouldn't. Instead you and she managed in a couple of days to undo six months' work. Robin's cure is back to Square One – Minus One, really, and I can't put off my return to Geneva any longer. I'll have to go tomorrow and persuade Robin to come too. Perhaps Chantal can undo the damage – let's hope so.'

'You're going tomorrow?' I felt curiously let down.

'Right. I'll leave you and Dawson to continue your search together. If you don't mind me asking, what *is* your relationship with him?'

Almost automatically I trotted out the old lie, the conditioned reflex. 'He's my surrogate brother. We've been friends ever since we were children.'

'You really believe that?'

I stiffened. 'Of course.'

There was quite a long silence, then he said, 'So Paul Lomax was right when he told me you had an incredible capacity for self-deception.'

I felt as if I'd been punched in the stomach. *Paul* – the rat! How dared he kiss and tell? Coldly my brain supplied the link between them: Paul was Ben Henschel's accountant, of course it was perfectly natural that he and Richard should be friends. But to discuss *me* . . .!

'He was pretty cut up when you left him,' said Richard.

'He walked out on me.'

'Because you made it clear that's what you wanted. Paul's not a man to stay where he's not welcome.'

I asked with a sarcasm that should have penetrated the hide of a buffalo, 'What other gems of information did he give you about me?' The thought of the pair of them dissecting my character made me boil, but at the same time I had an awful compulsion to know what Paul had said.

After a moment's silence, he said, 'Well, there was the self-deception bit. And he said you were extremely obstinate.'

'Rubbish.'

'He also said that the man who could dislodge Charles Dawson from your heart would be a lucky fellow. Is that rubbish too?'

'Unmitigated.'

'I wonder.'

'Do go on,' I said tightly. 'I find these unsolicited testimonials absolutely fascinating. Seeing myself as others see me. I'd no idea Paul was such a big mouth.'

'Don't blame poor old Paul. Better blame me; I winkled it out of him. I thought it might help to get you out of his system.'

'Well . . . *thanks!*'

'Of course I had to discount most of what he said.' I was almost sure he was laughing. 'He's inclined to lay it on a bit thick. In fact when it comes to some of the things he told me, I'd need a personal demonstration to convince me that Paul wasn't fantasising.'

'You're not likely to get that,' I said coldly.

'Not after coming all this way with you on a fool's errand?'

I said despairingly, 'Don't you *believe* Rowan was here? Do you still think I'm making it all up?'

'Not all. Not after seeing Casavargues. But it isn't going to be easy to produce *that* piece of evidence now, is it?'

'Why did you agree to come?'

He considered. 'Impulse, I suppose. Curiosity – oh, that fatal curiosity of mine! I've been curious about you ever since you turned up here in Rowan's wake. How did a girl like you come to get mixed up in her sordid marital intrigues? It beats me. An attractive, talented girl like you, of apparently stainless character . . .'

I said dryly, 'I thought Paul was the one who laid it on thick.'

A plank in the fire flared, and I was aware of his eyes watching me, assessing my response. 'I suppose you get tired of being told you're beautiful?'

'It's not,' I said carefully, 'a thing one tires of easily. Neither is it something one can take much credit for. One face, Standard Issue, take it or leave it.'

'Oh, I'd take it. Definitely. I can't think why it hasn't been snapped up before . . . or was that Dawson's doing?'

His proximity disturbed me. Abruptly I got up and crouched beside the fire, hugging my arms round my knees. Even fully dressed, outside the nest of hay the cold bit savagely.

'Come back. You'll freeze.'

I busied myself pushing firewood together and raking the embers into a glowing heap. I didn't want to return to the nest's insidious cosiness. I could create my own body heat, thank you very much. I looked at my watch's luminous dial and my heart quailed. It was still only ten o'clock. Nine hours to go till daylight.

'Paul usually goes for the fluffy dependent type,' said Richard conversationally. 'Pretty little kittens who purr when they're stroked. It must have given him quite a shock to find he'd shacked up with a tigress.'

'Me? A tigress? Hardly!'

'Maybe you're right. On second thoughts, you're more like a bushbaby: all big eyes and innocent cuddliness, but capable of doing the most amazing amount of damage in an astonishingly short time.'

That was definitely below the belt. 'You don't seem to realize,' I said bitterly, 'that I was only trying to help.'

'Ah yes: the famous last line, *I did it for the best*. I'm sure you know what the road to hell is paved with.'

I was silent and he said in a completely different tone, 'All right, you're kicking yourself and you'd like to kick me too, but that isn't going to solve any problems. What I want to know is, *who* are you trying to help? Rowan, or your pseudo-brother?'

'Both, of course.'

'Given that their interests conflict, which of them commands your support – let's say, your affection? Come on,' he said when I didn't answer, 'I really need to know.'

'I don't accept that their interests conflict,' I said angrily, and he sighed.

'I see. Are you determined to die of exposure out there?'

'I'm all right.'

'Well, I'm not.'

'That's tough.'

I knelt before the blaze, congratulating myself on the superior heat-retaining properties of female subcutaneous fat. We could tolerate lower temperatures than men. Swimming the Channel, surviving a blizzard, keeping house on an ice-floe . . . a woman could always stay warm and cheerful when men were shivering.

I said, 'When the going gets tough, the tough get – ' Too late I heard the hay's warning rustle. He pounced on me, one arm round my shoulders and the other scooping behind my knees. knees.

'Come along, my talkative hot-water bottle, you're neglecting your duty,' he said cheerfully, and dumped me back on the heap of hay.

'Let me go!'

'Not till you've restored me to some semblance of warmth. You don't suppose I pulled you out of that drift for nothing, do you? Stop thrashing about. We can't afford to lose any of our bedclothes, such as they are. God, it's cold! There's no need to carry on as if I'm going to rape you. That's the last of my priorities just now.'

I'd have been glad of this assurance if I'd believed it, but there's something about being held in close proximity to a man you hardly know that triggers doubts in the female mind. 'Then keep your hands to yourself,' I muttered.

'And risk another punch in the belly?' But his hold slackened and I moved into a more comfortable position against his chest, my head beneath his chin, knees drawn up less in defence than to conserve my own warmth. There was no denying that this was an improvement on crouching by the fire.

We lay in silence, adjusting to this new accord. I tried to keep my mind on higher things, but it was uphill work. I'd be the last person to describe myself as sex mad, but one's body often sees things differently from one's brain – or even one's heart. For some unaccountable reason mine found Richard's almost irresistible. An interesting exercise in self-discipline, I thought, grimly counting sheep.

'Well?' he said softly, after a longish interval.

I made a noise supposed to indicate surprise, sleepiness, and complete unconcern, though in fact I felt as keyed up as a sprinter in the starting blocks.

'How about it?'

I yawned. 'About what?'

'That personal demonstration.'

'Sorry.'

'Why not?'

'I'd hate to disappoint you after the big build-up.'

'I wouldn't be disappointed.'

'How d'you know?'

'Perhaps I'm psychic.' His hands moved slightly. My skin tingled in anticipation.

'No!' I said loudly.

'Oh, come on, forget Charles Dawson. He's no good for you. You're wasting yourself, sweetheart. Deceiving yourself.'

'Leave Charles out of it. And keep your hands to yourself. The answer's No, I tell you.'

'*Really* No?'

'Really.'

He sighed. 'What a waste. What a bloody awful criminal waste. Now I see what poor old Paul was up against.'

He turned over to face away from me, hunched his shoulder and appeared to fall asleep instantly. I lay for a long time, staring into the embers of the fire while my thoughts chased each other in a dismal circle until at last sleep claimed me too.

Chapter Ten

An overflowing ashtray was balanced on the arm of Charles' chair. It went flying as he sprang up, blue eyes blazing, and the acrid smell of burnt-out stubs filled the living room.

'Where have you been? Why did you vanish without a word? I've been going mad worrying about you.' He caught me to his chest, and the relief of feeling his arms round me, the old certainty that he'd be able to put things right, nearly made me burst into tears.

'What's the matter?' He held me at arm's length, his eyes searching my face, and what he saw there must have given him a glimpse of the truth because his arms dropped suddenly to his sides.

'Oh, no!' he said. 'Tell me what's happened. You didn't . . .?'

'She had gone.' With an effort I controlled my voice. 'I went to the barn and she wasn't there. She'd been taken away. There wasn't a sign of her.'

His hands came up again and tightened on my shoulders, biting into the muscle. I felt he was only just restraining himself from shaking me like a rat. '*Why didn't you wait?* You damned interfering fool – why couldn't you do as I asked? Oh God, what have you done? I told you not to go anywhere near that place without me, and you – you – ' His fists clenched as if to strike me, and he turned away suddenly towards the window. I stared at his rigid, furious shoulders and wished the earth would swallow me up. I bent and collected the scattered stubs, my hands shaking.

'Why did you do it?' He had himself under control again. 'Leave those damned things alone and tell me everything. You mean you went there by yourself?'

'No. I couldn't cross the glacier on my own. And she was too heavy for me to move. I – I asked Richard Labouchere to come with me.'

'Labouchere? You mean the one who paints?'

'His brother.'

'Oh, I know. The lawyer. Crooked as a corkscrew. What did you tell him? What reason did you give that shyster for wanting to be escorted across the glacier?'

'I had to tell him the truth,' I said miserably. 'He didn't believe me until we found where Didier's body had been hidden.'

Again I thought he would explode. 'You found *what?*'

'The body of the guide who took me there in the first place. It – he – was buried under the cliff.'

'I see. So that convinced Labouchere that you were telling the truth, did it?'

I hesitated. 'I'm not sure. Even then he didn't seem to believe that Rowan had really been kidnapped.'

Charles sat very still. 'Why not?'

I said with difficulty, 'He seems to think you and I have – have got some reason for pretending . . .'

Only the rapid ticking of a pulse in Charles' throat betrayed how hard he was thinking. 'Has he gone to the police?' he asked at last. 'Are we going to see the whole story in banner head-lines?'

At least I could reassure him on this point. 'No, I managed to persuade him not to – for Rowan's sake. He said he'd give me the benefit of the doubt and not say anything without asking me.'

It had been a major concession for which I'd argued long and hard as we slogged back across the glacier, but in the end Richard had agreed, since the evidence was buried beyond immediate recovery, to give me a few days' grace.

Charles said, 'I don't trust Richard Labouchere.'

'But he's Ben's solicitor!'

He shook his head. 'Ben's not the man he used to be or he'd never leave his affairs in the hands of a shady lawyer. Labouchere's sharp, I tell you. Up to all the tricks. The way he acted in poor Jenny Ardenti's case was a disgrace.'

The name rang a bell. I tried to remember what had hap-pened to Jenny Ardenti. For a few days, a few years back, her case had dominated the scandal pages. Though the details had blurred, memory resurrected certain headlines: *Minister's Daughter on Drugs Charge. The Teddy Bear Case.* There'd been pictures of a weeping girl – pretty, slender, very young – trying vainly to shield her face from the cameras. She'd tried to smuggle cocaine through the Customs, hidden inside a child's teddy bear. She'd claimed the toy wasn't hers; someone had asked her to look after it. The old story.

'She should never have been convicted,' said Charles angrily. 'She hadn't a clue what she was carrying. Someone made it worth Labouchere's while to see that she took the blame.' He lit a cigarette. 'So our lawyer friend has agreed to conceal the fact that a murder's been committed? That's going it a bit, even for him. How did you manage to persuade him?'

I explained about the avalanche and the night in the barn. Charles listened, frowning, tapping his fingers on the arm of his chair. When I'd finished he drew me to him, holding me tight.

'Don't think I blame you, darling. I know you thought you were acting for the best. But please, *please* promise me you won't do such a thing again.'

'I couldn't leave Rowan there another whole day. You were miles away, and I was only trying – '

He put a finger against my lips. 'Darling, I know, I know. You don't have to explain. But you didn't think of me, did you?' His smile was sad. 'I've lost Rowan. I can't afford to lose you, too.'

'Don't say that. You mustn't give up. You'll get her back, I know you will.'

He shook his head. 'In a purely physical sense, perhaps I will. I'll certainly keep trying. But emotionally I've lost her. There's no love left in our marriage. It's hell to admit it. I've kept up the pretence as long as I could, but I've never been able to hide the truth from you.'

I was silent, unable to find words to comfort him. Then he said in a different, brisker tone, 'But none of that alters the fact that I'll do my damnedest to save her. Where's Labouchere?'

'He had to go back to Geneva.'

'Good. There's something you must listen to. It's pretty harrowing, I warn you, but at least it tells us she's still alive.'

I caught my breath. 'Another tape?'

'The receptionist handed it to me when I got back to my hotel. That's how I knew you must have gone off to find her without waiting for me.'

138

'I'm sorry.'

He gave my hand a brief squeeze and stood up. 'Say no more. Now listen.'

Above the whirring of the portable recorder, Rowan's voice was weak and querulous, the consonants so slurred that it was difficult to understand her.

'Why don't you hurry, Charles? Why don't you do as he says? I'm cold and tired and hungry. Why won't you come and fetch me? You don't care what happens to me, do you? You don't love me any more. You want me to die . . .'

A pause, a click, and then the kidnapper's voice, clipped and accented. 'You heard your wife speak, Charles. Why don't you do as she asks? You are playing a dangerous game, you and that English girl. Oh yes, I'm watching her, too. She's worth watching. But she won't find anyone in Villoutrey's barn – no one alive, that is! Now listen carefully, my friend. I shall give you two more days. Just two, if you want to see your wife alive. I repeat your instructions. When the money is ready, put a notice in the *Locations* window, saying you have an apartment to rent in the Sorcière Block, Staircase B, Number twenty-nine, and invite offers. You understand me? Sorcière Block, Staircase B, number twenty-nine. I shall look for it, Charles. Do not disappoint me.'

Another click, and the tape whirred emptily.

'Play it again,' I said. 'There's something about the voice . . .'

He ran the tape through several times until it had lost all impact and was simply a collection of sounds.

I sighed. 'It's no good, I can't place it. Still, at least she's still alive. Where there's life there's hope. What about the money? Can your father-in-law pay up?'

Charles grimaced and stubbed out his cigarette. 'Of course he could. He could pay it at the drop of a hat if he wanted to.'

'But he *must* want to!'

He sighed. 'I'm afraid he's deliberately making difficulties. I've spent the last two days trying to get him to see sense and agree that mine's the only way: pay up and shut up. There's no feasible alternative. Anything else is too risky.'

'You mean he doesn't agree? He'd rather risk her life?' I

139

couldn't believe Rowan's father would dice with the safety of his only daughter.

'You know Ben. He made his pile by outwitting people and he thinks he can play this the same way.' He paused, then said quietly, 'He wants to bring in the police.'

'Oh, no . . .'

'I'm afraid so. I've argued for hours, trying to persuade him. What's money beside Rowan's life? But you know how obstinate he is. He's incapable of taking advice, especially from me. He thinks that if he tips off Interpol they might be able to put the finger on this maniac.'

'But the risk!'

'I know. It scares me.' He hesitated, drawing deeply on another cigarette, then said, 'I've been thinking . . . I wonder if he'd pay more attention to you?'

'I hardly know him. Well – I used to, of course, but I haven't seen him for a long time. I don't suppose he'd take *my* advice.'

'You used to get on well with him, though?'

I nodded. 'I suppose so.'

'I wish I could say the same,' Charles said wryly. 'He respects you.'

'Oh, I doubt it . . .'

'He does. You've built up your own business, just as he did. You're both self-made men.'

I'd never thought of myself as a self-made man. Charles went on, 'Far from respecting me, he thinks I'm a parasite and a Philistine. I suppose you can't blame him. He's never seen – never chosen to see – the price I pay for living off my wife. The sacrifice of my career, my commission, even my self-respect . . . to Ben that's nothing. He despises me, I'm afraid, so he's more or less conditioned to disagree with anything I suggest.'

I knew he was right. Once Rowan's father made up his mind about a person, nothing would change it. I said quickly, 'If I play him that tape and get him to realize what danger she's in, he may agree to pay. After all, I'm the only person who's seen her imprisoned. Yes, I'm *sure* I could persuade him. I'll go tomorrow.'

I felt a surge of new energy. If I could talk Ben into providing the ransom money, I'd have done something to redeem my earlier blunders.

'You can take Rowan's car.'

'Right. I'll be off first thing. What about you?'

'I'd better stay here in case there's any new development. Another message, possibly.'

I smiled tentatively. 'Like Box and Cox?'

'That's right. "One goes up and t'other goes down –"'

'"You'll get to the bottom all safe and soun'."'

We grinned at one another. Then a new thought sobered me. 'There's something I must do before I go. I'll have to tell Didier's mother.'

'Surely it can wait?'

'No,' I said regretfully.

'All right, I'll come with you.'

'Thanks.' On such an errand, I longed for moral support.

We strolled arm in arm through the twisting streets of the old village and despite our mission I felt happier than I had for a long time. But when we halted in front of the Café Belle Hélène's peeling brown-painted door, the curtains were drawn, the place deserted.

'It's Sunday,' Charles pointed out. 'Lots of little restaurants close for Sunday lunch.'

The sign on the door confirmed the guess. *Fermé*. I looked up and down the alley. 'Bubu lives in one of these houses. I don't know which.'

'You can hardly try them all.'

'I don't see why not. At least I know her name, now.' I rapped on two or three of the shut, secretive doors, but got no response. 'How odd. Where can they all be?'

Charles grinned. 'At church, you heathen. Come on, it's a beautiful day and this may be our last chance to ski together. Let's make the most of it.'

'Oh, but I've got to –'

'No excuses,' he said firmly. 'I've got one or two things to do first, but let's meet at the Sun Bar by the Col du Diamant in –' he consulted his watch – 'an hour and a half. At two o'clock – all right? Don't keep me waiting!'

'When have I ever kept *you* waiting?' I retorted, and hurried back to my apartment to bathe and change.

141

It was when I took my skis from the locker to keep my rendezvous with Charles that I remembered they weren't my skis at all, but the long thin trekking models lent me by Didier. I'd left my own trusty Heads in the rack at the summit restaurant, and I hoped most fervently they were still there. Hiring skis was expensive enough: to pay for lost ones would strain my finances to the limit.

So instead of joining the queue for the Col du Diamant chair-lift, I changed course and began the awkward shuffling trudge across to the big *téléférique* where Gina had accosted me the previous morning.

I'd agreed with Charles that it was a beautiful day, but then we were both lucky in having complexions that tanned rather than burned. People with fairer skins were finding the Alpine sun combined with a cutting wind rather too much of a good thing, and many had muffled themselves against ultraviolet rays until they looked like creatures from outer space. Waiting in line for the lift, I amused myself trying to guess age and sex and nationality of some of the heavily goggled and greased skiers around me. My own face felt more than comfortably warm after the morning's trek across the glacier. Though I don't usually bother with sun screens or barrier creams it seemed sensible to take the chiffon scarf from round my neck and knot it loosely in a gangster's mask over the bridge of my nose, anchoring it beneath the lower rim of my goggles. I immediately felt more comfortable.

The lift swung down and we crowded in, the first in line being shoved forward and jammed against the windows as latecomers jostled for space.

I was trying to disentangle my ski-sticks from those of an enormously tall crew-cut German, without losing my few hard-won inches of standing room, when I happened to glance beneath my neighbour's raised arm at the last man entering the big lift. He was ruthlessly shoving his way into the packed bodies, trying to avoid the closing automatic door. An unremarkable figure, spare and whippy, less than medium height, with huge goggles and scarf that hid his face, but at the sight of him my heart seemed to slow, then start thumping with heavy, rib-shaking beats. I'd been wrong when I thought I wouldn't know him again. Though I was well hidden in the press of bodies and he wasn't even facing me, I felt as scared and vulnerable as I had two days ago on the glacier, waiting for him to leave the barn.

I couldn't be sure. Reason told me there were hundreds of men who looked like him but instinct, stronger than reason, insisted he meant danger. His clothes were different: he wore a pale green padded anorak and woolly red hat pulled well down to meet his collar. As he stood with head bent, clasping a pair of long racing skis to his chest, apparently indifferent to his surroundings, I could almost persuade myself that I was mistaken, that this was a stranger who meant no more to me than I did to him. Almost, but not quite. For as he turned to speak to a girl beside him who was apparently protesting against being pushed, something in the quick, darting movement of the narrow head confirmed my fears. This was Rowan's kidnapper, Didier's murderer: could it be coincidence that he'd chosen to travel in the same *téléférique* as me?

I thought of abandoning my quest. I would let the crowd leave and then travel back by myself in the empty lift. But that, I realized, would make me even more conspicuous. What if he jumped back into the empty lift at the last moment? My best hope of avoiding him was to hide in the crowd.

As the lift swung steadily upward from one pylon to another, I watched covertly from the shelter of my neighbour's arm, but the man in green never glanced in my direction. He seemed absorbed in the view, the panorama of knife-edge ridges across the valley, each crowned with its blobs of colour – deckchairs, restaurant, bar – marking the top of its lift-system.

In one of those deckchairs opposite, Charles would soon be sitting if he hadn't already arrived. Glass in hand, he'd wait for me to join him. He'd give me forty minutes or an hour's law, I guessed, before shrugging and deciding I wasn't coming. It would have taken me less than half an hour to collect my skis, zoom down to the valley floor and up the other side, if only the green-clad man hadn't appeared.

Why was I always alone when trouble loomed? I wondered desperately. All morning I'd had Richard's protection; then I'd spent an hour or two safe with Charles. But the moment I went out alone, the killer followed. The sinister explanation had to be that he was, as he'd claimed, watching me all the time, waiting to catch me on my own. At the memory of those strong, sinewy hands gripping my shoulders, trying to hurl me over the precipice, I felt sick with fear. Like a rabbit mesmerized by headlights I didn't know which way to run.

The lift bumped and grounded. People grasped their skis and sticks and moved towards the door like a solid wave. The green-clad man stepped out and strolled towards the exit and, hemmed in by the crowd, I had to follow. First in, last out, I thought, just like the French law of primogeniture regarding twins: then I saw, with almost hysterical relief, what had pushed that idea into my subconscious. A bright blue anorak with silver chevrons, topped by a silver skid-lid, appeared at my right shoulder, another on my left.

'*Bonjour, Catherine*,' exclaimed the chief ski instructor's sons in unison. They shook hands warmly, apparently delighted to renew our acquaintance. Two sunburnt noses shone above two wide white grins. Never in my life have I been so glad to see friends.

'Will you ski with us this afternoon?' asked Jean-Louis, taking the initiative as usual.

'Papa wants us to practise our English,' explained his twin. 'We thought we might learn something from you, a few phrases to please the examiners.'

'It would be a pleasure,' I said with perfect truth. From the corner of my eye I saw the man in the green anorak bending over to put on his skis. His goggles were turned towards me, but I couldn't tell if he was watching us or merely looking in that direction. When he had them attached, he didn't slide away down the gentle slope but stood looking at the signpost, as if debating which run to follow. I knew with a sinking feeling that he was waiting for me.

'Come on,' urged Jean-Louis. 'We will be your guides.'

'No, let's have a drink first and talk about what I can teach you. Look, there's an empty table.'

Nothing loath, they stuck their skis in a snowbank. 'Why are you using trekking skis, Catherine?' asked Claude, casting a knowing eye at the cumbersome pair I'd just put beside his.

'Oh, a friend lent me these to try. I'll put them back – my own are over there in the rack,' I said hastily. I went across to it and to my astonishment and relief, there were my Dynastars, lightly powdered with snow, just where I'd left them. I carried them back to the table.

'That's not very safe, you know, to leave your skis where anyone can take them,' said Jean-Louis disapprovingly; but when I gave him the menu and invited him to choose a drink, he forgot my lapse of security and turned his attention to more important matters.

I'd placed myself with my back to the restaurant wall in order to command a view of the whole verandah as well as the slope below. As we drank our hot chocolate and discussed the requirements of language examiners, I kept a close eye on the skiers passing the restaurant, but the man in green had vanished. Perhaps I'd been mistaken after all. The slopes were full of slim men of medium height and athletic build. By degrees I relaxed my vigilance and began to worry instead about keeping Charles waiting. As he'd said, it might be our last chance to ski together, and I was spoiling it for him.

'D'you know if there's a way to reach the Col du Diamant without going down to the bottom station?' I asked the twins. 'I told a friend I'd meet him at the Sun Bar at two, and I'm afraid I'm going to be late.'

They exchanged glances. '*Mais oui, naturellement*. It is not necessary to descend first. Much simpler to cross the ridge. Two o'clock, *oh la-la*! That doesn't give much time. We will show you how to get there.'

They drained their cups and pulled down their goggles decisively.

'It won't be too difficult for me, will it? I'm not very good.'

'Look, see for yourself.' Jean-Louis pulled a crumpled map from his pouch. With a stubby, none-too-clean finger he traced the route. '*Voyons*, here we are at the start of *Tulipe Rose*. We follow to this corner, cross to *Asphodel*, then *Pensée*, turn right and up the drag-lift to *Gentian*, over the ridge on *Tulipe Noire* . . .'

'That's Black,' I interrupted. 'I can't manage Black runs.'

They registered polite surprise. 'Don't be afraid. We will go very slowly, very gently.'

'Isn't there a way round?' I knew my limitations.

Again they conferred and nodded. 'It is longer, but it avoids the *Tulipe Noire*.'

'Let's go that way then,' I said.

We set off in single file, Jean-Louis leading, me in the middle, and Claude bringing up the rear, but soon I found that fear of holding Claude up made me go faster than was either comfortable or safe, so we swapped places and both boys went ahead, with frequent stops to check my progress.

As in any sport, the pleasure is doubled when you're guided by an expert. The twins were every bit as good as Jerome, and far better in that they offered advice with smiles and encouragement, instead of shouting orders in fractured English. Following them as closely as I could, watching where they turned, where they braked, where they allowed speed to build up, I found I was covering the snow faster and more rhythmically than ever before. It was exhilarating. The wind stung my cheeks, the snow hissed softly under my skis, and although we were taking slopes I'd never have dared to tackle on my own, the bumps proved easy and the steepest *Schuss* held no terrors with the twins in front to guide me.

'*Formidable!*' Claude exclaimed as I drew up beside them, glowing and panting after a long series of swooping turns. 'Keep that up, and we'll soon be at the Sun Bar.'

Off they shot again, their natural exuberance gradually getting the better of their promise to go slowly. To them this descent probably seemed snail's pace, whereas for me it was the outside limit of speed.

We had reached the wind-facing slope of the Sorcière, which had to be crossed in order to go round the head of the ridge and down the south slope of the Col du Diamant. Here the powder-snow had blown into drifts, exposing bare ribs of rock interspersed with sheet ice. Sometimes one's edges bit into it, and sometimes they clattered over the ridged surface in alarming skids. Some of the piste-markers were buried up to the discs in drifts, and it was difficult to see the proper track. The twins were getting too far ahead.

'Stop a minute!' I called breathlessly as we reached a steep gully quilted with icy moguls just above the tree-line. I braked hard, but my skis didn't respond; it was only after a couple of dangerous lurches that I managed to halt among the boulders on

146

the extreme edge of the piste. Rather shakily I manoeuvred my skis round to face the other way, and saw the twins, travelling fast and whooping like cowboys, shoot on round the corner and disappear.

For a moment I stood recovering my breath, enjoying the solitude. Presumably because of the icy conditions, no one else had chosen this run. Then – as if to contradict this guess – a lone skier appeared on the slope above me, silhouetted against the sky, and something in the line of his crouching body prompted me to press closer into the lee of the boulders, waiting for him to pass.

He vanished and reappeared, vanished again. I stayed stock still, scolding myself for shying at shadows, yet unable to bring myself to move. It was ridiculous to imagine that every man I saw on the slopes was a homicidal maniac, and yet . . .

The man in green glided over the ridge and down through the tight-packed moguls, taking a straight line, knees flexing and straightening like steel springs, skis clattering viciously on the ice. Once again his face was muffled, but there was the look of a hunting animal in the way the goggles turned questingly from side to side as if following a scent . . . a hungry, implacable predator.

Don't let him see me, I prayed. Oh, God, don't let him look this way.

Where the moguls flattened out, a hundred yards below me, he stopped with a flick of his heels. There was a signpost showing the choice of runs; for a moment he considered it, as if uncertain which to follow. I'd seen the twins take the right-hand fork, and I willed the man in green to choose the left. He slid a few yards forward into deep snow, peering intently downhill then, to my dismay, poled away down the right-hand piste.

My thoughts darted here and there like fish trying to escape a net. Claude and Jean-Louis had probably stopped by now, wondering what had become of me. When the man in green came up to them, he would realize I was behind him. Perhaps he had realized already, and was waiting in ambush. I shivered.

The only way to avoid him was to take the left-hand piste, but the discs marking it looked ominously dark. Cautiously I went as far as the signpost, and my heart sank. The left-hand run was

Tulipe Noire, and crossed markers indicated that it was closed. All the same . . .

I shuffled forward, assessing the difficulties. First a narrow, icy, and extremely steep descent between close-set pines, where it would be almost impossible to brake; then the markers spread out in a long curve across the bowl of a valley, where one would be as conspicuous as a fly on a tablecloth.

I cursed my stupidity in getting separated from my guides, but there was no help for it. Closed or not, *Tulipe Noire* it had to be.

I took the first fifty yards on skis, the second on my back, and the final stretch of that icy *Schuss* upside down. When eventually I unscrambled myself from the tree in which I'd come to rest and tested for damage, I was surprised to find everything in working order, including my skis. It wasn't the recommended way of getting down a Black run, but at least that top stretch was behind me and the track ahead looked more inviting. It curved through the trees in a long serpentine, and though rather steep and narrow it hardly seemed to present the problems you'd associate with a Black run.

I started down it confidently enough, and soon discovered my mistake. Although easy enough to ski on, it was impossible to stop, and I was going faster and faster. Like most middling to bad skiers I need a piste wide enough to allow me to brake by pressing my heels out in a snowplough, or else room to reduce speed by turning. *Tulipe Noire* was deeply rutted and too narrow for either.

Corner succeeded corner relentlessly, and once launched on my downhill path I couldn't slow down at all. Crouching like a half-open penknife, uttering muffled yelps as I ricocheted off grooves and bumps, I rocketed down through the trees, peering ahead desperately, believing every second must be my last. The black mouth of an underpass yawned before me, and there was no way to avoid it. In I shot, deprived of my last vestige of control as my skis slipped into the two deep grooves left by more expert skiers. It was like riding a bicycle along tramlines: any attempt at deviation could spell ruin.

Disaster struck as the gloom of the underpass gave way once more to daylight. A snowbank loomed ahead, but I was going too fast to follow the track round it. I felt my skis leave the ground. The tips ran violently into the deep snow and stuck, and I fell forward across them.

Compared to my last fall, this was a soft one. I was still sitting in the hole, much relieved to have stopped moving, when I heard the hiss of skis above me. Looking up, I saw the man in green emerge from the trees to my right, about fifty yards away, and glide over the roof of the tunnel from which I'd just surfaced. I hadn't realized that the two runs crossed at this point. He was moving fast, using a long skating shove from one ski to the other to increase his speed, and he nearly flashed past without noticing me.

Then the huge goggles turned and spotted me on the piste below. He flicked to a halt; for a moment I feared he was going to jump straight off the parapet on top of me. My snowbank was about forty yards from where he stood, but there was also a drop of some twenty feet and this, thank God, was enough to deter him.

He glanced back up the track as if wondering whether it would be easier to cross above the tunnel, decided against it, and before I had even moved he set off downhill again.

The next instant there was a flash of blue – and another – and the twins came hurtling over the tunnel.

'Stop!' I shouted. 'I'm here.'

They, too, flicked into immobility. They peered over the parapet at me. The freckled, snub-nosed faces registered mixed emotions: surprise, relief, indignation. Questions sprayed down on me.

'What happened? Are you hurt? Why did you take *Tulipe Noire?* Didn't you see it's closed? How did you get down there? Isn't it broken after all?'

'I'm sorry,' I said. 'You went too fast for me. Isn't what broken?'

'The liar!' spluttered Claude. 'That *type* – he said you'd broken a leg.'

'The man in green? The one who just went past?'

He nodded vigorously. 'We asked if he'd seen you and he said you were hurt. You'd had a bad accident. He told us to go quickly to the *Poste de Secours* to fetch the blood-wagon.'

'What a liar!' said Jean-Louis disgustedly. 'He was making

fun of us. We'd have looked proper fools if we'd fetched the Mountain Rescue team for nothing.'

'Papa would have been angry,' added Claude, and they both looked sombre.

'Never mind, you'll have the last laugh,' I said quickly. 'I saw that man go past me just now in a great hurry. He probably didn't want to meet you again!'

'He was going to the *Tulipe Noire* drag-lift . . . What are you doing?'

I had sorted myself out by now and, shuffling across to the side of the tunnel, I attempted to climb the steep bank to join the boys. Claude leaned over, extending his ski-stick, but it was just too high for me to grasp.

'*Viens*,' he said to his twin. 'Give me your stick too. We'll tie them together – '

Jean-Louis didn't answer. He was staring fixedly to his left at something I couldn't see.

'Come on,' said Claude impatiently. 'Wake up. What's the matter?'

'There's the green man. Look – he's just getting on the lift now,' said Jean-Louis. 'He's going back to the top. Let's wait here and catch him when he comes down.'

'*Going back to the top?*' All my fears returned with a rush. Fear – and a chilling explanation of why the man in green had pitched the boys that story. He had sent them – not on a wild goose chase, but to fetch the blood-wagon he knew would be needed. Now he was returning to make sure there'd be a casualty for them to rescue: a casualty or a corpse.

'Stop him,' I said urgently. 'Delay him as long as you can. Don't tell him where I am. I – I must go.'

There wasn't time for explanations. If they delayed him only a minute or two it might be enough to throw him off the scent and give me time to hide among the homegoing skiers. The next stretch of *Tulipe Noire* looked easier . . . He wouldn't hurt them. He wouldn't dare.

'Wait!' cried Jean-Louis. 'What is it? *De quoi s'agit-il?*'

'I'm frightened,' I said, almost without meaning to, and left them leaning over the parapet, mouths open, eyes round with shock.

With two strong shoves I pointed my skis downhill, and now

it wasn't a question of trying to go slower, but of outrunning that menacing green-clad skier who, if he gave chase, could overtake me as easily as a Grand Prix car overtakes a taxi. The slope ahead was smooth and plainly marked; I crossed it at such speed that my eyes stung with tears and my short skis flapped protestingly.

But fast as I went, I knew with sick conviction that it wasn't anything like fast enough. My only hope, and it was a slim one, was to catch up with another skier and cling to him or her until we reached the populated lower slopes. Normally a run like *Tulipe Noire* would have attracted a sprinkling of daredevils keen to test their skills on the worst it could offer, but since it was officially closed the only person I was likely to meet would be another law-breaker, and the last thing he'd want would be my company.

The brilliant afternoon had turned a leaden oppressive grey. Small frozen snowflakes lashed against my cheeks and the icing-sugar surface of the upper slopes began to give way to heavy crunchy crust. My heart was beating so fast that I found it difficult to breathe, and resolutely I resisted the temptation to stop and look back.

The man in green must have reached the top by now and started down *Tulipe Noire* after me. Would the twins be able to stop him? Would they even try? From the look on their faces it seemed likely they thought I'd taken leave of my senses.

I caught an edge and fell; got up, and fell again. This time I risked a look behind, and what I saw confirmed my worst fears. A black dot – a pin-man – was speeding down the long serpentine cut out of the trees, scorning to follow the piste but simply leaping from one mogul to the next, heading directly for me. He was going to cut me off . . .

The ugly buildings in the valley looked so far away. I couldn't possibly reach them before the man in green swooped down on me. It was like the worst kind of nightmare, straining every nerve to escape from the terror behind, knowing it is coming closer by the second. There was another mogul-studded slope ahead, and I tumbled down it anyhow, hardly knowing if I was on my skis or my back, desperate to reach the shelter of the trees. There was a chair-lift to my right, with a few skiers waiting to board it. I turned off the piste and ploughed through deep snow up to my knees, crouching beneath the bank that marked the last curve of *Tulipe Noire*, and saw the man in green travelling at speed, shoot past once more.

It wouldn't delay him long. He would realize what had happened as soon as he reached a straight stretch and saw his quarry had vanished. Forgetting all inhibitions I shoved past the small queue and grabbed the handle of a T-bar before anyone could protest. As I was borne away up the hill again, I turned to look for my pursuer, but he was out of sight.

I sagged back against the T-bar, gasping for breath. Sweat was trickling down my spine under my layers of clothes, but my hands and feet were lumps of ice and I had lost a glove in my last fall.

By degrees, as my breathing returned to normal, I began to wonder where I was, and what had happened to the twins. The intense relief of having shaken off the man in green made me want to sing. I hadn't used this drag-lift before, but there'd be a map at the top of it to give me my bearings: I had a feeling that I'd strayed too far from the head of the valley.

I stared around, trying to recognize landmarks, my gloveless hand stuffed in my pocket and the other clutching the T-bar. Another line of pylons ran parallel to the ones along which I was being towed; I noticed that the few skiers coming up on this one were moving nearly twice as fast as I was. Several empty 'meat-hooks' passed me, then a small girl in a fluffy hood and an elderly couple shouting over their shoulders in German.

The towing cables were about five yards apart. They reached the top of a slope, dipped gently, and began another ascent. Staring at the ridge ahead, I realized why it looked familiar: pure chance had directed me back to the summit of the Col du Diamant from another direction. I could actually see the sun-deck of the bar where I'd meant to meet Charles. Too late now, of course, but he *might* have waited . . .

Hardly daring to hope he had, I scanned the deckchairs as I approached. I was conscious of yet another skier about to overtake me on the parallel drag-lift, and remember feeling vaguely surprised that the lines appeared to have drifted even closer together.

'*Attention, Catherine!*'

The shrill cry reached me a split second before I felt the hands on my throat. I swung round and looked straight into the goggles of the man in green. I gasped with shock, and instinctively released my hold on the T-bar as I tried to tear away the steely fingers gripping my windpipe. The next moment he had jerked me backwards off my lift and we were grappling savagely in the deep bank of snow at the side of the track.

I couldn't breathe. My eyes felt as if they would fall from their sockets. I clawed at his face, catching the silk scarf and jerking it loose. A mouth like a nigger-minstrel's, thickly smeared with grease, opened to spit a single vicious curse as he shifted his grip and forced my face down into the smothering snow.

There was roaring in my ears, a confused jumble of sounds which told me with awful certainty I was about to black out. I struggled and kicked, but he was incredibly strong. Even as I fought for dear life, at the back of my mind was a sense of astonishment that this could happen. A man was strangling me in broad daylight, beside a ski-lift and in full view of a restaurant swarming with people, none of whom was going to lift a finger to help me.

Just as I thought I was finished, miraculously there came a reprieve. In a sudden violent flurry of movement, I realized that other hands were battering my assailant; shrill voices flung at him every foul name known to *lycée* scholars, while an aluminium stick flashed as it belaboured the green back and shoulders.

'*Cochon! Salaud!* Let go. Leave her alone!'

'*Espèce d'ordure!*'

'Get off! Let go!'

The furious combined assault was more than my attacker could cope with. The pressure on my gullet suddenly eased, and I drew a shuddering breath. The world was a dark, whirling void shot with bright streaks of light. Dizzily, as if from a great distance, I heard the twins urging one another on.

'Give him another!'

'Hang on. Don't let him escape!'

'Help us, Catherine!'

With a great effort I rolled over in time to see the man in green handing off Claude and Jean-Louis like a rugger player, as he sidestepped and scrambled back to the only packed snow for a hundred yards: the track beneath the drag-lift.

He can't go down there, I thought, aghast.

I was wrong. For an instant he stood poised like a diver over the steep double groove: then with a little hop and a stab of his ski-sticks, he launched himself down it as if on suicide bent. Suicide and mass murder. Shoulders hunched, legs flexing like springs, he bore down on the ascending skiers like a fire engine racing down Oxford Street, scattering traffic right and left. People on the lift veered wildly to either side to avoid him, but the track was narrow and bounded on each edge by deep banks of snow. I could hardly bear to watch. Some dropped their T-bars in terror and collapsed beside the track. Others continued uphill, apparently oblivious, and he passed them so close that their clothes must have brushed his.

'*Complètement fou!* Absolutely crazy!' exclaimed Jean-Louis, watching open-mouthed. There was a wistful, almost admiring note in his voice.

In seconds, the man in green had vanished. Stiffly I stood up and brushed off my clothes. The twins recovered my skis and I put them on. My throat ached – I ached all over – and my teeth wouldn't stop chattering. During our struggle we had rolled quite a long way down the bank flanking the drag-lift, and were no longer in sight of the Sun Bar, which went some way to explaining why no one else had come to my aid. If it hadn't been for the twins . . . I shivered.

'Thank you. Thank you very much,' I croaked. 'You saved me.'

Claude waved an airy hand. 'It was nothing.'

'On the contrary, it was a lot.'

They shifted uncomfortably. 'Perhaps we should have stayed closer. Richard told us – ' Jean-Louis paused, looking a little embarrassed.

I turned sharply to face him. '*Richard?* Richard Labouchere?'

'*Mais oui* . . .'

'What did he tell you?'

Again he hesitated. 'You wouldn't be pleased to hear. It's not very flattering . . .'

'Tell me what he said.'

Jean-Louis said reluctantly, 'He promised to give us a lesson on the Delta – the hang-glider – if we looked after you. He said you weren't – well – very good on skis and might – er – get into difficulties.'

'How kind of him. How very thoughtful.'

They observed me anxiously. 'He was right, *n'est-ce pas?* Without us you would have had *des ennuis* – some difficulties? We didn't waste our time?'

I did my best to smile. 'Far from it. I'm sorry to have been such a trouble to you. You've been very patient.'

'Everyone has to learn,' said Claude philosophically. The impish grin transformed his face. 'And from our point of view it was worth it. It's not every day one gets offered a hang-gliding lesson!'

Furious though I felt with Richard for interfering in my affairs and putting children in danger, there was no point in saying this to the twins. They had done their job: now they could claim their reward. I only hoped it wouldn't prove as hazardous as looking after me.

Rowan's father lived in one of those solid, well-built turn of the century houses with immaculately scrubbed doorsteps, so typical of Geneva's residential suburbs. I reached it soon after two o'clock, and since Charles had told me that his father-in-law was invariably driven by Mario to lunch at the Anglo–French Club, I took the precaution of waiting just across the street until I saw the black Citroen glide sedately down the tree-lined avenue and halt in front of the house. Mario opened the rear door and transferred his master to a wheelchair, which he manoeuvred carefully up a ramp beside the steps. They disappeared into the house, and a few minutes later Mario reappeared alone.

I gave him time to garage the car and remove his chauffeur's cap before crossing the street and ringing the dazzling doorbell. Waiting for him to answer, I glanced up and down the street to see if anyone was watching me, but though a few people hurried past, no one seemed to pay me any attention. The air was warm and soft; well-ordered municipal flowers bloomed between the carriageways. It was a disorienting leap forward into spring for one fresh down from the winter-white mountain landscape.

'*Prego?*' Mario had opened the door, burly and blue-chinned as ever and with the same slight air of wanting to repel intruders. I smiled at him but he didn't respond.

'Hello, Mario; how are you? May I come in? I saw you bring Mr Henschel home a few minutes ago and I'd like to speak to him. It's rather urgent.'

'One moment, please.' It was plain that Mario would have preferred to tell me his master wasn't at home, but after leaving me on the step for a couple of minutes, he came back and said that Mr Henschel would see me. 'He is drinking coffee in the long Gallery,' he added. 'Please follow me.'

Though I hadn't entered this house for years, I scarcely needed a guide. Nothing, it seemed, had changed since my last visit ten years ago. To the left of the gloomy hall was a dining room panelled in dark oak; to the right Ben's book-lined, equally dark study, and straight ahead up a single flight of stairs the lightest and most agreeable room in the house: a picture gallery which Ben had built out over the garden to display his ever-increasing collection of oil paintings and bronzes. According to Rowan the old man now spent most of his waking hours up here, reading or simply gazing at some favourite picture while his still-agile brain mulled over new ways of making money grow. When Mario announced me there he was, with a sheaf of papers and a pocket calculator on the table at his elbow, staring at the canvas in front of him while coffee cooled on a tray beside him.

I'd been prepared for a change in Rowan's father. The semi-invalid life he'd been forced to live since his heart attack last spring had aged and faded him physically. His big head with its strong curved features so like Rowan's now looked top-heavy on his frail body and he didn't rise as I entered, merely turned his head in my direction. Then he smiled, and my fear that he might not recognize me was quickly dispelled.

'Catherine, my dear girl! Come in. How kind of you to call.'

To my relief I saw that he meant it. I smiled too, and went forward, then stopped involuntarily as I took in the change in the contents of the gallery. What had been a conventional collection of portraits and landscapes seemed to have been replaced by a nursery school art exhibition painted by children who were, if not actually delinquent, at least severely disturbed.

156

Huge garish canvasses with swirls and whirls of primary colour apparently applied with a spatula were interspersed with tiny black and white geometric designs of eye-baffling complexity. The effect was bizarre, almost shocking. More canvasses were stacked against the walls. I saw that Ben Henschel was into Modern Art.

'You must forgive me for not getting up. Doctor's orders,' he said with a little grimace, extending a hand of frightening transparency. 'Sit down and share my coffee. Mario, another cup, *per favore*.' As the soft-footed Italian padded away, Ben said with a trace of his old vigour, 'Well, Catherine, this is a terrible business. Have you any news? I had my solicitor here this morning, and he told me all about your trip across the glacier. He agrees with me that it's high time we called in the police. What are your views? Please don't tell me you've come to press my son-in-law's case for paying this ransom. I am totally opposed to such a policy. It would set a most dangerous precedent. What guarantee have we that my daughter will be released unharmed? None. What guarantee have we that she is alive even now?'

Mario returned with the extra cup and bent over Ben's chair, saying something I couldn't catch.

'He tells me I mustn't talk too much or get excited. *Si, Mario, capisco. Va bene.* You cannot imagine the frustration of sitting here helpless while my son-in-law mishandles the whole affair. What with fear on the one hand and frustration on the other, I am liable to go off my head. What was I saying? Yes: I ask you how Charles can possibly imagine that this criminal – this murderer – will be content with a single payment? Of course he won't. He will ask for more, then more, then he will threaten my grandchildren, my other dependants. He will squeeze me like a lemon until there is no juice left, and what will he give in return? Nothing! Yet my poor Rowan, my daughter . . .' His voice cracked.

'She *is* still alive,' I said quickly. 'Charles was sent another tape. I've got it here, if you want to hear it.'

For an instant he hesitated, as if bracing himself; then he indicated the built-in hi-fi at the far end of the gallery. 'Play it to me by all means.'

When Rowan's voice filled the room he seemed to flinch and

grow smaller in his chair. The high-quality equipment brought out nuances that Charles' portable machine had blurred, and again I had the tantalizing sensation of knowing – or almost knowing – the kidnapper's voice. When the tape was finished Ben shook his head.

'I will not allow that – that *canaille* to profit from his crime. There must be some way to frustrate him.'

It was a viewpoint I sympathized with. Charles had none of his father-in-law's subtlety: to his straightforward mind it was inconceivable that if he kept his part of the bargain the kidnapper wouldn't keep his. But Ben was right. If he met one demand there might be another, with no certainty of seeing his daughter safe at the end of it. Yet I dreaded the police and the inevitable publicity. In a place like Val du Loup there would be no hope of keeping the matter quiet, and if the hunt came uncomfortably close the kidnapper had an easy way out. One injection too many and his hostage would tell no tales.

I said tentatively, 'There's one lead we haven't explored properly.'

'What's that?'

'I think that Didier's mother – the woman I told you about – may have an idea who the kidnapper is. After all, she put me on his track in the first place. He must live in or near Val du Loup. Only someone who knows those mountains well would choose that barn as a hideout, and it needs specialized knowledge to drive those piste-bullies. He could be an instructor from the Ski School.'

'Go on . . .'

I said slowly, thinking it out, 'My guess is that he actually lives in Val du Loup, and that limits the field considerably. Take away the winter sports visitors, and what are you left with? A community of three or four hundred at the most. He can speak English, but then most of the guides can, more or less. That accent – '

'It reminds you of something?'

I shook my head. 'I've tried and tried, but I can't place it. It sounds somehow *stagey*.'

'Interesting,' said Ben. 'Run it through again.'

I did, and the impression remained, though Ben shook his head. A picture was forming in my mind, a personality. A bit of a linguist, a bit of an actor. Greedy, unscrupulous, brought up in the mountains. I sighed. You couldn't build an Identikit on that.

'I might be able to find him,' I said, 'if you'd trust me to have another go.'

'My dear Catherine! Of course I trust you.'

Tears prickled behind my eyes. I said indistinctly, 'I haven't done much good. Everything I've done has gone wrong. I feel so . . . so guilty.'

Handing me his own handkerchief, Ben said quietly, 'There's only one thing you've ever done that I regret, and that's to introduce my daughter to Charles Dawson. They should never have married.' His smile was sad. 'They say like begets like. The more I told her so the more determined she was to have him. What could I do? No need to look like that, child. I know you've a soft spot for him. Maybe I'm not the only one who regrets that meeting, eh?'

'Maybe not.' What could I say in Charles' defence without giving myself away? Of course they were right, the people who sneered at him for living off his wife's money. They overlooked the fact that he was generous and kind and good company, and would have been a hard-working husband and father if Rowan had allowed him to be. Some of the old bitterness rose in my throat. Why, with the world full of starving geniuses and unappreciated intellectuals, had she chosen to marry Charles?

'You're thinking Rowan's to blame, aren't you?' Ben watched me with his old shrewdness.

'I suppose it's six of one and half a dozen of the other.' I wasn't going to bare my heart to him. It had scarcely recovered from the going-over Richard had given it. However, there seemed no harm in adding, 'He does love her, you know. He's desperately anxious not to do anything that will put her in danger.'

'So he proposes to throw a million pounds of mine into a murderer's lap?'

'Isn't she worth that?'

He glared at me, and belatedly I remembered that he wasn't meant to get excited.

'Sorry.'

He was silent for a minute or two, staring at the canvas

directly facing his chair. It looked like a great burst barrage balloon with odd-shaped liquorice allsorts spilling out of its innards and though the colours were hideous I could see that it had a certain crude vigour.

'What do you think of that?' he asked.

'Do you really want me to tell you?'

He smiled a little. 'That's one of the first pictures Robin Labouchere ever sold. I snapped it up under the nose of the Centaur Gallery. Amazing, isn't it?'

'Astonishing.'

'He's very gifted – both those boys are. Richard's built up a thriving legal practice almost from scratch, and Robin has this extraordinary vision. Of course he's had his troubles, but that's one of the penalties of genius.'

Robin – a genius? My surprise must have showed because Ben leaned forward to pat me on the knee. 'It's true. Richard has many talents, but Robin, I assure you, is a genius.'

'I'll take your word for it,' I said politely. I wanted to hear more about Richard. Charles' hint of sharp practice had alerted my suspicions; it suddenly occurred to me that Richard fitted my hypothetical picture of Rowan's kidnapper too closely for comfort. *Could* he have been both the driver of the piste-bully and my rescuer from the cliff edge? Certainly, came the answer. All he had to do was remove the black hood and pretend that another man had just left the scene. I'd been in such a state of terror that I couldn't be sure if there'd been one man or two. But if that was the case, why not finish me off when he had the chance? Because he only wanted to scare me? My mind churned.

'What's the matter?' asked Ben, frowning.

There seemed no point in beating about the bush. 'Do you trust Richard Labouchere?' I asked bluntly.

'Don't you?'

'I don't know. I heard someone talking about the Ardenti case – '

'That girl was guilty!' Ben said with surprising vigour. 'Just because she was pretty and silly, she had public opinion on her side, but make no mistake, Catherine, she deserved everything she got. I consider Richard did very well to get her sentence reduced to eighteen months. He did all he could for Jenny

Ardenti, and much thanks he got for it! I considered it all the more important to show my belief in his judgment after that. A little dirt goes a long way, you know, and Jenny Ardenti had powerful friends.'

Ben was getting dangerously excited.

'Richard puzzles me,' I said, hoping for further sidelights on him. 'He seems so hard. So cynical.'

'Hard? Yes, perhaps. Do you consider that a defect? Personally I prefer my advisers without soft centres. Cynical? That may be another charge to lay at Jenny Ardenti's door. He won't make that mistake twice.' He smiled slightly. 'I've always taken an interest in those boys, you know. Their father was one of my greatest friends.'

'Is Richard like his father?' I prompted.

'Not in the slightest. Harry was a daredevil – a man of immense charm who never gave the morrow a thought. One of the bravest men I've ever known. No, I'd say Richard took after his mother. She used to work things out, calculate the odds, you know. She was a very good backgammon player.'

I wouldn't have minded hearing more about the Laboucheres, but Mario came in and bent over his master's chair. '*Signore*, your siesta. The doctor insists.'

Ben sighed. 'Yes, Mario, I know. I know. Miss Catherine is just leaving.'

'But what shall I do? We haven't decided.' I realized I hadn't secured his promise not to bring in the police, either. 'Shall I try to get in touch with Bubu? Will you wait two more days? What shall I tell Charles – about the ransom?'

Again he studied the picture, pain on his sharp-etched profile. 'I have no choice,' he said at last. 'Sitting here, helpless, I have no choice. I can't condemn my child. My brain tells me that I shouldn't pay a single penny to this man. My heart replies that all the money in the world will not compensate for the loss of my daughter. So what am I to do? Tell Charles that in two days' time I will send Mario with the ransom money. I leave him to complete the negotiations as best he can.'

'Why two days? Why not at once?'

He looked at me sharply. 'You heard the tape? It allows two days' grace. I intend to take advantage of every minute of them. I have sent Richard to England to make enquiries. Don't be

161

alarmed: he knows how to be discreet. But I want his report before I commit myself.'

Enquiries? My heart sank, but if Richard had already gone there was nothing I could do. 'So that's all you want me to tell Charles?' I rose.

'Yes. That is all.'

'Goodbye, Mr Henschel.'

'Goodbye, Catherine.'

But before I could turn to go out, he grasped my hand with his bony claw and drew my head down close to his. 'That's all I want you to tell Charles, but entirely between ourselves, I would be interested to hear what that old woman has to say. You understand?'

'Bubu?'

He nodded. 'It's an outside chance, a very forlorn hope, but it's possible she knows something. It's worth a try. Good luck, Catherine, and thank you for coming.'

He looked very shrunken and dejected as I left, hunched into the big chair as if the force of life burned low in him. However, as I was about to open the door he glanced up, and the bright intelligence in those eyes told me that whatever the doctors said, age and infirmity hadn't got Ben Henschel licked yet.

'You can trust Richard,' he said. 'Personally, I'd trust him with my life.'

Chapter Eleven

Entirely between ourselves . . . Ben's choice of words nagged me as I hauled the car round the thousand hairpins of the mountain road in the gathering dusk. Did he mean he wanted me to interview Bubu *alone*? No, that was ridiculous, I decided. However low his opinion of Charles' brains, Ben would surely not deny his suitability as a bodyguard. Ben, who had a properly Levantine abhorrence for unnecessary exertion, found his son-in-law's passion for sport contemptible. 'Hitting a ball or chasing a fox – what kind of employment is that for a grown man?' Rowan had quoted him as saying. All the same I couldn't imagine that Ben would wish me to investigate anything without Charles' support.

I arrived back in Val du Loup around eight o'clock, tired and stiff after taking a whole hour longer to drive up the mountain than down it. The serpentine road had been busy; much of the way I had crawled behind queues of family saloons with skis clipped to their roofs, sapping their acceleration. My eyes felt as if they were out on stalks after hours of staring into dazzling headlights; I rubbed them as I took the public lift from the low-level car park to the phoney village square.

I hoped Charles might be waiting for me at the apartment, but he wasn't; after washing and changing I went to his hotel. To my disappointment the svelte receptionist who, like most women, had quickly succumbed to Charles' smile, told me Monsieur Dawson was out. I sat in the hotel bar for nearly an hour, fending off enquiries about Rowan; then, when he didn't appear, I embarked on a tour of all the likely eating-places. Again I drew a complete blank. Bursting with the news of my successful mission, I could hardly contain my chagrin. Nor my hunger. After missing both lunch and tea, the two gin-and-Frenches I'd sunk in the hotel bar were making me a trifle lightheaded. Dismally I renounced the hope of Charles' company and ate a solitary substantial meal of pasta washed down with Chianti.

Once more I returned to the hotel: still no sign of him. It was nearly eleven o'clock. I made one final round of the bars and cafés, hoping against hope to find him drinking with friends, and at last faced the inevitable. In forty minutes or so, the Café Belle Hélène would close. If I wanted to see Bubu tonight I'd have to go alone.

Skiers, by and large, are early bedders. There were few people strolling the streets of the condominium: fewer still as I crossed from the new village to the old. I wished with all my heart that Charles was with me. The memory of the pockmarked lout who'd tried to pick me up was all too fresh, and so was my recollection of manhandling by Bubu's surly henchman.

The street lighting was poor, and the dark little alley looked gloomier than ever. As I went down it I realized that this was because the windows of the Belle Hélène were shuttered, the door blacked out. The sign that on Sunday night had said *Fermé* was gone and in its place, stuck on at eye level, was a notice on stiff white official paper.

I struck a match and peered at it. It informed me that the Department of Health and Hygiene in the village of Val du Loup, Grandes Alpes, had formally closed the Café Belle Hélène, Rue de la Montagne, Val du Loup, pending investigations. All enquiries were to be addressed to the principal inspector. It was signed by the secretary to the Council, J. J. Petitpierre.

It took several of my matches to read it right through; with a sinking sensation I realized that this put the kybosh on my forlorn hope. My last line of enquiry had been cut off. Without the restaurant, how could I get in touch with Bubu? Without Bubu I had no means of unmasking the hooded man.

I stood there like a dummy, wondering if I had the resolution to start knocking on doors at this time of night, and imagining my reception if I did. Before I could decide, one of the secretive little doors opened, and an old man leading a dog came out. The dog was a bushy-coated, lean-jawed Alsatian. I wondered if it was the animal which had menaced my ankles on my last visit.

'*Monsieur?*' I said as they came abreast of me. The old man jumped. He hadn't noticed me standing by the café door.

'What d'you want?' he countered as grumpily as if I'd propositioned him. 'Can't you see I'm busy?'

'Could you tell me why the café is closed?'

'What does it matter to you?' he snorted. 'That's not a disco for tourists. Foreigners are nothing but trouble. They ought to eat in the places designed for them and not come bothering the likes of us.' He came closer, peering at me, asphyxiating me with garlic-laden breath. 'Weren't you here earlier?' he said suspiciously. 'Weren't you the one who caused all the trouble?'

That was a tricky question. 'What kind of trouble?' I asked.

'That kind!' His gesture took in the darkened café, the stiff official notice. 'The kind that cost my wife her job and myself the only bit of peace and quiet I'm likely to see. Now she'll be at home all day and all night too – nag, nag, nag, it'll never stop. All because some fancy foreign piece saw a microbe in her *cassoulet*.' He cackled mirthlessly.

'Is your wife Madame Casavargues?'

Now I'd said something really funny. The wheezing laughter intensified until I feared he might choke. I hoped most fervently that he wouldn't. It would be a toss-up whether I'd bring myself to revive him with the kiss of life.

'My wife? Certainly not, thank the good God. My wife's a decent woman, even if her tongue's a trifle sharp. Madame Casavargues! Heh-heh-heh.'

'Can you tell me where to find Madame Casavargues?'

He hawked and spat. 'Why d'you want her? She's cleared out. Gone to ground. She's been ordered to leave the premises while the damned officials run their microscopes into every nook and cranny. Can't upset the tourists, you know. Tourists? Scum, I call them. Ordure. All they've ever brought is trouble, and that goes for his High-and-Mightiness Emil Kronsky too. They come here like a plague of rats to do honest folk out of a living. Think they own the place. My father lived here and my grandfather too. Owned their land, kept themselves to themselves, owed no one a *sou*. Now you can't plough a hectare or feed a sow without a form in triplicate signed by some jumped-up jack-in-office still wet behind the ears. Come along, my friend,' he tugged at the dog's lead. 'We've got better things to do than stay here all night.'

'Can you tell me where Madame Casavargues is? I've got a message for her. It's important.'

'Why should I rack my brains for you?' he grumbled. 'How should I know where she's gone?'

All the same, I was certain he did know.

'Perhaps your wife can help me,' I said, and took a step towards the door from which he'd emerged.

Quickly he moved to bar my passage. 'I might remember . . .'

'Would this assist your memory?' Ten francs seemed a steep price for information that might be worthless, but unfortunately I had nothing smaller on me and guessed there'd be little future in asking this old curmudgeon for change.

'It might.' I could see his greedy eyes converting the money into bottles.

'Or perhaps I should offer it to your wife?'

'*Ça, non!*' He came to a decision. 'The son-in-law of Madame Casavargues is Gaston Charbonnier, who runs a *crêperie* – a pancake stall – at the Salle des Jeux. It is possible he knows her whereabouts.'

I waited for him to continue, but that seemed to be all my ten francs would buy, so I handed over the money which vanished as if it had never existed into some secret recess of his long, flapping coat.

'*Viens, Bayard.*' He shuffled off without another word, towed by the dog, while I retraced my steps in search of Gaston.

The Salle des Jeux took up most of one side of the village square, and if Val du Loup could be said to have a night life, this was where the action was. On the outside, posters and fairy lights promised every delight the dissipated teenager could desire, and through the swing doors one entered a long, brightly-lit gallery pulsating with the mind-numbing beat of heavy rock, where glassy-eyed youngsters in skin-tight jeans, studded jackets and cowboy boots, their hair every colour of the rainbow and then some, languidly eyed one another and punched the buttons of gleaming rows of one-armed bandits – fruit machines, Space Invaders, and every kind of electronic gambling game. At the far end of the gallery was a pingpong table; occasional shouts from the players penetrated the din. The atmosphere was both decadent and depressing: even the dim-

166

mest child must quickly have realized that this was simply the slowest way of losing the ten, twenty, or fifty francs with which parents had bribed him to keep out of their way until bedtime. I could well imagine those parents congregating in one another's apartments to sink litres of cheap wine and amuse themselves with strip poker, wife-swapping or games of bridge, happy in the absence of their bored and destructive young.

My mission weighed on my mind. Childishly delaying the confrontation, I stopped by an unoccupied Penny Falls – only it was a *Franc* Falls – which had an avalanche of coins clustered like swarming bees on the very lip of the top step, ready to cascade over the edge and make me rich; but I added all my loose change to the heap without precipitating the avalanche, administered the obligatory kick of frustration to the machine, whose metalwork was much dented from this treatment, and went on my way lighter of pocket. No one paid me the least attention.

There were several hot-dog stalls built into the gallery walls, but only one *crêperie*, where a strongly-built blonde in her early twenties, her handsome bosom encased in a tight embroidered basque and a tall chef's hat on her golden curls, was deftly turning and folding pancakes on a large griddle. She was pink-cheeked from the heat and doing a roaring trade. It took me several minutes to push my way to the front and attract her attention.

'*Mademoiselle?*' she enquired, glancing up in surprise when I didn't order.

'No pancake, thank you. I wondered, could I speak to Gaston?'

She gave me a quick, scared glance, and the spatula trembled slightly in her capable hand. 'My husband is not here, *mademoiselle*. Can I help you?'

If Gaston was Bubu's son-in-law, and this was his wife, it followed that this girl must be Didier's sister. I thought I saw a slight family resemblance in the heavy, rather broad face, but she looked quicker-witted than her brother. The queue of pancake patrons was building up behind me.

'What do you want?' she said again.

Decidedly she was nervous. My heart sank. I'd have preferred to break the news at one remove, via Gaston, but since he wasn't there it would have to be direct.

'I've been looking for Madame Casavargues,' I said quietly. 'I went to the café . . .'

'Is it . . . about Didier?' she interrupted in a low voice.

I nodded.

'You – you know where he is? Gaston has searched everywhere.'

I said reluctantly, 'I'm sorry, *madame*. I'm afraid I have bad news.'

'*Oh, mon Dieu!*' The tightly encased bosom quivered and I prayed that she would neither scream nor faint. Quickly she recovered herself. 'We have been so worried. Wait here one moment, please, *mademoiselle*.' Rapidly she took orders and dispensed pancakes to the immediate circle of customers, then came out from behind the stall and pulled down its grille, ignoring the loud objections of youngsters cheated of their defence against night starvation. She padlocked the grille and, as the disconsolate teenagers drifted away, opened a small door at the side. 'Come in, *mademoiselle*. Wait here. I will find my mother.'

The room into which she ushered me was in sharp contrast to the garish pleasure arcade. It was small, dark, efficiently soundproofed and rather comfortably cluttered, with onions and baskets and herbs and strings of dried fungi hanging from hooks in the ceiling. The chairs sagged invitingly; a scrubbed deal table occupied the middle of the floor, and a cat lay purring and kneading its paws on a goatskin in front of a pot-bellied enamel stove. There was a pervasive, not unpleasant smell of damp animal, garlic, and tobacco.

When Bubu entered silently through the street door on the other side of the room, it was clear that her daughter had already warned her of trouble. A black scarf covered her head and was tightly knotted to support the pallid folds of chin. She stood before me, stiff and squat, her eyes like small black currants in a large pale bun.

'*Alors, mademoiselle, racontez-moi.* Tell me what has happened.'

I kept it as short as I could. When I could think of nothing more to add, she sagged slowly onto one of the chairs pulled up to the table, put a gloved hand against her forehead and sat there

168

without speaking for what seemed a long time.

'My poor Didier,' she said at last. 'My poor son.'

The blonde girl began to weep, stifling her sobs in her apron. I had a strong feeling that my news had only confirmed what they'd already known in their hearts. After three days' silence, they must have guessed that Didier would not return.

I said, 'I tried to tell you sooner, but I couldn't find you. The café was closed.'

Bubu spat and the blonde girl looked anxiously at me. 'Have you told the police?' she asked.

I shook my head.

'Good,' said Bubu, raising her black, glittering eyes from the table. 'Leave this to me. You have done what you can and now you must let me handle affairs in my own way. I shall not rest until I have destroyed this animal who killed my son.'

I had no doubt that she meant it. Like the Hound of Heaven, with unhurrying chase and unperturbèd pace she would hunt down the man in the black hood in her own secret and remorseless way. I shivered.

'Do you know him?' I asked.

'No, but I shall find him.'

'I saw him, *madame*. Perhaps you will recognize the description.' I told her all I could remember: the hood, the padded shoulders with their silver-gilt epaulettes; a man of medium height, slim build; an excellent skier who spoke English fluently and knew the mountains well. I even mentioned the tune he had whistled. She shook her head.

'Will you tell me how your son came to know him?'

'Willingly. Stop snivelling, Jeanne. Tears won't bring your brother back. Now listen, *mademoiselle*, and I'll tell you what *I* know.'

Richard's guess had been correct: Didier Casavargues had lost his life trying to make a fast buck. The story was a simple one. Just over a week ago, Didier had come home in high spirits. He'd eaten at the Belle Hélène as usual, and spent the evening ordering drinks for all his cronies. The next day he'd cadged a lift down to Charleville-les-Abbayes, and come roaring back on a brand new Honda 500 which he'd long coveted. When his mother questioned him he refused to reveal the source of his sudden affluence beyond saying that by pushing two buttons he'd earned himself six months' wages, and why shouldn't he spend them as he pleased?

Knowing her son well, she didn't press for details, though she suspected the money was dishonestly come by. 'Didier was always secretive, always obstinate,' she said. 'He wanted it all for himself.'

Three days later, however, the picture changed. From her son's morose expression and muttered comments she gathered that the promised windfall – or at least part of it – hadn't materialized. Apparently whoever had bribed Didier to press those buttons had welshed on the deal. The garage in Charleville began to clamour for payment, and eventually Didier was obliged to return the Honda to them. He came back from his second trip to the valley full of drink and threatening revenge. 'I'll show that bastard. I'll teach him not to mess around with me. What if I did follow him? I was only guarding my own interests, wasn't I?'

. Beneath the bluster, Bubu had sensed that her son was nervous. He stopped eating at home, and instead installed himself with his cousin at the restaurant at the summit where, he said, no one could creep up on him. It was at this point that he enlisted the help of his mother to get in touch with me. He had instructed them to tell me that if I wanted to know the whereabouts of Madame X, I must meet him the following day, but I must leave the tall Englishman behind. 'A type like that asks too many damned questions,' had been Didier's reason for excluding Charles.

'Did you know that Madame X had been kidnapped?' I asked bluntly.

'It was a possibility. I was not sure of it.'

'So you asked me to pay for her safe return?'

She closed her eyes, then opened them and said, 'I regret it infinitely.'

'What made you think the tall Englishman was my lover?'

'I watched you. It was plain to see.'

'Your eyes deceived you,' I snapped and then, ashamed of my touchiness, added, 'Now you see why I don't want to tell the police. They will prevent us from paying the ransom, and Rowan . . .'

'The police – pah!' She made an extraordinarily expressive

gesture of contempt, pulling her nose between two fingers and spitting simultaneously. 'Keep those pigs out of this – I'll have nothing to do with them. Clumsy officious imbeciles. Dirty grasping swine! I've had my fill of them today. I don't want them to spoil my revenge.'

She sat brooding and toadlike, menacing in her heavy black clothes, her strong hands kneading the fur of the cat, which squirmed in ecstasy. There was something frightening about those hands: I could imagine them wringing a chicken's neck or cutting the throat of a squealing pig just as competently as they sought out the cat's ticklish places to scratch and stroke.

Jeanne, composed though still sniffing, poured me a tot of cognac, but her mother waved away the offer.

'You must be patient, *mademoiselle*,' she said at last. 'In this place I have many cousins, friends . . . all those who lived here before the tourists came. I need time to ask questions, spread the word.'

'Time's short,' I reminded her. 'The day after tomorrow the money must be paid. I don't think Charles can delay it any longer.'

'Be patient,' she said as if I hadn't spoken. 'I will do all I can. I will spread my net and see what swims into it. *Ne vous inquietez pas, mademoiselle*. Have no fear. He will not escape me.' The ugly toad's mouth worked briefly. 'When he is in my clutches, that man will wish he had never quitted his mother's womb.'

There was a savagery about her that was close to madness. I felt that no reasoning, no consideration for the laws of God or man would deflect this woman from her purpose. The English have never understood the blood feud: the taking of life for life until both sides are exterminated, but I knew instinctively that would be the code that Bubu and her family obeyed. She was no longer a grieving mother but an avenging fury, hard and pitiless as the mountains that bred her. So she would remain until the blood-debt was paid.

I'd hardly touched my brandy, but suddenly my head began to swim and I couldn't bear the claustrophobic room a moment longer. I stood up, grasping the table edge for steadiness.

'I – I must go now.'

'When I have found him, I will send Gaston to you, *petite*

Anglaise, and together we will hunt him down, *hein*? But be warned: no police. Agreed?'

'*D'accord.*' I murmured my condolences but although she bowed her head in acknowledgment, I sensed she was no longer listening. The spider had started to spin her web.

Jeanne opened the street door and thankfully I escaped into the crisp clear night.

One more try and then bed, I thought, trudging through the slush across the square to Charles' hotel. It had been a long day and a frustrating one. I had a panicky feeling that the whole situation was sliding beyond my control. More and more people knew that Rowan had been kidnapped; the ripples were spreading ever wider without bringing us closer to the kidnapper. Every lead I followed ended in a blank wall.

It was therefore with no great pleasure that I recognized the couple seated in a cut-out barrel in the darkest corner of the Hotel de la Sorcière's bar: Charles, together with Gina van Lawick, heads bent close in laughing intimacy, an empty litre wine bottle between them and brandy *ballons* in hand. I'd go farther: I felt a stab of angry jealousy so sharp that it was like a knife in the belly. While I'd been flying back and forth on mountainous roads, cajoling money from old Ben, forging alliances with the local Mafiosi, all in aid of securing Rowan's safety, what had her stricken husband been doing? Wining and dining a blonde, of course: how could I have expected anything else?

The gut reaction lasted only a second before I realized I was being irrational and grossly unfair. Charles might have any number of reasons for chatting up Gina; it was his evident pleasure in doing so that I resented. They looked as if they were having a lovely time tearing their entire acquaintance to shreds.

'Hullo, there!' I said to the absorbed heads.

They looked up quickly; not guiltily, but definitely startled. Though the cat-with-cream smile remained pinned to Gina's wide thin mouth, I had the impression that she wasn't pleased to see me. Charles was, though. He jumped up and hugged me, leaning across the table to the peril of the brandy glasses. 'Back me up, darling,' he whispered in the second when his head was clamped against mine.

'Hullo, Catta; back already? Don't tell me you've driven to Geneva and back in one day – I simply don't believe it,' Gina drawled.

'Oh, that's nothing to Catta. She's a woman of iron,' boasted Charles. I smiled at him; there was no mistaking the warmth of his greeting and the stab of jealousy ceased to trouble me. Over Gina's head I signalled with my eyebrows: You haven't told her? and back at once came the reassuring message: Of course not! What kind of a fool d'you take me for?

'We thought that Richard would take you out to dinner,' went on Gina. 'I thought he'd grab the opportunity.'

'He wasn't there so he couldn't,' I said as coolly as I could when I wanted to shake the teeth from the mischief-making bitch's head.

'Oh? Where is he, then?'

'How should I know?'

She digested that. 'He told *me* he'd be staying with Mr Henschell because he'd got a lot of work to do for him.'

'Perhaps it didn't take as long as he expected. Does it matter?' I was damned if I was going to tell her he'd gone to England.

Gina said with some irritation, 'I like to know where he is in case I need to get in touch. He's no business to disappear without telling me.'

'Catta, darling, you must be exhausted. What'll you have – brandy?' Charles signalled to a waiter. 'Tell me, how was the journey? I was just explaining to Gina that you'd driven Rowan down to stay with her father. A few days' rest is what she needs.'

So that was the story he wanted me to back up. 'Oh, it went fine,' I said lightly. 'We went quite slowly, you know what those roads are like.'

'She'll be back for the Ball, you said?' Gina looked at him sharply.

'Oh, Lord, yes! Nothing would keep her away from that,' Charles laughed. 'The famous Cleopatra dress, you know. If she misses the chance of wearing it here, I'll find myself forced to give a fancy-dress Ball next summer, to give that damned costume an airing. But she looks stunning in it, doesn't she, Catta?'

'Stunning,' I agreed. I wondered why Charles was bothering

to feed all this to Gina. Was he afraid that *she* had a hot line to the Press? I saw that he was watching me rather anxiously, and smiled my reassurance.

'How was my father-in-law? Amiable as ever?'

'He was very kind.' I gave him a straight look. 'Very helpful.'

Charles' eyes relaxed. He smiled. 'I'm so glad to hear it. One never knows . . . That really puts my mind at rest. Tell me more about the journey. Did you try that restaurant I told you about?' He gave a snort of amusement. 'We ought to tell her what *you* had for lunch today, Gina! It was partly her fault, after all.'

'What was my fault?' I looked from one to the other. Now I thought signals were passing between them: signals I couldn't interpret.

'I'll tell you. Gina agreed to dine with me tonight for the sole purpose of restoring her faith in *la cuisine française* which, thanks to you, took a rather nasty knock earlier today.'

'What *are* you talking about?'

'Give me a chance! I'm just explaining. Gina asked me if I knew anywhere local which would give her a decent meal. So I told her about that place you went to the other night – remember? You said the food looked terrific.'

'The Belle Hélène.' I looked thoughtfully at Gina. A fancy foreign piece, the old man had called her . . . it seemed a fair description.

'That's the place. So off goes Gina, hungry as hell, and all unsuspecting orders their set menu. After a longish wait, the garçon places a plate of soup in front of her, and what d'you think's floating merrily on the top, large as life and twice as natural?'

'A microbe?'

He gave me a quick, puzzled glance. 'Odd you should say that. No – in fact it was the *leg of a mouse*: at least that's what the analyst said.'

'Poor little thing,' I commented absently. My brain twisted and turned, looking for reasons why Gina should do such a thing. What was *her* connection with the Belle Hélène – and Bubu?

'I nearly died!' Gina took up the tale. 'There it was, floating on top of a bit of spinach or sorrel or something, with its claws curled up, ugh! It was all I could do not to scream.'

'What *did* you do?' I asked. 'Just for interest?'

My reaction – or lack of it – plainly annoyed her. '*Just for interest*, I did the only thing any sensible person would have done. I popped it straight into a plastic bag and took it along to the *Préfecture*.'

'Wasn't that a bit extreme?'

'My God, I might have been poisoned! Heaven only knows what the kitchen must be like, to have mice falling into the soup. It's probably alive with vermin. It's a positive health hazard.'

'So what was the official reaction?'

'Of course they were horrified. I stormed in and told them exactly where it had come from, and they said they'd investigate the matter right away. That sort of thing gets a holiday resort a bad name, and don't they know it! Actually,' she added with a touch of complacency, 'they weren't all that surprised. The man I spoke to said they've been taking an interest in that café for some time, and this was just the excuse they needed to crack down on the place.'

'So you were really doing them a favour, weren't you?' I said, smiling. 'By the looks of things the Belle Hélène won't be serving food with or without mice to garnish it for some time to come.'

'You mean you've been there – today?' asked Charles.

'Yes. The whole place was shut up.'

'You have to hand it to the French,' said Gina with satisfaction, 'at least their bureaucracy works. They must have moved pretty fast.'

'Tell me,' I said casually, 'do you usually carry plastic bags around with you when you go out to lunch – on the offchance of finding something nasty in your soup?'

She gave me a hard green stare. 'I don't much like that question. Why shouldn't I carry a plastic bag?'

'It seems almost too convenient.' When Gina coloured angrily I decided to needle her a little more. '*I* thought the Belle Hélène food looked delicious. Did you tell the waiter what you'd found? Or the *patron*?'

'Of course I didn't. They'd have whisked it out of sight and pretended I was making the whole thing up.'

'Which you weren't?'

'For heaven's sake, why would Gina do a thing like that?'

175

protested Charles, laughing. 'Spoiling her own lunch – it wouldn't make sense.'

'I'm not sure,' I said. 'It might if she had a particular reason for wanting to make trouble. To get the restaurant closed and its owner put out of business.'

There was a short silence. Then Gina said furiously, 'Sorry, Charles, I'm off. I'm not going to sit here and be called a liar to my face. Let me tell you, Catta – '

She stopped as Charles held up a hand. 'Steady on, you two,' he said. 'Don't let's get too intense about this. Personally, I think it's all rather a joke.' He turned to me. 'Look, darling, you've had the hell of a lot of driving today and I suggest it's time for bed. It'll all look different in the morning. Come on, Gina, drink up and we'll see Catta home . . .'

He went on talking, pouring oil on troubled waters, but I heard none of it. So there was to be no chance to tell him what I'd achieved today, or what I'd found out. He wasn't going to side with me against Gina; our special relationship no longer counted with him. *Didn't he care?* I caught the tail end of a wink passing between them and felt a deep regret. What had Paul called it? 'An amazing capacity for self-deception.' How could I have fooled myself into believing Charles hadn't changed? The Charles with whom I'd have cheerfully faced hell or high water was gone, buried in the rubble of his ill-fated marriage and here, wearing his skin, speaking with his voice, was a stranger.

It was like losing him all over again. I sat there in silent misery with my brandy, scarcely noticing that a page boy in uniform had come over and stopped at our table.

'*Monsieur Dawson? On vous demande au téléphone.*'

Charles grinned. 'No peace for the wicked, eh? All right, I'm coming.' He tipped the boy and said to us, 'Will you wait?' then rose and sauntered over to the door.

Gina and I sat in silence, neither of us willing to break the fragile truce. She lit a cigarette without offering me one.

The call did not take long, but when Charles reappeared he seemed to have aged ten years. He shoved carelessly through the crowded tables, ignoring protests from people he buffeted. With head bowed he made a beeline for me – for Gina. To my horror I saw that tears were pouring down his face.

'Charlie! What's happened?' Gina jumped up, guiding him to

176

his chair. Her arm went round his shoulders with easy profes-
sionalism; I remembered that she was a nurse.

His mouth moved but no sound came out.

'Drink this,' she ordered, putting her own glass to his lips.
He gulped obediently and shuddered, but the brandy steadied
him. Gina waited a moment, then said again, 'What's wrong?
Who was it?'

'It was . . . Mrs Chivers, our housekeeper. She – she said
she'd been trying to get hold of me all evening.'

'*Why?*' We spoke in unison, but already I had an inkling of
what the trouble might be.

Charles breathed through his open mouth, then said shakily,
'It's Ivan and Lorna. They – they didn't come back from
school. When the au pair went to fetch them, their teacher said
they'd already gone.'

'They can't have!'

'A man came to the school gate and said he was their uncle,'
Charles went on as if she hadn't spoken. 'They got into his car
quite happily.' He paused, then said with a note of suppressed
hysteria in his voice, 'What am I going to do? Mrs Chivers asked
what she should do, and I couldn't tell her. She – she wanted to
know if she should ring the police. She's been trying to get hold
of me ever since she realized what had happened.'

'But what *has* happened?' said Gina. 'Is he their uncle? Have
they got someone they call uncle? Or have they been – '

'Kidnapped,' said Charles, and his strong handsome features
suddenly blurred like melting chocolate. 'Both my children. Oh
God – what am I going to do?'

Gina was marvellous. Much as I disliked her, I had to admire
the way she coped. Charles went entirely to pieces: I could
never have managed alone.

Between us we got him to his room and into bed. 'There's
nothing you can do tonight,' Gina said firmly, and made him
swallow tranquillizers. She was right. The state he was in, he'd
have done more harm than good trying to find out anything
from anyone.

I left Gina to settle him and went to my own apartment where
I telephoned poor Mrs Chivers. She confirmed the story and
added more details. Ivan, it appeared, had handed his teacher a
note that morning, purporting to come from Mrs Chivers

herself. It said that both children were to be collected that afternoon by their uncle, who would take them to the dentist and then home. So when the 'uncle' appeared at the school gate, the young assistant teacher on duty had allowed Ivan and Lorna to go without a moment's hesitation.

Could she describe the man? I asked.

Unfortunately not. She'd been so busy dismissing the children and sorting out the regular school-runs that she'd hardly glanced at him. The only description Mrs Chivers had was from the Finnish au pair girl, whose English was uncertain, who confirmed that a man had met them on their way to school that morning and given a letter to Ivan, saying it was for his teacher. All she could say about him was that he was a normal man, a very brown man.

'A coloured man?'

'I don't know, I'm sure.' Mrs Chivers sounded on the brink of tears. 'What was she doing, talking to coloured men when she should have been taking the children to school? If I've told that girl once, I've told her a dozen times that she's supposed to be there waiting at the gate before they come out. Now look what's happened! I'm at my wits' end with worry. Mrs Charles gone off on holiday without leaving an address, and Mr Charles, poor gentleman, sounded knocked all of a heap. What should I do? I don't know if I should tell the police or what. Poor mites, where are they now? They hadn't a thing with them, only the clothes they stand up in and the guinea-pig Lorna had to bring home. And if that wasn't bad enough, there was this note I found pushed under the front door.'

'What did it say?' I felt suddenly cold. I remembered Ben Henschel saying that if he paid once, all his dependants would be at risk.

'It was just a typed note, telling me the children were safe and in good hands.'

'Whose hands?'

'It didn't say. Just that I needn't worry and shouldn't say anything to anyone. Well, I could hardly sit back with my hands folded while those poor mites were taken away, God knows where . . .'

'Who have you told?' I asked urgently. 'Who knows the children are missing?'

'Just me and Gudrun, Miss Catherine,' she said miserably. 'I didn't like to tell the school – I pretended there'd been a misunderstanding. Did I do the right thing? I'm that worried, I don't know which way to turn.'

I calmed her as best I could and told her to leave everything to me. I would get in touch with Mr Henschel: he would advise on the best course to take. I warned her against telling anyone what had happened, and suggested that she telephoned the school tomorrow and said that both children had colds and she was keeping them at home for a few days. She was pathetically grateful for positive direction and promised to do exactly as I said.

Then I tried to ring Ben, but not surprisingly since it was now a quarter to two, Mario wasn't answering. Heavy of heart and head, I decided to get a few hours' sleep, but barely had I washed and brushed my teeth than the doorbell to the apartment pealed twice.

I stood there in my nightdress, heart thumping, wondering who the hell it could be. A drunk? A sleepwalker? Gina?

I reached for the nearest sharp object, which happened to be the Sabatier chopping knife, and holding it concealed in the folds of my nightie I cautiously opened the door.

It wasn't a drunk or a sleepwalker. It wasn't even Gina.

'Hello,' said Richard, and walked past me into the living room. 'I wondered if you'd let me sleep with you for what's left of the night?'

Chapter Twelve

My nerves were strung too tight to appreciate the suggestion.

'No!' I exploded. Too late I saw from his satisfied grin that this was exactly the rise he had wanted.

'Sorry,' he said, not looking in the least sorry. In fact he had every appearance of being extremely pleased with life in general and himself in particular. 'Perhaps that was an unfortunate choice of phrase. I only wondered if your sofa was going spare for a few hours? It's hardly worth slogging all the way to the Eagle's Nest at this time of night. I wasn't really planning to turn you out of your downy couch.'

'It sounded more as if you planned to join me in it,' I said, still ruffled.

The grin widened. 'That would be even nicer, since you suggest it.'

'No!' I repeated, even more explosively.

'Pity.' His shoulders shook with laughter. 'Does that mean that Dawson's there already?' he enquired with the delicacy of a rogue elephant. 'I've been battering on his door for the past ten minutes without getting a peep out of him. It did just cross my mind that he might be fraternizing with you.'

'Well, it can just uncross your mind again.' I recovered my cool. 'If you want to talk to Charles, you're out of luck. He's in his room, all right, but he's out for the count after swallowing a fistful of Moggies.'

His eyebrows rose. 'Moggies?'

'To help him to sleep.'

'Strange. One had always supposed – from what one heard – that Dawson prefers more traditional methods of fighting insomnia.' He turned guileless brown eyes on me – too brown, too guileless by half.

A very brown man. I knew what the Finnish au pair girl had meant. Brown hair, brown eyes, brown face.

'Did you take the Dawson children away from their school today?' I demanded.

He laughed. 'Paul warned me you weren't just a pretty face! Yes, I did – and it's not an experience I'd care to repeat. Neurotic guinea-pigs aren't the easiest of travelling companions.'

I said angrily, 'Charles is nearly off his head with worry.'

He raised his eyes ceilingwards. 'Heaven preserve us from birdwitted housekeepers! I told her the children were in good hands.'

'Whose hands? How dare you snatch Charles' children away without a word to him or the woman who's in charge of them? My God, it's a criminal offence! And you have the gall to blame poor Mrs Chivers for raising the alarm! What did you expect her to do – hope for the best?' I was so angry that I found it difficult to get the words out. Richard held up a hand in a calming gesture.

'Just listen to me for a minute. And while you're at it, you might put down that knife. It makes me nervous.'

I was still clutching the Sabatier. I looked at it in surprise and replaced it on the chopping block. 'Go on. Explain.'

'That's better. Now, to answer your questions: yes, I did expect Mrs Chivers to do nothing. Perhaps it *was* asking too much of her intelligence and discretion – qualities with which she's not over-abundantly endowed. All right, all right, I know what you're going to say. Just simmer down. As to the legality of removing the children, I think it could be argued that in the absence of both parents it was natural that their grandfather should feel responsible for their safety. He was quite within his rights in sending his solicitor – *me* – to remove them to a more secure environment until such time as their father or mother was capable of resuming normal parental duties.'

'You mean they're with Mr Henschel?' My relief was too great for me to worry about his obvious attempt to provoke me by talking like a law manual. I hadn't enjoyed my recurring image of Richard's face behind that black hood.

'Well, no. As you saw, Ben's domestic arrangements are a bit overstretched at the moment, and I thought the addition of two lively children – not to mention a guinea-pig – would be too much for him.'

The wave of relief ebbed. 'Where are they, then?'

'Safe enough. With a cousin of mine, actually. She's got

children the same age, so she's used to coping. Don't worry, they're perfectly happy. That's what I came to tell Dawson, but since he's *incommunicado* I'll have to rely on you to pass the message on. Will you do that? I've got to be away by first light.'

I wanted to believe him. I wished I could rid myself of that grim recurring vision of Richard, who took after his cool, calculating mother, removing Ben's grandchildren to a place only he knew of, so that if his first attempt at the ransom failed, there could be a second . . .

'Mr Henschel *does* know where they are?' I pressed.

'More or less. He knows they're safe – just in case anything goes wrong with tomorrow's operation.'

'Tomorrow?' My heart seemed to jump.

'That's the other thing I wanted to tell Dawson. Against my professional advice and largely, I gather, because of pressure from you, Ben has decided to pay the ransom. I can't stop him. I understand his feelings, of course – '

'Do you? Can you?'

He ignored the interruption. 'But in my view it sets a deplorable precedent and a highly dangerous one. As I say, I can't stop him. I don't even want to. He's old, and he's ill, and he can't bear the idea of anything happening to Rowan. Once he would have fought every inch of the way, but not now.' He gave me a look that challenged me to disagree. When I declined to, he went on, 'All right, here are the details. I'll have to rely on you to pass them on to Dawson.'

'Why do you always call him *Dawson*?'

'It's how I think of him.'

'That's no answer.'

'It's the only one you're getting. Now listen carefully.'

'I am listening carefully.'

'Mario will arrive here on the afternoon bus, and bring the money. After that it's up to Dawson to complete the negotiations. Remember, it's absolutely essential to find out where Rowan is *before* handing over the money.'

'What if he won't tell us?'

'I think he will. All right?'

I felt it was very far from all right. I could see pitfalls in every possible move. The kidnapper held all the cards, I thought bleakly, and there was so little time. Mario coming tomorrow . . . *today*. Fear gripped my stomach.

Richard yawned. 'How about that sofa? Don't bother to wake up when I go. I'll grab a cup of coffee and let myself out.'

'What will you be doing while we're getting Rowan back?' I asked, cold and shivery at the thought.

'I'll be watching and waiting with Ben. Waiting for your telephone call to say everything's all right. Don't look so worried. Everything *will* be all right.' His smile flashed suddenly. 'You can tell me about it at the Hollenbergs' Ball.'

I was amazed that he could contemplate anything so frivolous. He saw my surprise and his eyes crinkled in amusement. 'I'm relying on you to be there. All work and no play makes Jack a dull boy – and not only Jack. You could do with a bit of fun. You look as if you've lost half a stone since this business began.'

I didn't want his sympathy. 'I won't be there,' I said. 'I don't like dances.'

'Oh, you can't fail to enjoy this one. It's unique.'

'You'd be surprised what I can fail to enjoy,' I said dryly. 'All right, sleep on the sofa if you must, and I'll give Charles your messages. I can quite see why you'd prefer to be gone before he wakes up. If I was him I'd kill you.'

'Would you? I wonder.' He moved very close to me and involuntarily I took a step back. I wasn't frightened of him: it was just a moment of weakness because I felt so drained, so deadly tired.

'Don't fight it,' he murmured. 'Don't keep trying to fool yourself,' and for an instant his hands rested lightly on my shoulders.

'Please stop telling me what to do,' I said rather shakily, 'unless you want me to tell you precisely what you can do with your advice.'

His hands dropped to his sides and he laughed. 'I suppose it *is* rather unfair to give you free advice when other people have to pay so much for it. The trouble is, as a professional, I find it very hard to stand by and watch someone making such a mess of her life without offering a few words of wisdom. But if you won't accept them, of course, that's your privilege – I almost said your funeral.'

I turned and walked quickly down the passage to my room, not trusting my voice to reply.

Charles woke clear-eyed from his drugged sleep when I succeeded in rousing him halfway through the morning. Hair ruffled, pyjamas haphazardly buttoned, he sat up in bed looking unfairly dishy for a man who'd had a heavy night.

'Oh God,' he yawned, 'don't say there's some new disaster?'

'On the contrary.' I was aware that I sounded over-crisp, schoolmistressy, the world's worker who toiled while others slumbered. I had the frenzied, frantic feeling that events were moving while we did nothing to stop them – that things were gathering momentum, sliding downhill out of control . . .

Rapidly I gave him a report on Richard's late-night visit, and saw the sleepiness drop from him like a discarded garment. He even smiled.

'Christ, what a relief! I should have know that's what the wily old bastard would do. Never let your right hand know what your left's up to – that's my father-in-law all over. Catta, darling, I could hug you.'

I suppose it was ridiculous of me to wish that he *looked* worried; since he showed signs of suiting action to words I withdrew to a prudent distance and perched on the windowsill to give him the rest of Richard's message. The news that Mario was arriving with the money brought Charles out of bed with a bound.

'Wonderful!' he exclaimed. 'So he's come to his senses in the nick of time. My God, I thought he never would. These last days have been a nightmare for me. I can hardly believe we're almost out of the wood at last.'

It seemed a shame to cloud his optimism, but I was far from sharing it. In my view, the exchange of ransom for hostage bristled with possible dangers, possible misunderstandings.

'D'you believe Richard?' I asked bluntly. 'You don't think he's spirited the children away . . . for some reason of his own?'

Charles laughed. 'Talk about suspicious minds! No. I doubt if Labouchere could dream up a scheme like that. He hasn't the imagination.'

'You told me he was sharp.'

'So he is. But he's hand in glove with my father-in-law and all

184

those vipers on the Henschels' board.' His voice sharpened with resentment. 'Sometimes I think they look on *him* as the heir apparent. He'd be a fool to do anything that might upset that particular apple cart. No: I think you can take it that Ivan and Lorna are just where Labouchere says they are: staying with one of his country cousins until this business is safely over.'

'*If* it's ever safely over.'

He gave me a curious glance. 'Still determined to look on the black side? Poor darling! You haven't lost your knack of dreaming up tall stories, anyway. D'you remember that summer when I had glandular fever and you used to pop your head round my bedroom door and ask if I wanted you to tell me a story? It used to send my temperature soaring.'

Of course I remembered. I was touched that he did, too.

He said reflectively, 'You were a sexy little thing, even then. D'you know what I really wanted? What I used to think while you were sitting on my bed, spinning those incredible yarns?'

'I can guess.' Abruptly I moved away from the encircling arm. I said, 'How will you get in touch? Where will you meet him, with the money? There isn't much time, you know.'

'Relax, darling, relax. Everything's under control.' He glanced at me sideways. 'I'm afraid I made an ass of myself last night. It was all . . . too much. And we'd – I'd – had a fair bit to drink. I rather went to pieces.'

'Good Lord, I'm not blaming you,' I said hastily. 'Anyone might have done the same. You've been under an awful strain. . .'

'Then why are you so stiff and starchy this morning?'

'Am I? Sorry, I didn't mean to be. It's just that you seem so sure everything's all right. You take it so lightly.'

'*Lightly!* Is that really how it looks to you?' His smile had a bitter twist. 'Then I must be one hell of a good actor, darling. My God, if I gave way to my real feelings I wouldn't be capable of rational thought. I'm doing my best to stay sane, and you accuse me of taking Rowan's danger *lightly*. I don't know whether to laugh or cry.'

'Charles, I wasn't accusing you.'

'That's damned well how it sounded. I'm beginning to think that our lawyer friend must have poisoned your mind against me.'

With alarm I recognized the tone. Unless I could reassure him I was in for a long harangue of self-justification. There simply wasn't time for it.

'Sorry! I didn't mean it like that, honestly.'

'Give me a kiss and I might believe you.'

I drew back. 'I can't. Not when Rowan – '

Suddenly, shockingly, his self-control snapped. 'Will you stop nagging me about bloody Rowan?' he burst out. 'I'm doing my best to save my bitch of a wife from the mess she's got herself into, and I won't be nagged and bullied and shoved around and told how to behave. Not by you or anyone else. I'm sick of pretending and I'm damned if I'll act the part of the grief-stricken husband just to please you. Do you really need me to spell it out? Don't you understand how things are with us? Listen: after the way Ro's treated me I don't give a tinker's cuss whether she's alive or dead, and if it wasn't for Ivan and Lorna I'd leave her to rot without lifting a finger. Get it?'

The angry flush faded from his face as he stared down at me and he said in a quieter tone, 'All right, don't look so shocked. I'm not going to freak out at this point. I'll do exactly as the kidnapper tells me and do my damnedest to get Rowan out of his clutches. That's what you want, isn't it? But I'm not going to pretend it's what I want, or that there's any love left between us. There isn't.'

'But, *Charles* – '

'Haven't I been punished enough?' he said tiredly. 'Must I go on for ever paying for that one mistake, that one moment when I chose the wrong track? It's your fault, Catta. You must realize that.'

'What d'you mean?'

'If you hadn't flung us together – if you'd never thrown Rowan at my head like that – none of this would have happened.'

Astonishment rendered me temporarily speechless. Was this – could this *possibly* be – how Charles remembered that fatal river party at Henley? A moment later it became clear that it was.

'If you hadn't spent the whole damned day making up to that hairy poet or painter or whatever he was, leaving me in the cold, Rowan would never have got her hooks into me.'

'But you offered to drive her home! You left *me*.'

'How could I refuse? You'd made it clear enough you'd had enough of my company. Not *creative* enough, I suppose! I wasn't going to play gooseberry, thank you very much. How d'you suppose *I* felt, seeing my girl go off with that bearded weirdo?'

His voice trembled a little, and the sound took me straight back to the even earlier day when our families had shared a holiday house in Norfolk and the news had come that Charles had failed his Common Entrance exam. Old Miss Glover, who'd coached us both, had been blamed.

'How could I answer those questions when we hadn't even *done* Pythagoras?' Charles had asked in the same trembling voice; and his father had said quickly, 'I know, old boy. It's not your fault. I blame myself for not realizing that silly woman's methods must be years out of date.'

No one had pointed out that Miss Glover's methods had been perfectly adequate as far as I was concerned. Everyone bent over backwards to be nice to Charles. My parents joined his in laying the blame on Miss Glover's thin shoulders, and of course I copied them. Now, finding myself at the receiving end of blame for another of Charles' failures, I wondered how the elderly governess had felt.

'D'you remember Miss Glover?' I asked on impulse.

'Who? Oh, the old trout who taught us maths? Of course I do. I used to spend her lessons wondering what you looked like without your clothes. I knew you were the only girl for me, even then.'

'So you married Rowan,' I said dryly.

He groaned. 'That's what I'm trying to explain – I only married her because you drove me to it. If you hadn't been so set on that damned career of yours, d'you think I'd have given her a second thought? I tell you, it nearly drove me mad, thinking of you in that art school, having it off with every man in sight.'

'I wasn't!'

'Everyone knows what art students are like,' he went on as if I hadn't spoken. 'Worse than medical ones. I didn't have to be told. I knew I'd lost you. Are you surprised that I turned to Rowan on the rebound? My God, I regretted that soon enough. On our honeymoon, to be precise. She's like one of those cannibal orchids, you know. Or a hairy black spider that sucks her mate dry and leaves the shell.'

'You're talking about my best friend,' I said coldly.

'I'm talking about my *wife*. All right, darling – ' his quick grin flashed ' – don't get on your high horse. That air of icy disdain doesn't suit you at all. Besides, we're wasting time. Mario arrives – when? Around three? Come on, let's get moving. We've a lot to do before then.'

He tore off his pyjama jacket and dropped it on the floor. Seeing that his trousers were about to follow, I beat a retreat.

'Are you awake?' said Richard against my jawbone.

I twisted the telephone round till the receiver was the right way up and stared incredulously at the hands of my travelling clock. This was *too* much.

'Have you any idea what time it is?'

'Just on a quarter past three,' he said as if this was a perfectly normal time to ring up for a chat. 'I wanted to make sure you weren't lying awake worrying.'

'Well, *thanks*!' I snarled. 'For your information I wasn't awake worrying but now I shall be for the rest of the night. All right? Satisfied?'

'Not entirely. I'd like you to tell me about today's hand-over arrangements. When and where and so on. I take it Mario arrived on schedule?'

'Yes.'

'And you've checked the cash?'

'We have.'

It had been like some mad game of Monopoly, counting and rubber-banding the used high-denomination notes as Mario, blue-chinned and taciturn, pulled bundle after bundle from his black attaché case and handed them over for inspection.

'Let's use a bit of system about this,' Charles had said at the outset. 'I'll count and put them in this waste-paper basket, and you check off the bundles and pack them into the haversack. All right?'

'Fine.'

Mario had simply grunted. We'd worked steadily, with the door locked and scarcely a word spoken except when Charles decided a note was too torn or dirty and Mario replaced it from the wad in his own wallet. Rapidly the money stopped being something real that you could buy things with, and became simply tatty scraps of paper whose sole value lay in their power to release Rowan. I even began to doubt that the kidnapper, however unbalanced, would be crazy enough to want a whole haversack full of this dirty confetti. It took over an hour and a half to complete the job to Charles' satisfaction, and then at Mario's insistence they'd gone together to lock both haversack and attaché case in the hotel safe before Charles left us to put the advertisement that would tell the kidnapper he was ready to deal in the window of the *Vente-Locations* office . . .

'Well?' Richard prompted.

I considered how much I should tell him. It worried me that he should persistently question me, rather in the way that one keeps banging tennis balls at the weaker partner in a mixed doubles in the hope that she'll give points away.

'Charles made the arrangements. Why not ask him?'

'I would if I could but I can't since he's not answering his telephone. So I'm asking you instead.'

I guessed Charles had had the sense to leave his receiver off the hook overnight, and wished I'd thought of doing the same. Even if he hadn't, at three in the morning it was hardly surprising that his room wasn't answering. I cursed my inability to sleep more soundly.

'Try him in the morning, then. I really don't *know* what he's arranged. It's all a bit complicated – I'd only muddle you.'

'Listen, Catta,' he said, and now there was a perceptible snap behind the reasonableness, 'I can't wait that long. I want to know *now*. Tell me what Dawson's fixed up about paying over the money and stop stalling, unless you want me to come and shake it out of you.'

'Aren't you in Geneva?' I said in alarm.

'No, I'm up at the Eagle's Nest. Shutting it up for the season. I'd have stayed another day to keep an eye on you if I could, but – ' fractionally he hesitated then went on ' – Rob's going through a bad patch. I've got to get back at once.'

'How bad?' I tried not to be pleased that Robin's troubles would keep Richard out of the way temporarily. All this popping up at odd times of night was a strain on my nerves.

'Pretty bad. The worst yet. Gina's just rung at panic stations to say she can't cope alone. He's more than she can manage. He's worried about Rowan – literally worried out of his mind. It's impossible to reason with him.'

'But – the doctor. That specialist you told me about. Can't she do anything?'

'Unfortunately Chantal's on holiday in Spain, and her locum seems to know very little about nervous diseases. No. I'll have to go and take charge until I find someone competent to look after him; that's why I'd be glad if you'd tell me here and now just what Dawson proposes to do about getting his wife back. Did he manage to make contact yesterday? Did the ad attract an answer?'

'Yes.'

'Another tape?'

'Yes.'

'How did Rowan sound?'

'Awful. Oh . . . really terrible. I can't describe it.'

'All right,' he said, and I was thankful he hadn't pressed me for her actual words, because the weak slurred voice, half choked by tears, had accused me and Charles of dreadful things. Of hating her and wanting her to die. Of deliberately delaying payment of the ransom. She had cried for her children, painful gasping sobs distorting her speech. Charles had listened with his face bleached beneath the tan and a grim set to his mouth.

'Then she's still alive. Thank God for that. Tell me what Dawson was instructed to do?'

'It's quite complicated. Really, you'd much better hear it from Charles.'

'*Tell me what you know* and for Christ's sake stop stalling. What's he got to do to get her back? Where does he take the money?'

'He's got to go to various different places and pick up messages,' I said reluctantly. 'Like a treasure hunt, you know, one clue leading to the next.' With sudden nostalgia I remembered the treasure hunts Charles used to organize for me and the younger children all round his parents' farm, leading us from loft to cellar, cowshed to coach house, sometimes on foot, sometimes on bikes, laughing and shrieking and trying to decipher cryptic little verses. They'd been the high spot of every Easter holiday as far back as I could remember.

'I see. Go on: where does he start? What time? Ben will want all the details.'

'At the top of the Sorcière lift at eleven o'clock. That's where he has to pick up the first lot of instructions. He's got to be completely alone, unarmed, unbugged, just what you'd expect.' I paused, then added, 'That's it, I'm afraid. That's all he told me.'

'It'll do.' Richard sounded pleased. I had a fleeting fear that I might have told him something I shouldn't. 'Now I'll be on my way and you can go back to sleep. Oh – just one thing: were you planning to take any part in this operation yourself? Any active part?'

'Well, no. Not exactly.'

'What d'you mean?'

'I thought I'd better stay on the sidelines. Just in case Charles needs help. Or . . . or Rowan.'

I'd seen myself in a supporting role: the little ray of sunshine, helpful yet unobtrusive, ready with the brandy and bandages. Charles' anchor-man, just as I'd always been.

'I want you to promise me you'll keep right out of it,' said Richard. 'I know it's a lot to ask, but I'd be happier if you stayed in your apartment until the whole operation's finished. Lock your door and don't open it to anyone until I ring to give you the All Clear. Will you do that?'

'I can't!' I exclaimed, dismayed. 'I'd go mad not knowing what was going on.'

'You won't know that anyway,' he pointed out, 'and if anything should go wrong – heaven forbid, but *if* it did – I'd like to know that you, at least, were safe.'

'I'll be all right,' I insisted. 'I can take care of myself.' The thought of spending long hours cooped up in this little box in lonely uncertainty brought me out in a cold sweat. I looked round at the walls, knowing it was as bad a mistake as glancing over one's shoulder on a dark night. As if to punish my foolishness the panelling moved a menacing pace inward.

'I *can't* stay here,' I said again.

'Listen,' he said urgently, 'it really is important that you should keep your head down until it's all over. I don't want any attempts to bump you off.'

'Why me?' I asked, and a nasty little chill touched my spine. 'It's nothing to do with me. I'm no – no *threat* to anyone.'

His laugh was not reassuring. 'Just like an ostrich. Stick your head in the sand and the danger won't exist. The danger's real enough, Catta, work it out for yourself. You're the only person who actually saw Didier Casavargues' murderer. You might be able to identify him.'

'But I can't!' Fear made my voice shrill. 'I told you, he was wearing that damned hood. I haven't a clue what he looks like. He must realize that.'

'I wouldn't bank on it. There's another thing. I didn't want to worry you with this, but if you won't agree to stay put today you leave me no alternative.'

When I said nothing, he went on, 'Until Rowan's safe, there's another person gunning for you, Catta. My brother.'

'Robin!' Now I was frankly incredulous. 'That's absurd. What have I ever done to him? I scarcely know him.'

'It's more what you've done to Rowan,' said Richard sombrely. 'Robin thinks – quite absurdly, I'm sure – that you and Dawson have a vested interest in her death.'

This was too much. 'For God's sake tell him that's untrue. She's my friend. My best friend. I'd do anything to save her. You – you can't believe such a thing.'

'What I can believe and what Robin can are two very different matters. Of course *I* don't believe it, but then I'm prejudiced in your favour. *I* don't think Dawson means any more to you than an outgrown crush – a surrogate brother. Right?'

'Exactly.' I was too relieved that he, at least, understood my feeling for Charles to examine that curious mention of prejudice.

'All the same,' he went on, 'for your own sake I've got to warn you what's in Robin's mind. If anything goes wrong – more specifically if Rowan gets hurt – it'll be hard to convince my brother that you're not to blame. Because of his trouble – his illness – he tends to get things out of proportion.'

'D'you mean he's violent? He'd attack me?'

'Let's say he's not subject to the normal taboos,' he said, and again the shiver ran down my spine. 'Don't worry, I'll do my best to make him see sense, but I can't keep him on a lead all the time, you know. Now, will you promise to stay in and keep the door locked? I won't incarcerate you any longer than is absolutely necessary, you know. But I'd hate you to get hurt.'

'All right,' I said reluctantly, 'but don't keep me there too long.'

'That's a deal.' He sounded satisfied. Mission accomplished. Agreement obtained. 'Now back you go to sleep, and try not to worry. Everything's going to be all right.'

To my surprise I did drop off again almost immediately, and by eight o'clock when Charles came hammering on the door, the whole conversation had assumed a dreamlike quality. I couldn't quite believe that either of us had said the things I remembered.

'Wake up. Open up!'

'Who is it?' I called, feeling like Little Red Riding Hood.

'Me, of course. Who else are you expecting?' he laughed. 'Come on, are you going to keep me standing here all day? We've got to have a Council of War. No time to waste.'

I had opened the door and let him in before it occurred to me that this was precisely what Richard had told me not to do. But of course he hadn't been meaning me to bar Charles from my apartment. It was the mysterious black-hooded stranger he was afraid of, and by God, so was I. I didn't need anyone to tell me to lock the door against him. Anyway, the rescue operation hadn't even started yet, I told my conscience. The hooded man would be fully occupied setting up his treasure hunt, leaving messages for Charles to find . . . When he'd gone off to his rendezvous, I'd lock myself in and start worrying, not a moment before.

Charles, however, had other plans for me.

'I want you to keep an eye on Mario today,' he said, when I'd made him a cup of coffee and he was comfortably ensconced in the only armchair. Against its buff upholstery he looked very handsome, very Technicolor, his eyes bright blue against his tanned skin. 'I wouldn't put it past him to try to tail me. That's the last thing we want. If the kidnapper should suspect that I'm trying to doublecross him, he won't come near the rendezvous and the whole operation will abort. It's up to you to see that doesn't happen. Thank God I've got you to rely on.' He looked grim. 'If anything goes wrong today, I wouldn't give tuppence for poor Ro's chances. So you stick to Mario like a burr and don't let him out of your sight – OK?'

193

I said awkwardly, 'Is there anyone else who could watch him for you? I'm awfully sorry, but I won't be able to.'

'What?' He looked at me sharply. 'Why on earth not? I thought you wanted to help. For God's sake don't let me down now.'

'Well, I do want to help, but the trouble is I've promised to stay here in the apartment . . . just until Rowan's safe.'

'*Promised?* Who made you promise?'

'Richard Labouchere.'

The blood rose darkly on Charles' cheekbones. 'That damned interfering shyster! What the hell business is it of his? How dare he tell you what to do? I thought he'd gone back to Geneva. Don't tell me he came here pestering you last night as well?'

'No, he rang up. He *has* gone back to Geneva now. His brother's ill.'

'Good riddance,' exclaimed Charles. 'At least that ought to keep him out of our hair today.' He frowned. 'I don't altogether trust Labouchere – in fact I don't trust him at all. There's something behind this. What reason did he give for telling you to stay clear?'

In the morning sunlight Richard's warnings and my own dark imaginings seemed equally ridiculous. I could hardly bring myself to admit them to Charles. I said offhandedly, 'Oh, he seemed worried that something might go wrong and the kidnapper might decide to have a go at me.'

'Why on earth should he do that? You're not exactly an heiress,' said Charles, with a grin that robbed his words of any sting.

I hesitated. It seemed absurdly melodramatic to claim that my life was in danger.

'The only thing that's likely to go wrong is if old Mario comes sniffing around where he's not wanted,' said Charles vigorously. 'We've got to keep tabs on him, and you're the only person I'd trust to do it. I'm relying on you. I *need* you.' His eyes pleaded with me. 'Don't let me down.'

I smiled at him but my heart felt empty. Richard was right: I had outgrown my love for Charles. For all his brash appearance of confidence, Charles needed me – and I no longer needed him. But I couldn't let him down.

'All right, I'll do it,' I said. 'I'll keep tabs on Mario.'

'That's my girl! And when this business is over, you and I . . .'

I hardly listened. I knew there was no point in listening. I had woken from a long sleep and my dreams had vanished. I looked at him dispassionately. The naked pleading look had left his eyes and the mask of confidence slipped easily into place again, but I had seen beneath it and knew that whatever he said, whatever he promised, there was no future for Charles and me. I felt no pain; nothing but this strange emptiness.

'Just explain exactly what you want me to do,' I said.

Chapter Thirteen

Charles needn't have worried: Mario presented no problem. When he and I had watched Charles swing aboard the Sorcière chair-lift, with the bright orange haversack showing up like a vitamin pill against his light blue anorak, Mario showed not the least desire to follow him.

'Now-a we wait,' he said stolidly, and led me to a café in the sunny slushy little square. He ordered coffee for me and grappa for himself before choosing a newspaper from the bundle under his arm and transferring his entire attention to the strip cartoons.

I envied his calm. I flipped rapidly through a copy of *Paris Match* without taking in a word. Then I stared about the square. It was a quarter to eleven, normally the peak viewing time for all the long-legged girls and ponces and playboys who were more interested in acquiring a suntan and showing off their pastel ski-clothes than sliding down the slippery slopes, yet today the *place* was almost deserted. The few late risers still strolling past our table were all directing their steps in the same direction.

When an amplified voice in the distance began calling out numbers and requesting spectators to clear the course, I realized why. This was the final day of the Ski Championships and all the world and his wife – not to mention his mistress – was there on the sunny north-facing slope of the Col du Diamant, waiting for the thrills and spills.

Today the Finals; tonight the Ball. My stomach muscles cramped into an apprehensive knot. There had been another paragraph in yesterday's London press, more gossipy speculation about Rowan's whereabouts and my relationship with Charles. I was almost sure the information must have come from Gina.

When the Ball opened tonight, Rowan would be safe . . . or dead. I forced myself to look squarely at both possibilities, but they seemed equally unreal. So did Richard's cryptic reference to himself being prejudiced in my favour. Why? I sat in a trance, half listening to the loudspeaker and the distant murmur of the crowd.

'You wanna see racing?' Mario looked up from his paper.

'No, thanks. Not really. Do you?'

He shook his head. 'OK, we sitta here.' He went back to his cartoons while I chewed my fingernails and tried not to remember how Rowan's voice had sounded. Could she still be alive?

By degrees I became aware of a feeling that someone was staring at me, trying to catch my attention. I glanced round. We were alone in the café; even the waiters had left their posts and congregated by one of the windows through which they could see the finish of the slalom course. A huge banner advertising sun oil spanned the finishing line. No one appeared to be watching me, yet the feeling grew stronger.

Then I looked over Mario's hunched shoulder and saw a flaxen head bob out from behind the bookstall and swiftly retreat. An instant later a hand made beckoning signals. With a sense of shock I recognized the buxom blonde from the crêperie, Gaston's wife. There could be only one reason for her to want to speak to me.

Dared I leave Mario? Would he vanish the moment I took my eye off him? It seemed most unlikely and anyway Charles had half an hour's start.

The hand waved again. With my heart pounding hard I swallowed my coffee and told Mario I was going back to the apartment. He nodded indifferently.

'*Va bene, signorina*. I stay-a here, drink-a grappa. If news comes, I tell-a you *pronto*.'

'Fine.' I got up and strolled across the square. From the corner of my eye I saw the blonde girl leave the bookstall and follow.

She caught me up just around the corner. She was wearing a long loden-cape with a high collar and inverted back pleat. Her cheeks were flushed and her breath came quickly. '*Mademoiselle! Catherine!*' she panted. 'You must come at once. We have found your friend.'

My heart gave a bump and then began to race. I could hardly get out the one word, 'Alive?'

Jeanne nodded. I felt an enormous surge of triumph: the overwhelming rush of relief and thankfulness combined that you get when a very long chance comes off. When the hundred-to-one outsider pips the favourite on the post.

'Thank God!' I said. 'Oh, *thank* you, God.'

She caught my arm. 'You must come. There is no time to lose.'

'Wait . . . Where is she? How d'you know it's my friend?'

'Gaston describes a dark-haired woman, perhaps twenty-five, thirty years, certainly English, bandages round her eyes, always calling for Charles. Charles, and Ivan, and Lorne . . . Lorne?'

'Lorna. Yes, that's her. Where is she?'

Jeanne waved in the direction of the Sorcière peak. 'Up there, completely alone. Gaston is watching the chalet. You must hurry . . . Oh, I thought you would never look up and see me!' She began to propel me along the narrow slush-covered pavement.

'Wait,' I said again. 'Where are you taking me?' Dimly at the back of my mind was the knowledge that neither Richard nor Charles would approve of me dashing off alone like this; but nothing venture nothing win, and if I'd followed their advice I'd never have had the chance to pull off this coup. I wanted more than anything else in the world to pull it off properly.

'I'll come,' I said, 'but first I must tell Mario.'

'Write him a note,' said Jeanne, and she whipped a pencil and notepad out of her bag as if she had foreseen this reaction. I noticed that it was the pad on which she took orders for pancakes.

'How far is it? How long will it take to get there?'

'Oh, perhaps twenty minutes, half an hour at the most.'

Charles would be at the top of the Sorcière now, searching for his first set of instructions. It seemed a safe bet that the kidnapper would put him through a number of hoops to make sure he was alone and unobserved before he told him where to leave the money. There might still be time to thwart him if Mario moved fast. After a moment's thought, I wrote:

Mario,
I have gone with a friend who knows where Rowan is imprisoned. If mission is successful, I will ring you in hope of stopping Charles handing over money. Wait at the café for my call.

Catherine

'Give that to a waiter,' I told Jeanne. 'Tell him to be sure to deliver it with the gentleman's next order.'

When she came back I said, 'Right, let's go.'

Her car was a battered yellow Volkswagen beetle which she drove like a chariot, slewing round icy corners as we tackled the steep hill out of the village. 'Gaston is waiting. He will be anxious,' she said nervously, and stamped her foot to the floorboards. The little car rocked and roared. I tried to look anywhere except at the drops below the hairpins.

'Who lives there?' I pointed to the well-spaced line of chalets whose pointed roofs just showed over the pine trees, high above the ugly grey mass of Val du Loup.

'Oh, those are the chalets of *les super-riches*: le duc de Normandie, Monsieur Kronsky, la marquise d'Avoine, Bardot, Jean-Claude de la Rue . . .' She went on reeling off names and I realized why the road was familiar: it was the horrid snaky route down which Robin had driven me after the Kronskys' party. Faintly through the car's open window I could hear the ski-race commentary, and see spread out below us the masses of spectators milling like multi-coloured ants on either side of the roped-off course. The *super-riches* in their luxurious chalets must be getting a grandstand view. As I watched, a tiny stick-man with an orange helmet hurtled down the course, zigzagging between barely-visible gates. The slope looked perpendicular.

'My God,' I murmured, 'how can they do it?'

Jeanne gave me a sideways glance. 'Three years ago my Gaston won the Hollenberg Cup. Today he sells pancakes to make a living.'

'That doesn't make him less of a hero.'

'*D'accord*.' She drummed her fingers on the wheel as if to hasten the car.

'Where is my friend? How did Gaston find her?'

From Jeanne's account I gathered that Bubu's claim to know everyone in the valley had been no idle boast. It had been one of her great-uncles-in-law, Pierre Lachasse, a retired woodcutter who worked as part-time gardener for the Marquise d'Avoine, who had reported hearing a woman crying behind the shutters of a room in the servants' quarters of the Chalet Ariane, which was shut up for the season since the owner was in Africa.

'Pierre looks after the garden, you see, but in winter, evidently, there is no work for him to do. He seldom goes near the chalet. But his wife, Tante Mathilde, wished for a sprig of jasmine to brighten her kitchen, so she sent him to clip a branch from the wall of the house. That was when he heard the woman cry.'

So slender a chance . . so delicate a chain of circumstance . . . I shivered. If Tante Mathilde hadn't fancied a vase of winter jasmine, Rowan's cries would have gone unnoticed.

'At first Pierre thought that Melusine, one of the Marquise's daughters, might have come with a boyfriend to watch the races without mentioning it to her mother. She's wild, you know. Unpredictable. It would have been quite in character. But then he looked through a small hole in the shutter and saw a strange woman with her eyes bandaged. He remembered what Maman had said, and sent word to Gaston. All yesterday Gaston watched the chalet, and saw nothing. But this morning a man came through the fence. He had a key.'

'Did Gaston know him?' I leaned forward eagerly.

Jeanne hesitated, then shook her head. 'He wore a mask – a black hood – completely concealing his face.'

I sighed. I should have guessed. 'Who owns the neighbouring chalets?'

'On the left the film director, Jacques Charballier. On the right an English milord, I don't know the name. Beyond that, Monsieur Kronsky. Here we are, now.' She turned down a narrow bumpy track between the pine trees, and a moment later the Chalet Ariane came in sight.

Though similar in size and shape to the Kronsky chalet I'd already visited, the Chalet Ariane lacked its air of glossy prosperity. It looked like a millionaire's toy of which the owner had tired, exuding melancholy and neglect from its peeling paint and sagging shutters to the leggy, unkempt shrubs clustered beneath their snowy shrouds. Evidently the retired woodcutter took his gardening duties lightly.

'Are you sure it's empty?'

Jeanne nodded. 'The Marquise no longer interests herself in winter sports. Once she was Emil Kronsky's *belle amie* and came often, but now – ' she shrugged ' – now she hunts other game. Since her son died she spends her winters in the sun –

Bahamas, Africa – she has properties all over the world.'

She swung the Volkswagen in a circle, ready for a quick getaway, and switched off the engine. Her hands were trembling. For a moment we sat staring at the chalet's secretive shuttered facade, in silence apart from the faint clicks of the cooling engine. The scrunch of boots over snow made us both start, but it was only Gaston, haggard and unshaven, with restless bloodshot eyes, who came and bent to speak through the window.

'You took your time,' he said roughly.

'I was as quick as possible.'

'*Mon Dieu*, it seemed an eternity. There's something about this place . . .' He left the sentence unfinished and scrubbed at his cheeks as if they itched. 'That poor creature, always crying! Come on, let's get on with it. Jeanne, stay in the car and keep watch. If anyone comes, sound the horn and start the engine. *En avant, mademoiselle.*'

Almost reluctantly I got out into the biting air. 'Where is she?' I asked in a low voice.

'Second window on the right. Luckily it's the ground floor. You can't see much through the shutter because of the sun, but you can hear her. Crying and moaning like a lost soul . . .' He paused then said, 'Pierre doesn't have the key. We'll have to break in.'

'Oh, God.'

'There's no other way.' He glanced over his shoulder. 'He may come back any time.'

'Quick, then.'

He led me to the shuttered window second from the right and, putting my eye to the crack between two warped planks, I tried to pierce the gloom within. It was impossible to make out anything definite; only vague shapes of grey and black, but after a moment I heard a faint sound, a sigh followed by that strange little mew.

Gaston was watching intently.

'It's Rowan,' I said. 'My friend.'

'*Bon. Allons-y.*' He took hold of the edge of the shutter and gave a strong pull. It didn't budge. 'Wait. There are tools in the car. He ran off, and came back with a hammer and a crowbar. Together we attacked the painted wood, struggling to wrench the shutter from its hinges. The noise of splitting boards was frightful, and we kept glancing round in case our activities were attracting attention. I prayed that the Marquise wasn't security-minded. An alarm would be the final straw.

But when we'd demolished the first shutter, the overgrown garden was still silent apart from the soft drip of melting snow and far-off gabble of the loudspeaker. Though it seemed incredible in view of the noise we'd made, no one appeared to have heard.

'*Merde!*' said Gaston, and attacked the second shutter. A few seconds later it lay smashed on the ground; cautiously we pushed up the sash window and crawled over the sill. I went up to the bed and stared in horror.

In the few days that had passed since my first attempt to rescue Rowan her condition had deteriorated frighteningly. Then she had been thin: now she was skeletal. There could be no doubt she hovered at death's door. With nervous haste Gaston sawed with his pocket knife at the bandages fastening her to the bed, and scooped her up, rugs and all, while I went back through the window to help him manoeuvre his burden across the sill.

'She's so light,' he whispered. 'She weighs nothing at all.'

Rowan's head, too big for her body, sagged over his shoulder. When I gently unwound the bandages covering her eyes they stared blankly at me, without recognition. A cold finger touched my heart. After all this, were we too late? My first elation had died. Rowan's life still hung by the merest thread. I couldn't spare the time even to ring Mario and tell him what had happened: the most urgent thing was to get her into intensive care.

Jeanne had run from the car to meet us. 'Where's the nearest hospital?' I asked.

She and Gaston looked at one another and then, doubtfully, at Rowan. 'Abbeville . . . but it's a long way. Two hours at least. Will she . . . can she . . .?'

'*Two hours!* There must be somewhere nearer. Where are injured skiers taken?'

'Anything serious goes automatically to Abbeville. It's a modern hospital, you know, with proper facilities. Here there is nothing. *Attendez . . .*' He frowned in thought. 'The only other place would be the hospice. It's just a small sanatorium, quite primitive, run by the Little Sisters of the Poor.'

It didn't sound very promising. 'How far is that?'

'Perhaps seven or eight kilometres.'

'We'll take her there.' One look at Rowan's pinched grey face was enough to convince me that she'd never survive a two-hour journey over mountain roads. As carefully as we could, we lowered her thin body on to the back seat and heaped rugs over her.

'How will we all get in?'

Gaston shook his head. 'Don't worry. I'll borrow Pierre's skis and take a shortcut back to the village. There's a direct route. I'll be there before you are.'

'Would you go to the café and tell Mario what has happened and where to find us? Oh, and leave a message at the hotel, too, in case Charles – M. Dawson – gets there first?'

Amazing though it seemed to me, only an hour had passed since I left Mario drinking his grappa.

'*Bon, d'accord.*' He turned to go.

'And thank you, Gaston. Thank you very much.'

He said gruffly, 'You don't have to thank me. That animal who shot Didier is going to pay for this. Pay in blood.'

'*Doucement*, Gaston.' Jeanne gave him a warning look and started the engine. As we drove gently down the rough track I saw Gaston wave and plunge confidently into the woods at the back of the Chalet Ariane.

It was a slow, agonizing journey. I dreaded every bump for its effect on Rowan, and though I squeezed into the back seat to cradle her head in my lap and hold her tightly, willing the weak flame of life not to flicker out, I could sense her vitality ebbing all the time.

'Hang on, Ro,' I urged her. 'Just a couple more miles . . . just a few more minutes.'

'*On arrive*,' said Jeanne with relief at last, turning into a cobbled courtyard. 'Wait here while I call the good sisters.' She jumped out, leaving the door open. I pulled the rug closer round Rowan, who lay frighteningly still.

'Just another minute,' I murmured. 'Just another minute and you'll be safe.'

203

The hospice of the Little Sisters of the Poor bore an unnerving resemblance to an opera set. In a high wall of rough-hewn blocks was an iron-studded door of forbidding solidity, and outside it dangled a huge metal bell which looked as if it was more for show than use. However its sonorous clang brought a prompt response from an elderly nun, her weatherbeaten complexion surrounded by a wimple. She wore a rusty black habit and boots. Jeanne addressed her urgently and after a moment they both disappeared within.

I waited. Rowan shifted in my arms and moaned, 'Charles.' It was the first word she'd spoken since we found her. I prayed that the good sisters would make haste, and almost before I'd finished the prayer two young nuns emerged carrying a stretcher, with Jeanne, still talking volubly to the old doorkeeper, close on their heels.

With soft exclamations of concern, the stretcher-bearers took Rowan from my arms and carried her through the gate, across another smaller courtyard and down a stone-flagged passage. Only when they had finally deposited their burden in a small bleak room more like a cell than a ward, furnished with a bed, a bowl and a crucifix, did I realize just what Gaston had meant when he said the hospice was primitive. It was positively medieval. Though the nuns were kindness itself, bustling about fetching blankets, mixing glucose solution, taking Rowan's pulse, it was abundantly clear that their nursing capabilities were rudimentary. They simply weren't equipped to handle any medical emergency.

'How long since *la pauvre* took any nourishment?' asked Soeur Angelique, the stout doorkeeper.

'I don't know exactly. Perhaps a week. Can the doctor – ?'

'My child, there is no doctor here. We are only a small community. Dr Grosjean attends us twice a week, and in urgent cases . . .'

'This is an urgent case, as you see. Can you summon him quickly?'

The nun's faded blue eyes under their wrinkled lids regarded me steadily. 'I regret, my child, that is impossible. We have no telephone. It would be quicker to fetch him yourself.'

I didn't want to leave Rowan. I had an absurd conviction that she was only hanging on to life because I'd told her to. The moment I deserted her she would give up. I consulted with Jeanne, who agreed to go in search of a doctor.

'*Any* doctor. In a place like this, there must be half a dozen if only one knew where to find them.'

In a place like this. Even as I spoke I realized that this was in no sense a normal place where you could expect normal services. Here a space-age playground had been ruthlessly superimposed on a medieval hamlet. A self-sufficient rural community which fed itself, policed itself and certainly did most of its own doctoring had been invaded by town-bred hordes demanding the modern amenities they considered their right: heating, garbage disposal, medical facilities. The trouble was, the hordes had arrived before the social services had time to catch up.

'Every doctor is doubtless watching the Championships,' said Jeanne.

'Of course! Get them to put out a call over the loudspeaker. Or try the trainers' stand – there must be doctors there. Only . . . please hurry.'

'I'll do my best. *Courage*, Catherine.' She smiled at me, and with a last glance at Rowan lying still and white in the glare of the overhead bulb, she hurried out, her heels beating a brisk tattoo on the stone flags.

I looked at my watch. A quarter to two. Surely Charles would be here soon? There was nothing more I could do to speed his arrival. He would get the message either from Mario or directly from Gaston. He had the use of Rowan's car. He might be here any minute.

I knelt beside the hard little bed, since there was no chair or even room for one in the narrow cell, and gently rubbed Rowan's hands.

'Charles?' she murmured again.

'Don't worry. He's on his way.'

This time when I unbandaged her eyes, they flickered open. I held my breath. They still had that blind, unfocused look, but I sensed that she was listening.

'Charles . . .'

'He's coming. And a doctor. You're safe now. You're going to be all right.'

All afternoon I stayed with her, talking, holding her hands, helping Soeur Angelique to feed her minute sips of glucose solution, waiting for the doctor. And Charles. I couldn't understand why he didn't come. But very gradually I began to see a change in Rowan. Her eyes opened more frequently, for longer periods, and the blurred look cleared from them. Her face looked less pinched, and I guessed that the effect of the last dose of sedative was wearing off. With renewed hope, Soeur Angelique and I again helped her swallow a mouthful.

'She should have a drip,' said the nun. 'It is best in a case like this. There's so little we can do.'

'I think she's improving.'

'Please God.' Again she left the cell.

Half an hour later Rowan's hand moved in mine. I looked up.

'Catta?' she said in a puzzled voice.

I nearly cried with relief. 'Rowan! I thought you'd never speak to me.'

Her eyes roamed the bare cell. 'Where am I? Where's . . . Goldilocks?'

'*Goldilocks?*' For an instant I was baffled; then my mind flew back to the other time she'd used the name. In my studio, when she was persuading me to come skiing with her. '*Goldie's always nagging Charles, trying to get his hands on my money.*'

She said muzzily, 'He covered his face, but I knew his voice. That tune he whistles . . . always the same. Charles doesn't know. I must warn him . . .' She sounded agitated. 'Why won't he come?'

'I've sent him a message,' I said soothingly. 'He'll soon be here.'

'I've slept so much and still I'm tired.' Her voice grew fretful. 'Don't know if I'm awake or asleep. He told me terrible things, Catta. Terrible things about you and Charles. He said you want me to die so you can marry him. Not true . . . tell me it isn't true.'

I swallowed. 'It isn't true.'

'I knew it wasn't,' she sighed. 'I told him he was wrong.'

'Who is he, Rowan? What's his real name?' The urgency in my tone made her flinch, and to my dismay her eyes clouded again. Her mouth trembled.

'I don't know. Don't ask me. I'm so tired. How can I sleep if you keep asking me questions?'

'Listen, Rowan I've got to know who he is. It's important.'

'The light hurts my eyes,' she moaned, and moved her head weakly, trying to avoid it. I switched it off beside the bed.

'Go back to sleep,' I said and eased her into a more comfortable position. 'We won't talk about it till Charles comes.'

A few minutes later, he came. I heard the engine stop and the clang of the great bell; then his quick steps striding down the passage, stopping in front of the door. He entered, followed by the flustered clucking of Soeur Angelique. I don't suppose anything so good-looking and uncompromisingly male as Charles had been seen in the hospice for many a long day. His large presence filled the cramped cell although he had stopped short, disconcerted by the gloom, his back against the door.

'Catta? Rowan? Are you there? What an incredible dump. Isn't there even a light?'

'Wait, I'll turn it on.'

He blinked in the sudden glare, and as he took in Rowan's appearance he looked shaken. 'My God!' he muttered. 'She . . . she . . . Is she alive?'

He moved forward and gingerly touched her hand, but she didn't stir. 'I'll kill whoever did this,' he said in a low, tense voice; and then, turning to me, 'Catta, you shouldn't have done it. You might have ruined everything. When I saw Mario coming after me, shouting at me, I nearly went berserk. Between you you almost caused a catastrophe.'

This was hardly what I wanted to hear. I rounded on him in fury. 'I rescued her! If I hadn't gone to look for her, she might still be lying in that awful spooky chalet like the Sleeping Beauty!' I said heatedly. 'She might be *dead*. Did you know where she was? Did *you* find her?'

'Stop it, Catta! I didn't mean that. You've pulled it off and I'm grateful, but . . .'

'You don't damned well sound it.'

'I only meant that you nearly bitched the whole operation by scaring the kidnapper away. Luckily Mario's not as fast on his skis as he used to be, and I managed to shake him off.'

I said bleakly, 'He was trying to stop you handing over the money.'

'Well, I'm afraid he didn't succeed.'

207

So that was that. There was a silence, then Charles said more gently, 'Come on, Catta, I'm not blaming you.'

'I should bloody well think not.'

'But you must admit you broke every rule in the book. Didn't I ask you to stay where you were? And not let Mario out of your sight? Can you imagine what a shock it gave me to see him pounding after me, shouting at me to stop? You could have caused a tragedy.'

'Where's Mario now?'

'On his way back to report to Ben – I hope. We've got to keep the whole thing very quiet. The police take a poor view of ransoms being paid without their knowledge. The fewer people who know that Ro's here the better. Who does know, by the way? Has she seen a doctor?'

I shook my head. 'Jeanne's gone to look for one. I think they're all watching the races: that's why she's taking so long.'

'Jeanne?'

'The girl from the crêperie. It was her husband who found Rowan.'

'I don't understand half of it,' he complained. 'Why did you keep me in the dark? Why didn't you tell me what you planned to do?'

I sighed. 'It wasn't planned. Oh, what's the use? I'll explain later. We had to bring her here because we didn't think she'd stand the journey to Abbeville.'

'Quite right.' He touched Rowan's hand again, more confidently.

I felt suddenly superfluous. I rose and squeezed past him to the door. 'I'll go and hurry up that doctor. There isn't room for all of us in here. If she wakes, give her a sip of that stuff – it's glucose and it's doing her good. Just a sip at a time. Don't overdo it.'

He followed me out to the passage and put a hand on my arm. 'Wait a minute. Has she said anything to you? Does she have the faintest idea who the kidnapper was?'

'Yes. She says she recognized his voice. She says you know him, too.'

His hand tightened on my arm. '*I* do?'

'She told me he's a friend of yours. She calls him Goldilocks.'

'*Goldilocks?*' He gave a short laugh. 'She's raving. Who the hell does she mean by Goldilocks?'

'You do know him,' I insisted. 'According to Rowan he's a – a special friend of yours. Young – ' I floundered under his burning blue gaze ' – and good-looking. With a rich father who keeps him short of money. She said he was always borrowing from you.'

'What else did she tell you?'

The muscle at the hinge of his jaw had tightened until it showed as a ridge. I couldn't bring myself to tell him of Rowan's accusation.

'That was all.'

'Don't lie to me.'

'It was. Really.'

'What a coward you are,' he said contemptuously. ' "*Special friend.*" I suppose you haven't the guts to say my wife told you he was my boyfriend?'

I was silent.

'That's what she said, isn't it?'

'I didn't believe her.'

'Loyal to the last. And you'd good reason not to believe her, hadn't you?' His laugh didn't sound amused. 'But you'd be surprised how many of her friends *do* believe it. Can you imagine what it's like for me, knowing my wife's spreading that kind of story and being powerless to stop her? Knowing that people like you are going to listen, and stare at me, and wonder?'

'I tell you I didn't believe her.'

'So you say. But I'll tell *you* that it's very easy to destroy a man's reputation. Just a few quiet hints dropped in the right ears can do the trick. Rowan's very good at dropping hints.'

This was getting us nowhere. 'I'm sorry,' I said, 'but – don't you see? – she must have dropped hints like that about *someone*. Someone she calls Goldilocks. Who is it?'

He said angrily, 'I tell you I *don't know*. It could be any one of half a dozen friends. People I go racing with, go to clubs with. People she's jealous of.'

'*Half a dozen?* Don't tell me you've half a dozen friends answering that description?' I was beginning to think he was being deliberately obstructive.

'Look, leave it alone, will you?' he said tersely. 'Rowan's safe, and that's all that matters for the moment.'

I wondered if Ben Henschel would agree with him. Or Bubu. Or even Rowan herself.

'It's important,' I insisted. 'You must remember who it is. We've got to find him. Quite apart from what he's done to Rowan, he's a murderer. I saw him shoot Didier Casavargues.'

'So you did,' he said thoughtfully. He stared at me as if for the first time I'd come into proper focus. 'So you did. Do you think you'd recognize him if you saw him again?'

I thought of the green-clad man chasing me on *Tulipe Noire*. I'd known him then, all right. 'I'm sure I would,' I said eagerly. 'His movements . . . the shape of his head . . .'

'But his face was covered, wasn't it? You couldn't see his features. Anything that would make him easy to identify?'

I was obliged to shake my head. 'No, but if Rowan calls him Goldilocks, he must have fair hair . . .'

'Not necessarily. She has these absurd nicknames for people. It's probably far more obscure than that. It could be something to do with liking bears, or eating porridge. She's quite illogical.'

I gazed at him, unconvinced. Rowan had a very literal mind. In my own mind a suspicion was forming that Charles *did* know whom she meant, but because he was a friend preferred to take no part in bringing him to justice. It was not a comfortable thought, but if Charles felt like that, why should I care?

The trouble was, I did care.

I said, almost at random, 'Well, let's hope the ransom notes were marked. I'm sure that's a precaution Ben Henschel would take.'

'They weren't,' he said shortly. 'I checked them all.'

'You sound pleased about it.'

'Of course I'm not, but I'd have been furious if I found my father-in-law was deliberately gambling with Rowan's safety.'

'He's paid out a million pounds.'

'What's that to him? Nothing. A flea-bite.'

I leaned against the wall, suddenly longing to be by myself, have a bath, take off my suffocating moon-boots. 'I must go.'

Again he detained me. 'Wait. Don't rush off. We haven't decided what to do tonight.'

'Tonight?' I looked at him in surprise. 'You may not have

decided, but personally I intend to sleep like the dead.'

'Have you forgotten the Hollenbergs' Ball?'

I said in utter astonishment, 'You can't be thinking of going? Not after this?'

'I certainly am. And so must Rowan.'

Now I knew he was crazy. 'It'd kill her. Don't you see, it's all *over*. What she needs now is rest and quiet . . .'

He said seriously, 'You're right there, but I'm not so sure that this business *is* over yet. So long as there's any chance of the kidnapper's identity being uncovered, Rowan will be in danger from him – and so will you. So keep your mouth shut about that Goldilocks business, right? It's vital that we keep her presence here a secret, and if she doesn't turn up at the Ball tonight, half the Press of Europe is going to start looking for her.'

'Oh, surely not.'

He said impatiently, 'They will. Rowan's *news* – you don't seem to realize what that means. Once the Press decides that someone's news, anything she does comes under the microscope. It gets blown up out of all proportion. Believe me, I've lived with it for long enough and I've learned to accept it. If word gets out that Rowan's recovering in a convent after a week in the hands of a kidnapper, and *she knows who that kidnapper is*, there won't be an editor in Europe who won't want an exclusive. In a one-horse place like this it wouldn't take them long to find her, either.'

'Then she'd better not stay here.'

He shook his head. 'If she was stronger, I'd get her flown home. But here . . . impossible. Can you imagine that old nun who let me in standing up to a grilling from a dozen reporters?'

I thought it over. 'She'd be safe in her father's house.'

'I know. As soon as she's fit to move, we'll take her there. Meanwhile, the only way to keep those jackals at bay is make them believe everything's normal. That there's no story.'

'How d'you propose to do that?' I asked, though I could see the way his mind was working.

'*You* must go to the Ball instead of her. No, let me finish. It wouldn't be as difficult as you think. People see what they expect to see and everyone's expecting to see Rowan dressed as Cleopatra. They won't really look at the person inside the costume. You'll pass as her all right.'

'But my voice! I don't sound like her . . .'

'That's easy. You've had a bad throat. You can speak in a whisper. I'll do the explaining. At that kind of do everyone's too busy thinking of his own appearance to worry much about other people's. Then, when the photographers have finished, you can make an excuse to leave early.'

I considered the matter carefully. It was mad . . . and yet it might work. Certainly it would cause less talk if Rowan put in an appearance at the Ball. And on a professional level, I wanted the Cleopatra dress to be seen. Its line was the basis for my new collection, and it was never too early to get your customers' eyes in to what they were going to want to wear in a few months' time. A lot of work had gone into the dress: it would be a pity to waste it completely. Nor, come to that, did I relish the thought of another lonely evening in my apartment, listening to sounds of revelry from the floodlit castle. I wondered where Richard was now and whether he had discovered my absence.

'How about it?' Charles urged. 'Are you game?'

'What will you do?'

'Oh, don't worry, I won't desert you. I'll be there. I'll dance with you all evening and start a new rumour that Charles Dawson and his wife have fallen in love again.'

'I only wish it was true.'

'Come on, you don't mean that,' he said quickly.

'Oddly enough I do.'

He moved very close to me, looking down with a half smile crinkling his eyes. 'What a tease you are, darling,' he said softly. 'But you'll do it, all the same?'

I swallowed with difficulty. 'Yes.'

A faint noise from the cell made us turn. Rowan had woken and was watching us through the half-open door. 'What are you talking about?' she asked fretfully. 'What are you planning?'

Swiftly Charles moved to the bedside. 'It's all right, my angel. Catta's going back to the village now, and I'm going to stay with you until the doctor comes. I'll keep you safe.'

'I don't want Catta to go.'

'I'm sorry, darling; she's got to. She's been here a long time, you know, looking after you.'

'I'll be back soon, Ro,' I promised, and closed the door gently. For a moment I lingered at the spy-hole, watching

Charles as he knelt beside his wife's bed, holding her thin hand in his large brown one. It made a pretty picture. With an unusual tightness in my throat I walked quickly away.

Chapter Fourteen

Flashbulbs exploded in a dazzle as I emerged from the hotel foyer on Charles' arm. The crowd lining the steps pressed closer.

'*Oh, la jolie! Qu'elle est belle!*'

'That dress – ravishing!'

'Who is she? The Grand Duchess?'

'No, that's the diamond heiress. The papers said she'd left her husband. What lies they make up, those journalists!'

There were scattered handclaps and sighs of envy from the women as they took in the full glory of my draped cloth-of-gold gown, dramatic gold necklaces, black wig and elaborate head-dress. Rowan and I had really gone to town on this one – no expense spared.

A leather-jacketed youth retreated down the red-carpeted steps as I advanced, his camera whirring, its lens aimed at my face. I tried to walk unhurriedly, unconcernedly, as Rowan would have done. She wouldn't flinch from the flashbulbs and outstretched hands. To her it would seem perfectly natural that all the people who hadn't been invited to Prince Hollenberg's Ball would want to gawp at those who had; to watch them saunter down the hotel steps and climb into the painted sleighs whose ponies were decked with red rosettes and ribbons and silver bells, and watch them whirled away up the snowy street to the Prince's fairytale castle where they would dance the night away.

Rowan would consider the gawpers had a perfect right to criticize the looks and costumes of the gilded jet-setters, and speculate freely on their private lives; just as she had a perfect right to flaunt before them the four-figure fancy-dress she'd commissioned for this one occasion. And because tonight I *was* Rowan and must think like her if our masquerade was to succeed, I slowed my step and smiled and tried not to shrink from those avid, envious eyes.

'Rhubarb, rhubarb,' said Charles, leaning over me as if deep in conversation. 'Let me do all the talking. They've got long-range mikes, so just keep smiling and look as if you love me. Great. Rhubarb, rhubarb . . .'

I smiled until my jaw ached. The retreating cameraman allowed us to pass and focused on the couple behind. A microphone was thrust under my nose.

'Nice to see you up and about, Mrs Dawson,' said a grey-suited man with a lined, sardonic face. 'Does this mean you and your husband are together again?'

I felt the warning pressure on my arm.

'I'm sorry, my wife's had a throat infection. She's been told to rest her voice,' said Charles confidentially. 'Yes, as you see, we're both very happy now.'

'Is that right, Mrs Dawson? Can you confirm that for me?'

'We're just good friends,' I whispered huskily, and the reporter laughed.

'How good?'

'The best.' I winked at him as Rowan would have done, and he grinned in a friendly way and let us go. There was a slight hold-up ahead as a stout Central European ex-royal and his equally well-upholstered consort were levered into their sleigh; more reporters fired questions at us.

'How much did the dress cost, Rocky?'

'Is it true you've filed for a divorce?'

'Can you comment on the rumour that you're living separately?'

'Where's Miss Chiltern tonight, Mr Dawson?'

Charles fended them off without a sign of irritation, though my face burnt so fiercely I was glad of the protection of my mask. Despite Charles' warning, I hadn't expected the sheer persistence of the gentlemen of the Press. We weren't the only targets for impertinent questions: behind us I could hear a rock singer getting a fair amount of flak, and several reporters had fastened onto a poor bewildered poet dressed as Socrates, who had been unwise enough to marry a budding film star young enough to be his granddaughter who had recently given birth to twins.

'How did you do it, Mr Luddington?' they said. 'What's your secret for prolonging sexual potency? Are you sure the babies are yours?'

Not a moment too soon for my nerves, the ponies towing the ex-royals' sleigh leaned into their collars and jingled away towards the castle.

Our turn next. Charles handed me into the sleigh and climbed in beside me. A footman in a powdered wig tucked a rug over our knees and under its cover Charles gave my fingers a reassuring squeeze. The ponies tossed their heads and the sleigh glided forward. I felt a sudden pang of regret that all these trappings of glamour and romance were being wasted on a sham. If only, I thought, this was for real. If only the man beside me was Richard instead of Charles. It gave me a curious pleasure to acknowledge this was what I'd have liked. Charles smiled into my eyes and pressed my arm tight against his body, and I felt nothing – absolutely nothing.

'You did that very well,' he murmured. 'Carry on like that and we'll have no problems. Just smile and follow my lead.'

'How was Rowan when you left her?'

'Ssh!' he cautioned, and lowered his voice still more. 'She was doing all right. Getting better all the time.'

'What did the doctor say?'

He shrugged. 'More or less what you'd expect. Give her time. Peace and rest and food will soon do the trick. She's in no danger.'

'Who's sitting with her?' I persisted. I felt uneasy about leaving her, even if it was in her interests that I'd taken her place. I wished Mario hadn't gone back to Geneva so promptly, or that I'd been able to get in touch with Richard before leaving. Still, he had said he'd be at the Ball. I clung to that thought.

'The fat nun – Soeur Angelique. Don't *worry*: she's all right. Look, we're nearly there. Let's see your best smile.'

The ponies' hoofs clopped hollowly on the drawbridge. The floodlit castle loomed above us, mysterious and beautiful with ice-crusted pinnacles winking like diamonds.

'Don't leave me,' I said, stifling panic. 'What if I don't recognize people? What shall I say?'

'You'll be all right. They won't allow any newshounds here.'

We followed the crowd through the castle door and into a big circular hall with a double staircase. Lights blazed from crystal chandeliers, footmen in kneebreeches and powdered wigs stood in well-drilled ranks round the walls, bare shoulders gleamed above rustling taffetas and silks. Many of the male guests had opted for uniformed roles: Nelson, Napoleon, the Iron Duke and the Iron Chancellor; a paunchy Prince Regent was deep in talk with Beau Brummel and Rupert of the Rhine's curling love-locks brushed the shoulder of a saucy Nell Gwyn.

The noise level rose as the chattering throng wound its slow way up the double staircase towards the landing where the Prince and Princess, splendid in high wigs as Louis XV and Madame de Pompadour, were receiving their guests. I realized that Charles was right: everyone was far too preoccupied with the effect he or she was making to question my identity. People waved and smiled and called out greetings, but there was no opportunity for anything but the most fragmented conversation.

I curtseyed to the Prince, who kissed me on the cheek, and again to the Princess who murmured, 'Beautiful! Delightful! So pleased . . .' and turned to the next arrivals. A blast of music hit us as we left that hurdle safely behind and moved through the gilded double doors to the ballroom.

'Will you dance, O Egypt?' asked Charles, sketching a bow.

I hesitated. As yet only a few couples had begun to waltz beneath the beautiful Dresden chandeliers. 'Won't we be a bit conspicuous?'

'That's the point. I want everyone to see you.' He put a firm hand on my waist and we floated off into the mainstream of the 'Blue Danube', the cynosure of all eyes, the handsomest couple on the floor.

It should have been a dream come true – but it wasn't. For two hours we danced and sipped champagne, and drifted from table to table as Charles directed, and all the time I worried about Rowan and searched with increasing anxiety for a glimpse of Richard. He *must* be here. He'd said nothing would keep him away. I'd relied on meeting him. But as we completed our circuit of the rooms without seeing him, I had to admit that he wasn't there. I felt unreasonably disappointed. The evening lost its last vestige of glamour and began to drag.

'Can't we go now?' I asked, as Charles manoeuvred me towards yet another group of friends.

'Wait a bit. It'll look odd if we leave before the fireworks. Look, there's old Lady Lawrence dressed as Queen Victoria.

She's a tremendous gossip. You'll have to say hello, at least.'

'Oh, hell.' I allowed him to lead me across the room.

'You naughty child!' scolded Queen Victoria, a plump little partridge who'd have made a convincing Widow of Windsor if she'd resisted the temptation to substitute diamonds for jet beads, 'you ought to have stayed tucked up in bed instead of coming here half naked, catching your death of cold. Couldn't bear to miss all the fun, I suppose?'

And the splendidly sporraned John Brown beside her rumbled, 'What'll you give me not to sneak to your father, eh, Rowan? He wouldn't like to hear you'd gone dancing with a throat like that. You ought to have kept her at home, young man,' he added, turning to Charles. 'Haven't you any control over your wife?'

'Have you?' Charles countered with a grin. 'Actually, you're right, Sir Gerald. We won't stay long. After we've seen the fireworks we'll make our excuses and siip away.'

'You take care of yourself, my dear,' said the old lady, bending confidentially towards me. 'Throats can turn very nasty up here in the mountains. I remember . . .'

She launched into a spate of clinical reminiscence, and I nodded and murmured and tried to stifle my yawns. More and more I longed for the evening to end.

At last the ballroom lights dimmed and there was a general move towards the balconies which overlooked a crescent of ornamental water below the castle terrace. Suddenly a cluster of rockets hissed skyward and burst into long multi-coloured fronds. As they flickered and died, a line of skiers carrying flaming torches swooped down the slope facing the castle. The band struck up a thumping reggae rhythm, and the torch-bearers began twirling round, skiing backward, passing their flares from hand to hand as they turned somersaults and backflips. I watched in amazement.

'Bravo!' cheered the guests on the balconies. 'Encore!'

'Ever seen this kind of thing?' asked Charles, lighting a cigarette. 'Hot-dogging – otherwise known as *le ski artistique*. This lot isn't half bad. Watch that chap in red.'

I watched, and with a sense of complete unreality I recognized Richard. It couldn't be anyone else. Even at this distance

I knew the way he moved, and though all members of the troupe wore bone-domes to protect their heads, I could see in imagination his daredevil grin, hear his shouts as he leapt and twirled like a dervish in the ever-changing light of flares, with rockets fizzing overhead.

'Beats me how they do it,' said Charles. He took my arm. 'Come on, we'll make tracks. No one will notice.'

'Let's just watch this.'

'I thought you wanted to go. Come on, we've seen the best of it. It gets a bit repetitive after a time.'

'Not for me.' He turned with a look of surprise and I laughed. 'Can't you see who's wearing the red helmet? It's Richard Labouchere.'

Through the eye-holes of his jewelled domino, Charles' gaze remained fixed on me. He said with a tinge of contempt, 'Yes, I've heard he makes a bit on the side at this kind of affair. I'm surprised you could recognize him at this distance.'

'I'd know him anywhere.' As I said the words, I felt a sudden surge of happiness. Another tiny link in the chain that had bound me to Charles seemed to snap. I was almost free.

'Well, well!' he said softly. 'So that's the way it is. Off with the old, on with the new. Come on, we'd better go. They're finished now.'

I didn't move. 'I've changed my mind. I think I'll stay a bit longer. Don't wait for me. I'll find my own way home.'

Though I'd foreseen that he was unlikely to be pleased by what amounted to a dismissal, I was unprepared for the intensity of his reaction.

'Have you forgotten why you came here?' His whisper was agonized. 'To keep those bloodsuckers off Rowan's trail – to give her a chance to recover. How d'you imagine they'll react if we leave separately? You'll ruin the whole plan!'

'No one will know. There aren't any reporters here – you told me so.'

'Maybe not, but you can bet your boots that the news that we've split up again will be in the morning editions,' he said grimly. 'I can't risk it. I won't let you ruin everything.'

I was silent. I wanted to stay. I wanted to talk to Richard and find out if this long-range magic operated at close quarters. I wanted to get to very close quarters. I felt as excited and uncertain as a girl on her first date – me, calm cool canny Catta . . .

Charles' voice changed to pleading. 'Please, *please*, darling, don't let me down now. I know it's asking a lot but I promise if you do this for me I'll never impose on you again.'

It was news to me that he was ever aware of imposing on anyone. I looked at his handsome profile with dispassionate interest.

'Just one last time,' he begged. 'Don't run out on me in the final furlong, within sight of the winning post.'

I willed the last link to snap, but obstinately it held firm.

'All right,' I said stiffly. 'I'll get my coat.'

'Bless you, darling. You won't regret it.' His relief was obvious. 'Wait in the hall while I organize some transport, and remember, above all, don't speak to anyone. We can't risk you being . . .'

I walked away while he was speaking. I felt angry, used, manipulated. Charles was right – this was the very last time I'd allow him to force me into doing something he wanted and I didn't. That last link was under considerable strain.

'*Madame* is going home so early?' asked the pretty little cloakroom attendant disappointedly. 'If I had the chance to dance in such a palace, I would not rest until dawn.'

'*J'ai mal a la gorge*,' I croaked, touching my larynx. 'I've run out of voice.'

'Oh, I'm sorry, I didn't mean . . . What bad luck!' She handed me the golden cloak and I tipped her with Rowan's characteristic lavishness. Should reporters try to pump her tomorrow, I thought, she would remember Cleopatra in her gold dress and necklaces.

The domed hall was empty. The footmen had gone upstairs to watch the figure skating that followed the hot-dogging display. Finally the Prince would present this year's Hollenberg trophies. I thought of Gaston, whose hour of glory had been so brief. One day a ski champion, the next a fryer of pancakes. *Eheu fugaces* . . . I settled myself on a spindly gold-legged chair in the shadows outside the chandelier's pool of light and waited for Charles.

Richard came first. I was rubbing my eyes, under the golden mask when I heard a quick step cross the marble floor and saw him hurry to the foot of the stairs. He hadn't changed out of the tight stretch salopettes and matching red poloneck he'd worn for the display. His hair, liberated from the casque, stood up in ebullient spikes and his skin glowed bronze with excitement and exertion. He looked tough, alive, alert: a different breed from those decadent gold-braided creatures languidly posturing upstairs. I watched him and found it difficult to breathe. Yes, I thought, I'm falling in love. How extraordinary! I had thought it would never happen again.

Don't speak to anyone. The temptation to call out to him was almost overwhelming but I mastered it. Motionless in the shadow, I watched him run lightly up the left-hand side of the staircase and vanish through the door leading to the ballroom. I wondered what the gold-braided fantasists would think of his attire.

Candles on the half-landing flickered. The domed roof from which the chandelier was suspended seemed miles away; beneath it I had the feeling of ant-like insignificance that comes over you in a cathedral. It wasn't cold but I shivered. Fairytale castles are spooky places to be alone in. Minutes crawled by, and then Charles appeared in the great arched doorway, looking round.

'Catta?' he called softly.

'Coming.' I rose and had begun to cross the slippery expanse of marble when a shout from far above made me look up. Three flights higher, where a gallery ran round the dome, Richard was standing. 'Wait,' he called. 'I've got to talk to you.'

Thrown by his sudden appearance, I lost my head and spoke in my normal voice. 'I can't. I've got to go with – '

'*Catta!*' He began to descend in long leaps.

'Come on,' urged Charles. 'Hurry!'

Watching Richard, I missed my footing, but before I could fall Charles sprang forward to grip my arm. 'Quick!' He hustled me towards the door.

I hung back. 'What's the rush?'

'It's Rowan.' He sounded distraught. 'She's asking for you. She . . . she's dying.'

'Oh, God!'

It never occurred to me to wonder how he knew, or question the likelihood of Soeur Angelique sending such a message.

221

Instead I let him hurry me across the courtyard to a waiting Mercedes whose exhaust puffed white smoke into the frozen night. The driver leaned across to open the passenger door for me, Charles jumped into the back, and the car purred away over the drawbridge.

I turned in my seat just in time to see Richard erupt through the arched doorway, but the automatic windows were closed and if he shouted I didn't hear. The car gathered speed.

'That was a close thing,' said Charles. His voice was quite different: relaxed, even amused. I twisted round to look at him and saw with astonishment that he was smiling. The street lights shone on his white teeth and crinkling eyes. 'Nice timing, Max.'

'It is more exciting that way,' agreed the man at the wheel, and his voice struck a jarring chord in my memory.

As calmly as I could, I said, 'How did you hear about Rowan, Charles?'

He seemed to be busy in the back seat, moving around, lifting something from the floor. A lock snapped open. When he didn't answer I added more loudly, 'Who told you Rowan wanted me?'

In the mirror I saw the men exchange a smile. 'Oh, that was Max. He brought me the message,' said Charles easily. 'You've met Max before, haven't you? I believe you gatecrashed his party. One way and another you've given poor Max quite a lot of trouble.'

For a moment I didn't understand. I stared at the driver's pale profile, taking in the handsome, vulpine features, straight nose, narrow jaw, wavy locks swept back from a high forehead. Red-gold locks. Goldilocks. I felt suddenly very cold. I remember Emil Kronsky's look of puzzlement and concern as he gazed at his son. Now I understood it.

My hand dropped to the door handle but before my fingers touched it Charles leaned over the back of my seat and suddenly a sweet, throat-catching smell flooded the car. A pad of material was pressed over my mouth and nose and I struggled vainly, holding my breath, trying to twist away from it. My ears began to roar as if I was drowning.

'Don't!' I gasped, flailing wildly.

The car slowed. 'Careful, Charles,' said the kidnapper's

voice. 'Don't let her bite you. A bitch like that may be rabid.'

I had to breathe or burst. As my lungs filled with the vile suffocating smell and my senses swam, I heard Charles say, 'Yes, you've given us a lot of trouble, but you won't get the chance to give any more.'

Then I plunged into roaring blackness.

I woke shuddering and stiff on a concrete floor. My head ached fiercely and my throat felt raw, as if I'd been screaming. Painfully I rolled to one side as my stomach heaved, then lay back drained and icy with the sour smell of vomit hanging all round. But stronger than any physical discomfort was the anger that burned in my very guts as I thought of Charles. 'You've given us a lot of trouble.' *Us*. How cynically he had exploited my old hero-worship, my old affection. How cold-bloodedly he'd used it to make sure I believed him rather than Rowan. Too late I saw that she had told me the truth and Charles had lied from the start. He had wanted to get rid of Rowan, not the other way round: to rid himself of a troublesome demanding wife but retain her money. And how well he'd succeeded. Even now Rowan believed that Goldilocks alone had kidnapped her. As she regained consciousness her first thought had been to warn Charles of his friend's treachery, not realizing that the ransom money would end up in her husband's pocket.

I lay and thought it over. After a week of sedation and privation, Rowan was confused and incapable of reasoning. But she was no fool. As her memory returned, the chances were that she'd put two and two together. With a stab of fear that dispelled all other aches and pains, I remembered my last sight of Rowan, with Charles bending over her. Such a pretty picture . . .

I shivered and sat up to take stock of my surroundings, surprised to find I wasn't bound in any way; also surprised to discover myself fully dressed in anorak, socks, sweater and jeans instead of the Cleopatra dress. The clothes weren't mine but they weren't a bad fit, either. I wondered who had effected the change and where I was and how Charles planned to dispose of me. He could hardly leave such a damaging witness alive. Oddly enough, the thought didn't frighten me but intensified my anger. Before Charles silenced me I'd give him something to remember.

I looked around for a weapon. The door of the long narrow room was locked, and its walls were lined with cupboards. The air was pervaded with smells of sweat, leather, sawdust, wax polish and damp wool in a blend that suggested a changing room. Beneath an inaccessible skylight was a workbench with a vice and a few small tools, none of them suitable for my purpose, but when I took a screwdriver and began opening the cupboards by removing their hinges, I struck gold.

In the first locker was a canvas bag with a drawstring neck containing a long slender bundle of struts and nylon which I had to spread out on the floor before I identified it as a collapsed hang-glider. In the second were shelves containing food and household supplies: soap, detergent, tins of fruit, sardines, condensed milk.

I removed one of my knee-length socks and looked thoughtfully at the tins before selecting the condensed milk and pushing it into the toe. I swung it to and fro: it made a serviceable sandbag. The discovery of the hang-glider told me I must be imprisoned in the workroom of the hang-gliding school attached to the Eagle's Nest: the sandbag might provide the chance to get out of it. Feeling more positive every minute, I shoved the canvas bag back in the locker, arranged the rugs that had covered me in a convincing sausage-shape, and considered the problem of the locked door.

It had neither handle nor keyhole on my side and was solidly constructed. I tried to insert the screwdriver between the door and the frame, but Alpine carpenters believe in durability and all my efforts produced were a few dents in the woodwork.

I was about to launch a second attack on it when the sound of approaching footsteps made me grab my sandbag and flatten myself against the wall where the opening door would conceal me. With a pounding heart I waited: a moment later I heard the protesting squeak of bolts. The door swung inward. With a violence born of fury I swung my sandbag at the figure coming through; only as it connected did I realize that the falling body belonged not to Charles or Max, but to Gina.

With a yelp she pitched forward and the tray she was carrying crashed to the floor. I looked at her crumpled form in consternation. The tin had caught her squarely on the back of the head but the damage looked superficial and she was still breathing. Around her lay the contents of her tray; a smashed plate, a phial of colourless liquid, and a hypodermic syringe.

After a moment's reflection I decided I'd rather be safe than sorry and removed her tights, tied her hands behind her back, then used the drawstring of the canvas bag to secure her ankles and tether them to the leg of the workbench. I gagged her with her own chiffon scarf and was glad I had when her eyes flashed open and she began wriggling and hissing at me.

Then I shook the tin of condensed milk out of my sock and replaced it. I had no desire to tackle snowdrifts barefoot. With a last look at Gina, I slipped out of the locker room and closed the door behind me. Cautiously I began to explore the chalet, my ears alert for the least sound.

The back door was locked and so were the windows on either side of it. The whole place was very quiet and the air had the faintly stale, musty smell of a house that has stood empty several days. Gaining confidence, I peered into a curtained, booklined study, then tried the bathroom. This looked more hopeful. A small window above the lavatory was ajar and I thought that when it was fully open I might be able to squeeze through. The snag was the snowdrift I would inevitably land in. I decided to try for an easier way out.

As I reached the entrance hall, my heart gave a leap of hope, for the front door was actually open, and beyond the cliff on which the Eagle's Nest stood, I could see the pylons of the Sorcière cable-car. Freedom so near and yet so far . . . The door to the right-hand front room was also open, and through it came the soft rustle and slap of paper. I knew the sound immediately.

'That's fifty thousand,' said Charles from the other side of the pine panelling, startling me by his closeness. 'Put that aside for Gina. Has she gone to do her Florence Nightingale act?'

'More like the Angel of Death,' said Max, and laughed. 'I doubt if he enjoys his job as much as she does.'

'Gina's no angel – still, I'm not complaining. She's earned her fifty thousand. Now she can go to hell on it her own way. Coffee?'

'Thank you.'

A chair scraped and feet crossed the kitchen. Silently I moved forward and put my eye to the crack in the door hinge. If they were counting money at a table, they might have their backs to me. The open front door beckoned.

Max was sitting at the end of the table, his red-gold hair falling forward a little and his long pale face absorbed as his hands sorted notes with businesslike dexterity. A moment later Charles walked across my line of vision, carrying two mugs, and seated himself, beside Max, facing the door. My hope of escape faded.

Max said thoughtfully, 'Hell hath no fury like a woman scorned. Will Robin Labouchere return to Gina, now her rival is removed?' He sounded clinically interested.

'Your guess is as good as mine. To tell you the truth, I don't greatly care,' said Charles. 'We've got what we want.'

The notes slapped and shuffled, shuffled and slapped. Charles began tucking them into two identical attaché cases.

'You don't care now what happens to Catherine?' Max's fingers paused in their work. A curious look crossed his pale face: avid, almost gloating. 'You let me do as I like with her?'

'Just as you like, but don't leave any marks. And remember, we'll have to be away by noon.'

'Two hours. Two hours to do as I please with your little slave,' said Max dreamily. 'She wasn't such an obedient slave as you thought, *hein?* She gave me some bad moments.'

'You shouldn't have started chasing her with heavy machinery,' said Charles with a trace of humour. 'Your love of drama ran away with you. I could have handled Catta easily enough if you hadn't tried to scare her off.'

'I'd have done more than scare her.'

'There was no need. While I kept an eye on her, she was no threat.'

Max murmured disagreement. 'I am not so sure. I think you made a big mistake about her. A girl like that is dangerous – like a dog who bites and won't let go even if you pull his teeth out. She was safe while you watched her – *bon, d'accord* – but what happened when you didn't watch her?'

'Treacherous bitch! I never dreamed she'd go back to that café. Maybe you're right. Maybe we should have got rid of her sooner, but I didn't want too many people disappearing at once. How're you doing?'

226

'Nearly finished.'

Max shuffled the last notes into a thick wad and snapped a rubber band round it. 'So. What's the programme now?'

Charles looked at his watch. 'It's ten o'clock and we want to be away by noon. That gives you time to dispose of Catta, and for Gina to clear up here.'

'And you?'

'There's one loose end I've got to tie up. We don't want that damned lawyer sniffing round in search of Miss Chiltern. I'll go back to her apartment, remove her baggage, and plant the necessary in her garbage can. A few used hypos, a couple of syringes, the odd trace of snow . . . Nothing too obvious.' He laughed. 'That should discourage his investigations. I don't suppose he wants a repeat of his experience with Jenny Ardenti.'

He locked the attaché cases. 'There. That's ready. Are you sure you can manage the drop?'

'No problem. I know just where I will take her.'

'Good.' Charles glanced round restively. 'Where's Gina? She's taking her time. Here, give me your cup . . .'

Chairs scraped, china chinked. They were coming out. I fled back up the passage, into the bathroom, closed the door softly and turned the key. Snowdrift or no snowdrift I'd have to risk the window. I pushed it fully open and climbed up on the cistern.

Footsteps echoed in the hall, stopped outside the door.

'You in there, Gina?' called Charles. 'It's time we were off. Max is just putting on his kit.'

As quietly as possible I lowered myself feet first through the window, but the back of my anorak snagged on the catch and I couldn't reach round far enough to undo it. I struggled silently.

'Gina?' Suspicion sharpened Charles' voice. 'Are you there?'

I had to answer. Suspended between heaven and earth, I tried to pitch my voice in imitation of Gina's high, little-girl tones.

'Won't be a mo.'

There was an instant's silence. Then he asked, 'Did you give her the jab?'

'Yes.'

The anorak ripped and I was free. I let myself hang to the full

227

length of my arms before letting go and landed softly and wetly in the drift below the bathroom window.

It was only when I tried to climb out of it that I realized how helpless I was without skis. The snow had piled head high round the walls of the chalet and the only way to flatten a track was to fall face down into it and then crawl along one's body's imprint. In two minutes I was soaked to the skin. In four I was in despair. In five they were after me.

I heard the crash as the bathroom lock burst open, then Charles' head appeared at the window, scanning the snow. I cowered behind the woodpile, aware that I'd left a track like an elephant's.

'She's got to be down there. She can't have gone far. Quick, Max, go round the front and cut her off. She mustn't reach the chair-lift . . .'

I had less than a snowball's chance in hell. Even if I'd reached the small lift that served the Eagle's Nest I'd have been no better off, for the chairs swung idly from their cable. I guessed that the machinery to start it was inside the chalet. Unless it was running – or you had wings – there was no way of joining the cable-car at the Sorcière restaurant.

High in the dazzling sky, a turquoise helicopter hovered like a dragonfly, too far away for me to hear its engine, much too far to attract its pilot's attention. With a sense of utter despair I crawled under the eave that protected the woodpile and waited for them to find me. I had reached the end of the road.

Chapter Fifteen

'Pull her out, Max! Pull her out and let me get at her!' shrilled Gina. I had just enough spirit left to wish I'd swung my improvised sandbag harder. Much harder.

'Don't worry. I'm coming out.' I crawled stiffly from between the piles of logs and straightened up. They closed round me like presidential bodyguards. I glanced at the sky but the helicopter had vanished.

'You bloody interfering bitch – ' Gina advanced with the clear intention of doing me a mischief, but Charles held her off.

'Steady,' he said firmly. 'None of that. If she's found she's got to be in a good state of preservation.' He grinned. 'All right, let's get on with it. Find her some gloves, Gina, and a helmet. Yours will probably fit.'

Gloves? Helmet? My legs showed a distressing tendency to buckle under me. 'What are you going to do?' I asked shakily.

The men exchanged a quick look. 'Shall we tell her?'

'Why not?'

'I am going to take you for a ride,' said Max. He was again wearing the black hood, and I thought: Of course! With his colouring he has to keep his face covered. An hour in the sun would flay off that white skin in strips.

'On the – the blood-wagon?'

'No, no. Never the same twice. The blood-wagon was for Rowan. You and I will fly through the air like birds.'

As his meaning sank in I stared at him in horror. 'No! You can't! I'd be terrified. I get vertigo . . . I'll do anything . . . *anything* . . .'

The hood stretched eerily as he smiled. 'Ah, but there's nothing you can do. Calm yourself, Catherine, you have nothing to fear. Gina can stop you being afraid. One small *piqûre* and in five minutes you will be happy as a bird. Flying over the glacier like an eagle – imagine it!' Through the slits in the mask, his amber eyes sparkled with malice. 'Then I will find a nice little crevasse to put you in. In some years – perhaps twenty, perhaps fifty – you will be seen again, perfectly preserved, a curiosity for geologists, anthropologists. You will be immortal, Catherine, doesn't the prospect delight you? When Charles and I have lost our beauty, you will still be young . . . though dead, naturally.'

I swallowed with difficulty. 'You're mad. You can't do it. Charles, you wouldn't let . . .'

'I think it's an excellent idea,' said Charles calmly. 'We've got to dispose of you somehow and it's always a problem getting rid of a corpse, especially when the ground's frozen. Rowan's body will be easy to account for, but yours . . . well, this seems the best answer.'

'So you killed her.' I felt a numb sorrow. Poor Rowan, what a waste. What a damned shame.

'You forced me to. It was your fault.' The note of self-justification filled me with angry disgust. 'If you'd done as you were told, none of this need have happened. All I wanted was enough money to get established and make a fresh start. God knows I'd earned it! Then you interfered, and things started to go wrong. If you hadn't begun poking and prying, spying on me, everything would have gone like clockwork. You ruined all our plans and this is the price you'll have to pay.'

'You won't get away with it,' I said. Something at the back of my terrified mind urged me to keep talking, to gain time. 'How are you going to account for Rowan being drugged and half starved before she died? That won't be easy to explain.'

He smiled. 'On the contrary, it's what a lot of our friends have been expecting for some time – ever since word got around that Ro had a drug problem. I tried to keep it quiet, but it got out – you know how these things do.'

'You mean you fed that story to anyone who'd listen.'

'Only my *closest* friends. They've been . . . very supportive. They know I did my best to get her to kick the habit but unfortunately, in the circle she moved in –' he shrugged '– drug abuse is pretty common, I'm afraid.'

'She never touched drugs!' I cried angrily. 'It's all a lie. You could hardly persuade her to swallow an aspirin.'

'Ask anyone,' he said indifferently. 'They'll all say the same. It was an open secret. And the post mortem will confirm it. I'm not blaming her. She tried to fight it, poor darling, but once

230

you're hooked, you're hooked. In the end the craving got too much for her. That, you see, was when *you* had the idea of bringing her here, hiding her in a mountain hut, and pretending to me that she'd been kidnapped. Oh, you were very clever, Catta, you played your cards well. Of course, *you* were the pusher who kept her supplied with snow – I've let that be known – discreetly, but once you're out of the way some enterprising reporter may make it the subject of an investigation. Poor Ro – she was putty in your hands.'

'Nobody'll believe it. Why would I do that to Rowan?'

'Because you fancy me, of course. You do, don't you? You've never been able to hide it.'

'You *scum*, Charles,' I said, feeling sick. 'You filthy lying murdering scum.'

'Language, language! Do be careful how you insult me – Max's temper is renowned for its low flashpoint. Now, Gina, have you got everything ready? Excellent. We'll find her some boots and then you can pop in your little jab. Don't you feel excited, Catta? You're about to have the thrill of a lifetime. What a way to go out!'

He turned to Max. 'Off you go, dear boy, and get your things together. Gina and I will rig the wing and take it down to the launch, so join us there as soon as you're ready. Say ten minutes?'

'*Bon, d'accord.*' Max went inside the chalet.

The next ten minutes were the worst I'd ever been through. Charles held me down while Gina shot me full of dope, and then they went off to assemble the hang-glider, leaving me locked in the concrete-floored locker room, waiting for the drug to take effect. I've never gone in for tranquillizers, so I didn't know what to expect. I kept looking at my arm where the needle mark showed red and angry and the surrounding skin felt bruised. If Gina was a nurse I pitied her patients. I waited and waited, but the promised euphoria didn't materialize. I felt icy cold and sick with fear. When at last they came to fetch me I was shaking so much I could hardly stand.

'Please, Charles,' I begged, 'don't do this to me. Don't kill me. I'll do anything you want. I'll give you time to get clear away.'

His mouth curved in the spontaneous grin I knew so well, but

231

his eyes remained cold as blue pebbles. 'Ah, but I don't want to get clear away. I want to live happily every after, in my own home where I can give my own children the best that money can buy. Who wants to spend his time skulking in some banana republic? That's where I'd have to take my three million francs if I let you live, my angel. You must realize that.'

'I'd keep my mouth shut, I promise.' Fear broke all my pride. I didn't want revenge: I simply wanted to remain alive. Surely, I thought despairingly, there must be some chord of affection I could touch?

Apparently not. Charles said brusquely, 'Don't be absurd. How could I enjoy my loot if I thought you were going to pop up some time in the future with a lot of embarrassing revelations?'

'I wouldn't. I swear I wouldn't.'

'You won't get the chance to. Come on, Gina,' he said impatiently, 'Max can follow us down when he's ready.'

They strapped a harness with a seat slung beneath it round my thighs and over my shoulders, pulling the webbing tight. Then Gina grabbed hold of the dangling clip and walked me down the short slope to the launching ledge, tugging me along like a dog on a lead. Charles followed, carrying the hang-glider. It looked horribly frail: far too spindly to be trusted with the weight of two humans. Beneath the curved blue and yellow wing were two tubes joined in a T. The short one extended forward to the nose-plate, the longer one from one wingtip to the other. At the junction of these tubes a triangular frame hung down, with bracing wires attached to it fore and aft to make a rigid structure. Only it wasn't really rigid. It billowed gently in the light wind, tipping from side to side as Charles carried it with his shoulders thrust through the triangular frame.

We stood on the ledge, waiting for Max. The air was cold and still. The blue sky arched above and the rocks glittered far below. Very far below. I felt the dizzying nausea of vertigo and my ears began to roar. I could hardly keep my balance, let alone pay attention to what Charles and Gina were doing, but from the way they worked it was obvious that they'd had plenty of practice in this sort of teamwork. I wondered where. Then I wondered who had subverted whom. Had Gina, smarting from Robin's rejection, incited Charles to get rid of his wife? Or had Charles coopted her into the conspiracy when he realized that

Rowan was in love with Robin? Whichever way round it had been, the result was the same: death for Rowan. Death for me. A carefree future for Charles with his money, his children, his lover . . . Rage rose in my throat, black fury at the injustice of it, at my complete helplessness to stop Charles getting away with it. Just as he'd always got away with everything.

'I'll haunt you,' I said. 'Damn you to hell, Charles. I'll curse you and haunt you for the rest of your life.'

'Ah, shut up,' he said indifferently. It was almost as if I'd already stopped existing as far as he was concerned. I was just a parcel to be tied up and dropped into an abyss.

They were checking over the hang-glider. The delicate struts quivered as the blue and yellow wing billowed in a breath of wind.

Charles turned and looked back at the chalet. 'Come on, Max!' he shouted. 'We haven't got all day!'

'Hold this a minute,' said Gina, handing him a rope. 'I'll run back and fetch him.'

'What the hell's keeping him?' muttered Charles. He took the rope, glancing once more over his shoulder. 'All right, Gina, clip her on. The wind's getting up. Make it snappy, will you?'

Like an automaton I moved arms and legs as she directed. I tried to think positively, to look ahead. Max wasn't a big man. Once we were down on the glacier I might be able to surprise him. I must fight for my life. I mustn't give up.

Then I heard a familiar whistle on the slope above. The black-hooded figure, now equipped with a helmet and carrying a second pair of skis over his shoulder, shot nonchalantly down the bank and pulled up with a flourish. I observed him covertly, and my spirits sank still further. Despite the impression of whippiness, he was more strongly built than I'd realized.

Gina seized my foot and forced it down on the ski-binding. 'Charles,' I whimpered, 'I'm scared . . .'

He turned from adjusting the anchor rope, looking as surprised as if a waxwork had spoken. 'How much did you give her?' he asked Gina.

'Enough to clobber a carthorse,' she said defensively. 'She must be slow to react.'

I felt as you do when the dentist reaches for his drill before his anaesthetic has deadened your mouth. 'Wait, *please*', I begged.

Charles took a pace forward, staring at me intently. Then he rolled back my eyelid between finger and thumb. He shrugged. 'Too bad. She'll have to go as she is. We can't hang about here any longer. Are you ready, Max?'

He was kneeling, still whistling softly between his teeth as he helped Gina attach my second ski. 'For God's sake,' exclaimed Charles. 'Is that the only tune you know?' For the first time he sounded edgy.

Max chuckled, and the sound made my stomach turn over. He was enjoying this. He was actually looking forward to launching off into space. He guided my hands to the control bar and my fingers fastened round it automatically.

'Ready?' said Charles. 'We'll pick you up at the mountain hut just after noon. That'll give us time to clear up here. OK? Happy landings!'

'*En avant!*' Through the hood the words were muffled, but I saw his mouth stretch in a grin.

'*Charles!*' I cried desperately.

Instead of answering he signalled to Gina and simultaneously they let go. My companion pushed out his control bar and the nose lifted. Instinct prompted me to crouch, bracing my legs, as we began to slide down the steep slope, faster and faster, until we reached the lip of the precipice and, with a stomach-abandoning swoop, lifted into the air. Up we soared and up again. I tried to scream but my lungs seemed to have collapsed. Even my breathing mechanism had seized up solid. I struggled for air. It was terrifying, exhilarating, the stuff of nightmares without the smallest hope of waking safe in bed. Beneath my skis the air felt almost solid, as water does when you're pulled up behind a powerboat. The straps cut into my shoulders, my thighs, my waist, the seat numbed my buttocks but I welcomed the pain since it alone convinced me that I was still alive and attached to something, however flimsy, that was supporting me above this horrifying void.

'Look ahead. Keep your head up. Don't look down!' My companion shifted his hands on the control bar.

I gasped. If I hadn't been trussed by the straps I should certainly have fainted. I thought that fright had finally addled my wits. In blank amazement I twisted my head round to stare at the black mask beneath the helmet.

234

'It's me. Richard,' he shouted against the rush of wind. 'Are you all right?'

I was all right. Even though I was hanging like a demented crane fly over a drop of several thousand feet, unable to move or breathe, I was all right. I was alive. 'Yes,' I croaked. 'Charles –'

'I know.'

'He killed Rowan.'

'I know,' he said again; or it might have been, 'Oh no!' The wind made it hard to hear.

'How did you . . .?'

'Wait,' he shouted. 'I'll tell you later. Got to land this thing . . . bit dodgy . . . hang on tight . . . scared . . ?'

'I'm not scared!' Amazingly, it was true. I was breathing normally again. Terror had retreated and in its place was a strange kind of exultation – even ecstasy. I had survived. I was on top of the world, and Richard was there to get us safely down.

The glider lifted again, veering to the right. As we turned gently away from the glacier to cross the ridge that lay between the Eagle's Nest and Val du Loup, I thought of Charles watching us through his binoculars, wondering what the hell Max was doing, and I felt a vengeful triumph. Now it was Charles' turn to worry and wonder. At last the tide had turned against him, too late to save Rowan; almost too late for me.

'What did you do to Max?' I shouted.

'Sorry . . . can't hear . . .'

The ridge was beneath us now, its grey rocks as spiky as a dragon's spine. Beyond it lay Val du Loup, curiously flattened, spread out across the dazzling white slope. Never had the ugly chocolate-block apartment buildings looked so attractive to me – or so inaccessible. Above the condominium the Hollenbergs' castle, with its frosted turrets and battlements, looked like the top layer of some fantastic wedding cake. The slalom course, still marked out with doll-sized flags, snaked down the white expanse to its left, and the great span of yellow bunting advertising Bergasol which formed the finishing line was reduced by distance to a narrow fluttering ribbon.

I turned my head again and met Richard's dancing eyes though the slits in the mask.

'Ever – done – this – before?'

'No!'

'Great. Enjoy the ride. Cost anyone else forty quid . . .' The rest of the sentence was lost in the wind. We were descending rapidly; it seemed to me that the ground, which had looked so steady from the top of our launch, had begun to shimmy and jiggle in the most alarming way. The snow was coming up to meet us at high speed and what had looked flat was now revealed as full of rocks and ravines. My shoulders ached from the drag of the straps and I couldn't see anywhere that looked suitable for landing. Richard was moving his weight about, adjusting the trim, doing his best to keep the sail level.

'Where are you going to – ?' I started to shout, then realized it was too late.

The snow whizzing past our skis was only thirty feet, fifteen feet . . . six feet below us. Richard pushed the control bar forward, raising the nose to a steeper angle as he headed for a smooth stretch of snow to the left of the Sorcière chair-lift.

'Keep your tips up! Bend your knees!'

I made a great effort to hold my dangling skis level with his, ready for the shock of landing. They seemed as heavy and unwieldy as telegraph poles. First I had one level, then the other would sag out of line. My thigh muscles felt as if a redhot bar had been driven through the back of them.

'Here we go.'

I almost managed it. For a second as we touched down I felt the ground smooth and level beneath my skis and experienced a mighty surge of relief. Then my left edge caught a bump and I spun helplessly sideways, dragged along by our momentum, bringing Richard down on top of me in a tangle of struts and flapping nylon. It was like capsizing in a gale. I tried to struggle free of the enveloping folds, felt an agonizing wrench in my knee, and then something hard and heavy, probably the cross-tube, caught me on the side of the head.

Memory came and went in flashes.

There were people all round, blotting out the sky, and Richard's voice telling them not to push, to give me air.

Another voice cut in, officious and demanding. '*Etes-vous assurée, mademoiselle?* Are you insured?' which made me want to laugh because in Val du Loup it was a standing joke that the

Mountain Rescue teams would leave you to perish in your snowdrift if you couldn't convince them that you were insured. But before I could begin to laugh or even speak, consciousness faded away entirely.

I woke to find myself in a clean white room with cheerful flowered curtains and the unmistakable smell of a hospital. My left leg was encased in plaster and suspended from a pulley hoist. My foot wore a baby-pink bedsock.

Richard was sitting beside the bed, reading a document whose pages were tied together with narrow green ribbon. I felt very drowsy, very safe, and utterly desolate. All our efforts had been for nothing because Rowan was dead. My best friend. My Terrible Twin. Tears filled my eyes and began to slide down into my hair. I sniffed and groped on the bedside table for a tissue. Richard looked up.

'What's the matter? Does it hurt very much? D'you want some more dope?' He took my hand, squeezing it hard. 'I'm so sorry. It was nearly a lovely landing. And then to smash your leg – '

'It's Rowan. I could have saved her. I should never have left her. I wouldn't let myself admit . . .' I gulped.

'Admit what?'

'That Charles would kill her.'

'He didn't,' he said quickly; and then, as my mouth opened in disbelief, 'It's true, I swear it. She's alive.'

'*What?*' I moved too quickly and yelped as my knee tweaked. 'But he said – he told me – '

'Steady on,' said Richard. 'Let's get this straight. He certainly meant to kill her and may have believed he had, but he was wrong. Rowan's very much alive. She's back in Geneva with her father, but she's determined to come and see you as soon as she's allowed to.' He paused, regarding me steadily. 'It *is* true. I was talking to her on the telephone only half an hour ago.'

After my certainty that Charles had killed her, the shock of relief was almost too much. I swallowed and said weakly, 'I can't believe it. I left him with her. He was bending over her, and when he told me he'd killed her he sounded so sure. I thought . . . I thought . . .'

'He thought he'd given her a lethal injection before he left her to die. That's what he meant to do. But luckily the syringe Gina gave him wasn't full of morphine.'

'But – ?'

'I'd had my suspicions of Gina ever since I discovered she'd been giving Robin injections the doctor hadn't prescribed. I took the precaution of raiding her room at the Eagle's Nest and emptying all her little phials. I refilled them with distilled water. That's what she gave Charles when he went to the hospice to finish Rowan off.'

There was a silence while I thought this over. 'So that,' I said with sudden illumination, 'is what she gave me, too.'

'Gave *you?*'

'Yes. They didn't want me struggling on the hang-glider, so she gave me a jab. She said it was a tranquillizer. I kept waiting for it to work, but I just went on feeling more and more scared.'

He moved from his chair to the bed and put his arm round me. 'Tell me about it.'

'No, you tell me first. How did you guess where I was?'

He grinned. 'Inspired guesswork plus the fact that Max Kronsky had spent a lot of time up at the Nest this winter. Robin let him have the run of the place because he was crazy about hang-gliding. He used to take paying customers when Robin didn't feel up to it. So I rang Ben and persuaded him to hire the helicopter, so that I could take a look. The moment I saw the door was open I knew my hunch was right. I'd left it locked and no one but Gina had a duplicate key.'

'Why did they risk it?'

'I suppose they thought there wasn't much chance of me coming back. With Robin half out of his mind, Gina must have been sure I'd go straight back to Geneva after the Ball. She did her best to get me to cancel our display, but I didn't want to let the Prince down. When I came in and saw you in the hall, dressed in Rowan's costume, I really thought I must be going mad. You see, I *knew* she was in the hospice. I'd left Mario there looking after her. Then I realized what Dawson was up to. He wanted to pin the blame on you every way he could. He'd spread it all round that you were the pusher who kept Rowan supplied with drugs. God, for a few days I believed it myself! He was going to put up another smokescreen, pretending you'd impersonated her at the Ball.'

238

Smokescreens: Charles' specialities. I said, 'What will happen to him? To all of them?'

He shrugged. 'That depends on Rowan. And on the police, of course. Attempted murder. Kidnapping. Demanding money with menaces. GBH. There should be enough to put them all away for a good long time.'

I wished I hadn't asked. It was difficult to imagine Charles in prison, deprived of freedom, possessions, exercise, all the things he'd gambled for and lost.

'Stop feeling sorry for him,' said Richard. 'Remember what he tried to do. He did his damnedest to kill you both.'

'I can't help it.' However hard I tried to push them away, images of Charles revolved like a kaleidoscope in my memory. Charles pulling the boat to shore. Charles smiling at me in the hotel room. 'Lots of girls don't like it at first.' Charles telling me he loved me – had loved me all along. Lies, nothing but lies.

I said bitterly, 'What a fool I've been. A blind, stupid fool. Why did I trust him? Why couldn't I *see*?'

'Because he's a con man,' said Richard slowly. 'A con man's stock in trade is his ability to inspire confidence. Don't look like that. You weren't the only one he took in – not by a long chalk. Think of all the other people who preferred to believe him rather than Rowan.'

'You needn't be tactful, I don't need you to make excuses,' I said bleakly. More memories flooded back. Memories of how, this past week, I'd hugged to myself the secret conviction that he loved me more than Rowan. Had always loved me most. I felt unclean, degraded. I covered my eyes with my hands.

'Would you prefer me to call you an idiot?' he said gently, and pulled my hands away so that I had to look at him. 'All right, you're an idiot. A stupid, headstrong, and extremely loyal idiot, and I love you.'

The scar of Charles' betrayal was too fresh. I flinched. 'Don't say that,' I snapped. 'It isn't true.' I couldn't stand any more soft soap. I'd had enough to last a lifetime.

A pretty nurse put her head round the door. 'I regret, *monsieur*, but *mademoiselle* must rest,' she said, smiling.

'I'm just going,' said Richard, but he didn't move and after a moment she withdrew her head.

239

'It's quite true. I do love you,' he said. 'You'll have to get used to the idea.'

'Damn love,' I said shakily. 'It always ends in tears.'

He smiled. 'Not always.'

His face was very near mine. I could see the white line of the scar bisecting his eyebrow, and flecks of gold in the stubble on his cheeks. It struck me that he looked tired, and I wondered how many hours he'd spent sitting here by my bed, waiting for me to come round. Charles wouldn't have done that, I reflected. Any fool can be uncomfortable, he'd have said. He'd have charmed the duty nurse into finding him a place to sleep while he waited, and probably into sharing it with him.

'It'll be different this time,' said Richard. 'Quite different. From the moment I first ran into you, I *knew* it was going to be.'

Ran into was right. I said, 'I can't start all over again. It – it hurts too much.'

'All over again? You haven't even started. Where's that famous spirit of adventure?'

'Dead,' I said, and turned my face away.

There was a short silence. When I looked at him again he was standing by the window, watching thick soft cottonwool flakes float lazily down to settle on the sill.

'Spring snow,' he said. 'In a week or so this valley will be green. Time to put away skis and think ahead. Don't worry. I won't rush you . . . I'm coming to London next month. Will you send me a ticket for your show? Rowan says it's a must.'

'I'll reserve you a place in the front row,' I promised.

'And dine with me afterwards?'

I thought it over. I couldn't see any reason to refuse. 'If you like.'

'Good. Then we'll take it from there,' he said, and went smiling out of the room.